SPICY CHOCOLATE

BOOK 3 OF THE ALCOTT FAMILY ADVENTURES

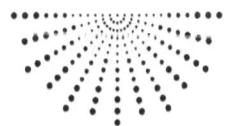

DAWN GREENFIELD IRELAND

ARTISTIC ORIGINS

Spicy Chocolate by Dawn Greenfield Ireland

Published by Artistic Origins Inc.

Copyright © 2018 Dawn Greenfield Ireland

All rights reserved.

New cover design by Brandon White/Victory Laurel (10/2022)

Interior layout by Yours Truly (me), Corrections 5/16/2026

ISBN 978-1-940385-12-9 (eBook)

ISBN 978-1-940385-13-6 (Paperback)

Publisher's Note:

This is a work of fiction. Names, characters, places, and incidents either are the product of the author's imagination or are used fictitiously, and any resemblance to actual persons, living or dead, business establishments, events, or locales is entirely coincidental.

Sign up for my newsletter to get the latest news and announcements first: www.degreenfield.com

Every word I have written and published is from my noggin (brain, in case you don't know what noggin means). My fiction is all make-believe, from the deep dive into my wild imagination. All my nonfiction books have been researched until my brain has scrambled.

Nonfiction	
The Puppy Baby Book	Mastering Your Money (2022)
Puppy Adoption and Beyond	Writers Preparation Handbook
Mastering Your Money (2008)	What's Breaking Your Budget
Online Classes	
Writers Preparation Handbook	How to Format Word Docs Like A Pro
Cozy Mysteries	**Sci-Fi-Fantasy**
The Alcott Family Adventures	**The Thol Series**
Hot Chocolate	Prophecy of Thol
Bitter Chocolate	Gifts From Thol
Spicy Chocolate	Love of Thol
Nutty Chocolate	King of Thol
Katz' Cat Series	Earth Calling Thol
Katz' Cat	**Sci-Fi Romance Adventure**
Bill Hill's Pills	Forced Dreams
The Detectives	**Dystopian**
The Pact	The Last Dog
Discreet Conversations	Texmexzona
Books by my Alter Ego ~ DG Ireland	
Bonded Shapeshifter Billionaire Series	
Bonded	
Tothars	
Tilted	
Unforeseen	
Connected	
Need A Notebook?	
See my 54 themed notebooks on my website www.degreenfield.com/notebooks	
Screenplays formatted as books	
Plan B (Dark Comedy)	Where's Ralphie? (Family Comedy)
The God Child (Action Adventure)	Standing Dead (Drama/Tragedy)
The Far Corner (Sci-Fi/Psychological/Creatures)	
Screenplays as TV Episodes	
Hot Chocolate ~ Episode 1	Prophecy of Thol ~ Episode 1
Bonded ~ Episode 1	
See my screenplays and awards on my website: degreenfield.com Filmfreeway, ISA Network	

ACKNOWLEDGMENTS

I'm very grateful to my son Brandon White/Victory Laurel for the redesign of the cover. Now it feels right.

No published author has made it to completion without an editor or an editing team. Many thanks to Paris Powers for tackling *Spicy Chocolate*. She gracefully read Hot Chocolate and Bitter Chocolate to get the flow of the story and characters. Paris, you made me stretch beyond my borders. My work would be in shambles without you.

A big thank you to Jon Goldey, Forensic Instrument Specialist, SPEX Forensics. He didn't think I was a nut-job when I hunted him down with my bizarre questions. I just hope I understood properly and have everything in order.

Many thanks to the following people/organizations for these recipes:

- Tiramisu Martini was created by The Cocktail Lady www.ayearofcocktails.com.
- Pumpkin Spiced Martini was created by Chad Tackett http://fitera.com/
- Chicken with Riesling from Food & Wine February 2003
- Perfect Roast Pork by Cook the Story http://cookthestory.com/

Thanks to all my Facebook pals for sharing my moments.

And my Twitter universe—those wonderful Tweethearts who pass along my Tweets. Thanks so much!

Those who stick around through thick and thin, year after year, and who lend support also have to be mentioned. Because without these incredible people in my life, I'd be lost.

So, many thanks to Margaret Rustan, Ann Starr, Dave Richards, Sandy Penny, Joseph Lawrence Thompson, Angela Moore, Ann Hilborn, Vicki Bigan, Colin Talbot and scores more.

Robert Beddow does it again with this terrific family tree—in full living color! Now you can see when characters were added for different books. The paperback will have a black and white family tree.

Many thanks to Ramon Ferro for his help with the Spanish translations between Chiquita and Manuela. He tweaked my Google translations to make them more accurate.

If you find any bloopers, send me a message so I can fix them!

Onward and Upward!

DEDICATED TO

The blazing love of my two sons:
Brandon Clay White
George Thomas White

In Memory Of
My parents, *George* and *Dorothy Daigle Greenfield*, and my big
sister, *Robin*.
You are missed so much
And
Shasta Annie Ireland who was my doggie sidekick for 16-1/2
years

FAMILY TREE

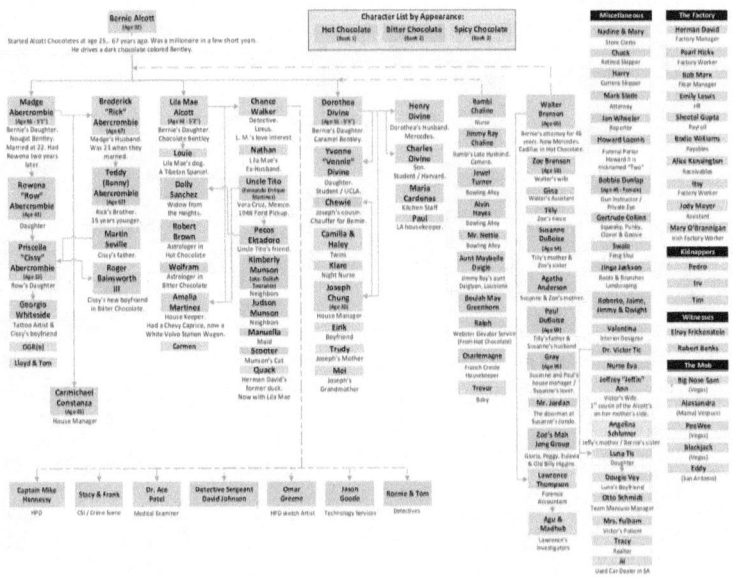

CHAPTER ONE

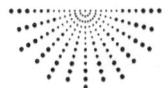

*E*very chair in Lila Mae Alcott's dining room was occupied by family and extended members in attendance for a scrumptious Sunday brunch with a Valentine's Day motif.

Lila Mae sat at the head of the table in a silk lilac pantsuit with a beige tank top, lightly scented with Dior's Poison, her favorite perfume. She smiled as she watched the family exchanges around the table. Her trim figure and unlined face made her look more than a decade younger than her sixty-two years.

Chance Walker, Lila Mae's handsome beau and a Houston police detective, sported a nice tan. He swiped a pecan off Lila Mae's plate when he thought she wasn't looking. She swatted him, somewhat territorially, but playfully. They giggled at the transgression and smooched.

The three youngest members of the Alcott chocolate empire were asleep in their strollers. Camilla and Haley slept like angels in their Valentine's attire, including pink headbands. Dorothea Divine, Lila Mae's baby sister, kept a hand on her daughter's twin stroller. Soon to be fifty-seven, Dorothea was recovering from the shock of this late-life motherhood experience.

Louie, Lila Mae's fluffy, champagne and white Tibetan Spaniel, lounged on the dining room floor amid the strollers, just as peaceful as can be.

Bernie Alcott, the patriarch of the family had built Alcott chocolates from the ground up to a billion-dollar world-renowned, privately owned company. Bernie, a new father at ninety-two, stuffed a wedge of pink buttermilk pancakes into his mouth.

Chewie, Bernie's attendant, chauffeur, and walking weapon, nudged Bernie. In addition to having black belts in several martial arts, Chewie was the Alcott sisters' electronics wizard.

"Slow down!" Chewie whispered. "No one's going to steal your food!"

Chewie flicked imaginary crumbs off his impeccable jacket and took a sip of fresh-squeezed pink orange juice. His uniform, which was hand-tailored for a "Kato of Green Hornet" look, was a dark hunter green and fit like a glove.

"Pink orange juice just looks wrong," Chewie said. He shook his head as he looked into the glass.

Bambi, sitting on the other side of Bernie, sipped a café mocha while she listened attentively to Dorothea, her former boss, now best friend. Trevor Alan Chaline-Alcott, born thirty minutes after his nieces, slept with a smile on his tiny face at her side, oblivious to the giant heart on his tiny shirt.

Bambi's voluptuous figure prior to her surprise pregnancy only changed one dress size, to Dorothea's chagrin. The tiny blonde was still the same sexy, curvy woman with the squeaky voice the Alcott girls were forced to take into the fold because of their father's transgressions. Over time, however, the Alcott clan discovered what a jewel she was, and they were happy to have her.

"Camilla doesn't like to be swaddled! I guess she feels

trapped," Dorothea said. "Haley doesn't care. She sleeps like a log."

Madge, the eldest Alcott sister, soon to be 67, gazed adoringly at the babies with full understanding. "Didn't Charles fuss if he was too confined?"

"Yes, that child had a PhD in whining!" Dorothea grumbled. She dabbed at her lips with a linen napkin.

"Trevor likes to keep to a schedule," Bambi said. "I think it's a genetic thing with the way your dad conducted business."

Carmichael and Amelia sipped the traditional Alcott café mocha, fingers entwined, looking like the lovebirds they were.

The Alcott lifestyles and attitudes never fit into the swanky River Oaks socialite circle. Those snobs would be appalled to sit elbow-to-elbow with staff at the table. Alcott employees were like family. The benefits alone kept them happy, loyal and close to the family.

Louie's ears went up and he jumped to his feet with a little *ruff*. He raced to the kitchen, barking. All three babies jerked awake and screamed in surround sound as Louie ran back to the dining room, then returned to the kitchen door, barking each way. He stood guard at the French doors, sounding the alarm.

Lila Mae and Amelia raced to the kitchen door and peeked through the windows.

"Louie! Sshh!" Lila Mae snapped.

Louie looked at his mistress with a questioning expression. He was doing his job, and a treat would have been appreciated. Seeing that none was forthcoming, he harrumphed loudly.

"Are we expecting company?" Amelia asked.

"No, we're all here," Lila Mae said.

They watched as a taxi pulled up and parked in back of the three Bentleys.

"Who would be arriving in a taxi?" Amelia asked.

They watched as shapely legs emerged from the back seat of

the cab, and pedicured toes peeped out of flaming red stiletto-heeled sandals.

A young Spanish woman in her late twenties grabbed her purse, bumped the door closed with a trim hip, and waited as the cab driver lumbered out of the front seat and retrieved her luggage from the trunk. Once she had her rolling luggage and cosmetic case, she pressed money into the driver's hand and sashayed toward the kitchen door.

Amelia and Lila Mae shared a look.

"Who is that?" Lila Mae asked Amelia.

Amelia shrugged. "Never saw her before."

"Who's here?" Madge bellowed over the screeching babies as she came up behind Lila Mae and Amelia. She peered out the door at the newcomer. "Who is that?"

"We don't know," Lila Mae said. "But if you give it a moment, we're about to find out."

The dining room emptied as Chance and Carmichael got up and followed the women. Bernie pushed aside the walker Chewie thrust upon him. They scowled at each other, and Bernie relented, grabbed the device, and plowed into Carmichael.

"Watch what you're doing!" Chewie scolded. "Are you okay, Carmichael?"

Carmichael feigned a limp. "I'm suing!"

Bernie muttered something under his breath while Chewie and Carmichael shared a chuckle.

Dorothea and Bambi rolled the strollers to the kitchen table and cooed to their babies trying to settle them down once again.

The stranger stood on the other side of the door popping her gum, one hand resting on the handle of her rolling luggage as she waved at Amelia and Lila Mae through the French door windows.

"Are you going to open the door?" she asked with a melodious, accented voice as she spied the family members craning their necks to see out the door.

The newcomer wore a skin-hugging, bright floral print skirt. The ruffles at the hem went over her knees in the front and dipped to her ankles in the back. The skirt was topped with a halter that tied behind her neck and dipped in the front. Her face was perfectly made up with beautifully arched eyebrows and penciled lips.

"Who is that?" Lila Mae whispered again.

"I don't have a clue," Amelia said. She squared her shoulders and opened the door. "May I help you?"

The woman gripped the luggage handle and lumbered forward. The sea of curious family members parted.

"I'm sorry I'm so late. The flight from Mexico was very bumpy, then Hobby Airport was very crowded with travelers, but I'm here now," she said.

She headed over to the kitchen island with Louie following. He sniffed at her every step. He wagged his tail approvingly. She plopped her cosmetic case on a barstool and dumped her purse on top of it. She rested the luggage handle against the island.

The young woman bent and scratched the top of Louie's head, straightened up and turned to the stunned family. She waved to Dorothea and Bambi. "Ladies!" She clutched her hands to her heart, went over to the strollers and looked at the three babies. The babies had quieted to bursts of whimpers.

"Oh! What beautiful little angels!" she said. "When were they born?"

"Four months ago," Bambi said.

Dorothea and Bambi unashamedly gawked at the sexy vixen. Bernie's eyes were glazed with lust. Bambi got up, grabbed Bernie's arm, and almost jerked him off his feet. She led him to the table and pushed him into a chair.

"Behave yourself," Bambi said in her squeaky voice.

Chewie and Carmichael snickered. Bernie glared at them.

Lila Mae and Amelia came forward. Lila Mae was all business. "I'm sorry, but please explain who you are and what you're doing here."

The woman looked shocked. "I'm Chiquita! Didn't Uncle Tito tell you when I'd be here?"

Amelia's shoulders drooped. She looked at Lila Mae. "Are you firing me?"

"Are you crazy?" Lila Mae asked Amelia. She turned to Uncle Tito's niece. "Chiquita, I'm Lila Mae Alcott. Uncle Tito mentioned you a long time ago, but why are you here now?"

Chiquita slapped her forehead. "Ai!" She rattled off a long string of words in Spanish.

"Don't ask me to translate that!" Amelia said, her cheeks turning pink.

"I'm here to train for when Amelia goes on her honeymoon," Chiquita said as she directed her eyes to Amelia.

"My honeymoon?" Amelia and Carmichael exchanged surprised looks. "We haven't even planned the wedding yet!"

"It's okay," Chiquita said. "You're stressed! Let me make some flan!" She grabbed her purse, cosmetic case, and the handle to the luggage and rolled toward the butler's closet. The sexy minx ducked inside the closet as if she knew the layout of the place.

She went into the open area on the opposite side of the wall from where the stove was in the kitchen and placed her luggage against the wall. She plunked her purse on top of the luggage and set her cosmetic case on the floor.

Amelia and Lila Mae followed Chiquita.

Bernie attempted to stand, but after a warning scowl from Bambi, changed his mind.

"This is perfect! We can put a little bed right here and the bath is close by. Maybe a little wall hanger so I can hang my clothes?"

Lila Mae stated. "You can't live in my pantry!" She made a frightful face at Amelia, who shrugged her shoulders.

Chiquita tut-tutted, rushed past, looked at the stock in the pantry, snagged a few items, returned to the kitchen and deposited her bounty on the island. She pulled open drawers until she found an apron and slipped the neckpiece over her head and tied the strings at her tiny waist.

"Go visit!" she shooed both Amelia and Lila Mae. "This is a long process, but you will love this flan!"

With that, she started singing in Spanish. She went to the refrigerator, grabbed the carton of eggs, returned to the counter, found a bowl, and did a little shimmy dance. Her skirt seams threatened to pop. The ruffles shook. She went about preparing the flan, singing and shimmying as everyone watched in dumbstruck silence.

Amelia's phone rang. She ignored the screen and answered, in a state of shock. She glanced at Lila Mae. "Uncle Tito! Yes, Chiquita just arrived. Hold on." Amelia shoved the phone toward Lila Mae.

"Uncle Tito? A little warning would have been great." Lila Mae glanced at Amelia with a hurt expression on her face.

Amelia mouthed, *what?*

Lila Mae shook her head as she continued to listen to Uncle Tito. "Okay, we'll take good care of her."

She handed the phone back to Amelia.

"What's going on? Lila Mae looks upset!" Amelia said. She listened. "No, I'm not! Where did you get that idea? You did? Well, maybe your info is wrong."

Everyone watched the drama unfolding. Madge stood and marched over to Lila Mae. "Will you tell us what is going on, and who this woman is?"

"Amelia's going to quit soon!" Lila Mae said, flabbergasted. "Uncle Tito sent Chiquita to replace her."

Jaws dropped. Mouths hung open.

Carmichael spread his arms wide toward Amelia in a *what's the deal?* questioning expression.

Amelia waved her hand, dismissing Lila Mae's statement. "For once, Uncle Tito is way off."

"He's never wrong," Chiquita said in a sing-song voice.

Amelia stared hard at Chiquita. "What side of the family are you from anyway?"

"I'm your mother's cousin Elsie's third daughter," she said. "If you'd come home to visit every once in a while, we would have met a long time ago."

Amelia's eyes turned to slits.

Carmichael, sensing a potential temper eruption of volcanic velocity, hooked his arm around her shoulders and steered Amelia into the dining room.

"How about seconds?" Carmichael asked.

CHAPTER TWO

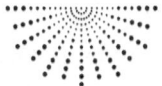

*L*ila Mae sat propped up in bed, reading a mystery
novel. Louie snoozed in his dog bed in his allocated
corner of the room, making soft whimpers as he ran
in his sleep.

The phone rang.

Louie startled awake and jumped up. He glanced around and
barked once.

"It's only the phone, Louie," Lila Mae said. "Go back to sleep."

Lila Mae glanced at the clock on the nightstand. Nine-forty-
five p.m. "Who would be calling at this time of night?" She
grabbed the portable house phone and checked caller ID.

"Jeffie?" she said. "Is everything okay?"

Jeffrey Ann Schlumer Tic, nicknamed Jeffie, was Lila Mae's
first cousin on her mother's side, and Doctor Victor Tic's wife.
Lila Mae waited for the current disaster news of Jeffie and
Victor's wayward daughter, Luna.

Lila Mae listened to Jeffie. She heard a noise downstairs. She
put her hand over the mouthpiece of the phone.

"Chiquita? Is that you?"

"It's me," Chance called out. He came up the stairs. He saw

she was on the phone, creased his forehead in question as he motioned to his watch, then kissed her on top of the head. Chance entered the closet.

"Well, at least she called, Jeffie," Lila Mae said.

Chance stepped out of the closet in his boxers and t-shirt. He waited for more information. *Jeffie?* He mouthed silently. Then whispered *Luna?*

Lila Mae whispered *yes.*

Chance shook his head and returned to the closet.

"She's bringing him home to meet you and Victor?"

Chance popped out of the closet holding his police revolver. He walked to the bed and deposited the gun in the top drawer of the nightstand on his side of the bed.

"Oh, no!" Lila Mae said. She made a scary face at Chance. "He's much too old for her!"

Chance shook his head and went into the bathroom and shut the door. The shower water ran.

"Let me know if you need us to stage an intervention," Lila Mae said. "We'll come over and tell her *what for.*"

She listened some more. "Get some sleep. Okay. 'Night." Lila Mae disconnected the call and shaded her eyes with one hand. "Oh, Lord. Here we go again."

* * *

WHEN CHANCE EXITED the bathroom in his white Turkish robe, Lila Mae was reading. She saved her place with a yellow index card and put the book on the nightstand.

"Should I even ask?" Chance asked.

"She called Jeffie and told her she's engaged to some character named Dougie Vey. He's older than Victor!"

Chance propped his two standard-size pillows against the carved headboard, then shifted the covers to the center of the bed. He slid onto the white, heavenly soft Egyptian cotton sheets and rested his head against the pillows. He let out a sigh of contentment.

"Where's she been for a solid year?" Chance asked as he turned slightly to face Lila Mae.

"Evidently, she went to New Orleans for a few months, then she *caught a ride* to Las Vegas," Lila Mae said using finger quotes.

"Oh, boy, I'm not sure I want to know what she means by that," Chance said. "Neither of those cities is the best place for someone with gambling problems."

Lila Mae flinched at that spoken truth. "The falling out between her and her folks was terrible. She has a lot of nerve just showing up as if nothing was wrong."

"What's she been doing there, or should I be too afraid to ask?"

"Singing," Lila Mae said.

"Do you mean she went from singing at the mega-church here to singing in a casino?" Chance asked.

"At first Jeffie said Luna told her she was a *performer*," Lila Mae said.

"Performer?" Chance blurted. "Did she really say that? I'd interpret that to mean stripper."

"Then she said Luna was a singer at this Dougie Vey's casino," Lila Mae said.

"She's about as messed up as Tilly used to be," Chance said.

"Well, what would you expect if your parents named you Luna and your last name was Tic?" Lila Mae said. "Astrologically, that sets up a roller-coaster of chaos."

"Changing the subject, what did you do with Chiquita?" Chance asked.

Lila Mae scowled. "I gave her fresh linens and let her loose in the apartment over the garage."

"You need to make sure she has papers to legally work here," Chance said.

Lila Mae's jaw clenched. Chance felt a definite climate change with the current subject, so he let it drop.

* * *

THE NEXT MORNING, Lila Mae woke with a start. She was alone in the dark bedroom. Through the glow of the LED nightlight, she noticed both Chance and Louie were missing. She heard clanging and banging coming from the kitchen. She leaned over and squinted at the alarm clock on the nightstand.

Five-thirty a.m.

"What in the world? Does she get up with the chickens?"

Lila Mae sat up and slid out of bed, right into her slippers. She retrieved her robe from a hook inside the closet door, exited the bedroom, and went down the stairs. The clanging and banging sounds escalated as Lila Mae walked down the stairs to the kitchen.

Chiquita was on her hands and knees with baking pans, cookie sheets, and cooling racks on the surrounding floor. Short bursts of Spanish spewed through her clenched teeth.

"English, Chiquita," Lila Mae said. "We only speak English in this house. Amelia can barely speak Spanish."

Chiquita banged her head when she backed out of the cabinet. She rubbed the top of her head. "Oh, sorry, Ms. Alcott," she said. "I hope I didn't wake you. Mr. Chance had coffee and left. Louie's outside."

As if on cue, Louie scratched on a bottom window pane in the French kitchen door.

Lila Mae opened the door, and Louie trotted into the kitchen and stopped at his raised feeding station. His bowl was empty. He glanced up at Lila Mae hopefully.

"Don't even think about it, Louie," Lila Mae said. "You're not getting breakfast before seven o'clock!" Lila Mae turned her attention back to Chiquita. "What exactly are you doing, Chiquita? " It's five-thirty in the morning!"

Chiquita appeared slightly embarrassed. "I'm sorry for starting so late."

"Late?" Lila Mae said, trying to control her temper. She came around the corner, wiggled her fingers toward Chiquita's hand and pulled her to her feet. She led her to the kitchen door. "Go back to bed. We don't start until seven-o'clock."

Chiquita pointed to the pans on the floor.

Lila Mae shook her head, opened the French door, and shooed Chiquita outside. She shut off the lights, retraced her steps to the staircase, and went back upstairs with Louie at her heels.

* * *

AMELIA UNLOCKED the kitchen door and entered Lila Mae's kitchen. She flipped on the switch and the room flooded with light. She walked to the butler's pantry and deposited her purse in a basket on a bottom shelf.

Amelia perused the coffee containers, grabbed one then snatched up the container of Alcott's Organic Hot Chocolate. She returned to the kitchen and stopped in her tracks. She stared at the clutter on the floor between the kitchen island and the stove.

"What the...?"

Amelia noticed a squiggly key ring on the counter. She pursed her lips until they puckered tightly. Her lips moved, silently cussing.

There was a *tap, tap, tap* on the kitchen door. Chiquita waved at Amelia.

Amelia deposited the coffee and hot chocolate containers on the counter and stormed over to the door and wrenched it open.

"What is the meaning of this mess on the floor?" Amelia jabbed a finger in the general direction of the baking utensils several times.

Chiquita slipped around Amelia and hurried to the mess in question. She stooped down and began gathering the bakeware, making a racket.

"I was trying to arrange them…"

"There was nothing wrong with the way they were arranged!" Amelia exploded. "They happen to be sorted by usefulness and use."

Lila Mae and Louie hurried into the room. "Now, ladies…"

"We need to have a *come to Jesus* meeting," Amelia thundered. "Chiquita can't push her way into my kitchen and take over!"

"Calm down, no one is taking your place," Lila Mae said.

Louie barked. He stood at the door, waiting for someone to notice that he wanted out.

Lila Mae hurried to the door and opened it. "Sorry, Louie."

Louie snorted his opinion, then trotted outside.

"Okay," Lila Mae said. "Chiquita, I know you are eager to please and excited about being here, but your arrival was quite a surprise yesterday."

Amelia stood with arms tightly crossed at her chest and a scowl on her face.

Chiquita left the bakeware on the floor and stood with a fearful expression on her face. "You're not sending me away, are you?"

"Of course not," Lila Mae said. "We just have to set some rules. First, put those things back into the cabinets where they belong. We need to have coffee and breakfast before any serious discussions."

* * *

LILA MAE SAT at the kitchen table sipping cafe´ mocha and nibbling on breakfast tacos.

"Unless there's an emergency, we start around seven in the morning, Chiquita," Lila Mae explained. "Amelia and I have a routine and you'll have to observe for a few days to understand how we work together. After watching—and helping out for a while, you should fit right in."

"And until I win the lottery, drop dead, or something else that will permanently remove me from this position, don't even think of rearranging anything!" Amelia blared.

Chiquita quivered with fright.

Lila Mae kicked Amelia's foot under the table.

"Ow!" Amelia belted out.

Lila Mae gave up. "Tone it down a bit. This isn't a hostile takeover."

Amelia was out of her element. She sputtered a few times and decided to keep her mouth closed.

Chiquita watched the women interact while she sipped her cafe´ mocha.

"Now, Chiquita," Lila Mae said, somewhat uncomfortably.

Both Amelia and Chiquita focused on Lila Mae.

"We need to get some paperwork out of the way. Do you have a work Visa or a Green Card to work in the United States?" Lila Mae asked.

Chiquita waved her hand aside. "I have a Green Card from working in Brownsville and McAllen, and I have a bank account in McAllen."

"That makes things much easier," Lila Mae said. "You can probably open a bank account at a local branch."

"What exactly is your official name?" Amelia asked. "Chiquita's a nickname."

"Elena Consuela Martinez, but I've been called Chiquita since I was five years old," Chiquita said.

* * *

AMELIA MADE a note on the planning calendar in the butler's pantry. "Chiquita?" she called. "Let me show you something important."

Chiquita entered the pantry and stood beside Amelia.

"This is the planning calendar. It shows all events, whether they are here at the house or at one of the sisters' houses, or somewhere else."

Chiquita looked at the sheet of copy paper hanging by two black clips on the wall that depicted the current month. Some squares contained typed data, others hand-written data, and others had a big black X through the information to show the date had passed.

"How come most of these are typed?" Chiquita asked.

"We always write new appointments in red ink so we can see a new event that wasn't planned when we printed the sheet," Amelia explained.

"Oh." Chiquita lightly placed a manicured finger on the red square Amelia had filled in moments before. "This dinner at Victor's (she pronounced it Veek Tor) and who's this? Jeffrey? Are they gay?" she shot a questioning look at Amelia.

Amelia snorted, amused. "Oh, I can't wait until you meet Joseph." She sighed heavily. "That's Lila Mae's cousin, Jeffie. Her husband Victor is a doctor. They have a daughter named Luna, and the dinner is to introduce Luna's fiancé to the family."

"But we're not cooking for them, so why do you have it here?" Chiquita asked.

"Sometimes we have to lend a hand," Amelia explained. "Quite a few family members and extended family will be in attendance, and sometimes it's too much for one or two cooks by themselves."

"What do you mean by *extended family?*"

Amelia thought a moment. "Uncle Tito is a good example of

an extended family member. He's not related to the Alcotts, but he's important to them, so he's in that category. When he comes to town, he's always included. In the Alcott family that would also include Walter Branson, the attorney for the Alcott estate, his wife Zoe, and most likely her sister Suzanne, Suzanne's fiancé Gray, and her daughter Tilly."

Chiquita tried to follow her cousin's line of thought.

"Then there's Gina, Walter's assistant, who is dating Chewie, Mr. Alcott's man." Amelia counted on her fingers. "Madge's brother-in-law Teddy, who used to be Benny, but he changed his name; he's dating Tilly."

Amelia saw Chiquita's eyes glazing over from the litany of names and relationships. She rested her hand on Chiquita's shoulder. "It's okay. You'll get to know them all and who they belong to."

Chiquita shook her head. "I don't know... I'll try."

"Why don't you take the recycling outside? The green bins are on the other side of the garage," Amelia said. "That will clear your head."

* * *

THE ROOTS and Branches truck pulled up at the curb in front of Lila Mae's house on Del Monte in River Oaks. Five men piled out and proceeded to remove lawn equipment from the attached trailer.

Chiquita came out of the house carrying a full bag of plastic, aluminum and glass products. She sashayed from the kitchen door, across the parking area in front of the garage to the side of the garage, humming a tune.

Her flounced turquoise skirt whipped back and forth with each step. Chiquita deposited the bag into the first green bin and rubbed her hands together. She glanced at the curb and saw Jingo Jackson staring at her like a love-struck dog. She waved.

Mesmerized, Jingo walked right into the opened truck door and smacked himself.

Chiquita covered her mouth and snickered. She hurried back to the house, making an adjustment to her off-the-shoulder embroidered peasant blouse.

Jingo stood gawking, dumbfounded and watched her until she disappeared inside. He shook his head as if trying to clear an apparition he just imagined.

* * *

THE KITCHEN DOOR swung open and Chiquita stepped inside, fanning herself with her hand. "Aye yi yi!" she said. "Who's that good-looking man with the long hair?"

Amelia put down the paring knife by the vegetables on the cutting mat and walked to the kitchen door and looked through the French panes. "You mean Jingo?"

Chiquita shrugged. "Is that his name?"

"Yes. Jingo Jackson, but you're here to work, not fill your social calendar!"

Chiquita spewed off a string of Spanish faster than Amelia could keep up to interpret.

"Amelia! I'm not a slave here. I have private time after work," Chiquita said. "That man is gorgeous!"

CHAPTER THREE

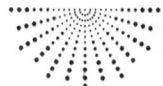

*L*ila Mae pulled the Bentley into the circular driveway at Victor and Jeffie's ostentatious house. A hired attendant rushed to the car, opened the door, and held out his hand for Lila Mae. She accepted the valet's help and eased herself out of the car as a dark chocolate-colored Bentley pulled into the driveway behind her vehicle.

Lila Mae stepped aside, pressed a button, and separated her car key from her house keys. She handed the car key and fob over and received her ticket from the valet. The man jumped into her car, and the Bentley zoomed away.

Chewie pulled Bernie's Bentley up close to the valet station, popped the trunk, and got out of the car. As usual, Chewie was meticulous to a fault.

"Hello, Lila Mae," Chewie said as he tipped his hat to her.

"Hi, Chewie. Is he behaving?"

Chewie tittered as he turned to the passenger door. "Sort of."

The valet rushed up and grabbed the rear door handle. Chewie wrenched the valet's arm away from the car.

"Thank you, but I will help Mr. Alcott out of the car,"

Chewie said in an authoritative tone. "Please retrieve the walker from the trunk."

The valet gave Chewie the once-over and huffed to the back of the car and pulled the folded walker out.

Chewie opened the door and assisted Bernie out of the car. He fretted over the elder Alcott like a mother hen.

"Don't get your suit wrinkled," he whispered.

Bernie gave Chewie a stern look. "It's too late to go home and change. We're here."

The valet presented the walker to Bernie.

Chewie claimed the walker and handed the car keys to the valet. When the Bentley and the valet were out of the way, Chewie turned the walker around and held it out to Bernie.

Bernie shot daggers at Chewie.

"It's either the walker, or you hang on my arm all afternoon," Chewie said. "Which will it be?"

Bernie scowled and grabbed the walker and clomped up to Lila Mae with Chewie at his side.

Lila Mae assessed her father. For ninety-two, her father was in pretty good shape. He dressed well and always demanded quality.

"Is that a new suit?" she asked.

"Yes. I called Arthur and put in a rush order last month."

Lila Mae rubbed the material on Bernie's sleeve. "I love Gieves & Hawke. The bespoke tailors of Saville Row know menswear."

"You look lovely, as usual," Bernie said. He appraised Lila Mae's favorite peach silk pantsuit and lilac shell. He puckered up and kissed her cheek.

A yellow Bentley pulled into the driveway and parked in back of Bernie's car. Bambi got out of the car and went to the back seat. After a few moments of wrestling with the restraints, she managed to unsecure the baby carrier. Bambi backed out of the rear door with the baby carrier and joined the group.

Trevor cooed happily, and his arms and legs flapped.

Lila Mae fussed over the carrier. "He's such a happy-go-lucky little guy."

Chewie fawned over the baby.

Bernie held one of Trevor's feet and smiled contentedly. "That's my little Taca."

"Taca?" Bambi asked. "What does that mean?"

"Those are his initials. I made it up," Bernie said.

Chewie and Lila Mae looked at each other, weighing the name in their minds. Lila Mae cringed.

"Taca," Bambi said again, rolling it around in her brain. She frowned deeply. "Sounds like caca, which is short for poopy. You're not calling our son that. It would stifle his intellectual growth, and his classmates would bully him!"

"Oh, I hadn't thought of that," Bernie said.

Lila Mae beamed proudly at Bambi.

"Let's go inside," Lila Mae said. "Victor and Jeffie are most likely wondering what's going on out here."

"You go ahead," Chewie said. "I'll stay here with the cars until the valet returns."

* * *

JEFFIE ANN and Victor drifted from one guest to another, making everyone feel welcome in their home. At fifty-three, Jeffie had retained her girlish figure, along with a beautiful complexion that was the envy of other women who paid for the same look. Her dark, glorious hair was thick and wavy and free of any chemicals. She believed in *au natural*.

"Oh, no." Lila Mae recognized Jeffie's pasted-on smile as her cousin made eye contact across the room. This was a warning sign of a precursor to another impending disaster regarding Luna. There were not enough fingers and toes to count the number of legal retainers Victor and Jeffie had to secure from the time Luna was fourteen until she took off a year ago to places unknown. They had probably paid for one of Walter Branson's Cadillacs.

The rowdy girl had been bailed out of one bad situation after another. She had no common sense and didn't stop to think things through. Lila Mae could only guess at the financial hits each episode had cost her cousin. It was no wonder Victor had no plans to retire anytime soon.

Lila Mae crossed the room and one-arm hugged her cousin. "It'll be okay, Jeffie."

Jeffie gave Lila Mae a grievous look. "I don't know how this situation will ever get better."

"Is it that bad?" Lila Mae asked.

"You tell me," Jeffie said. She hooked her arm through Lila Mae's and gently repositioned her as her daughter entered the room with her fiancé in tow.

Lila Mae took one look, clamped her mouth shut and turned her back on the couple. *Oh, My God,* she mouthed at Jeffie. "Is that him? It can't be! What could she ever see in him?"

"He must have deep pockets," Jeffie said. "They'd better stay deep if he wants to hang onto her because we all know she'll dump him as soon as the last quarter is spent."

Victor cleared his throat. "Now, Jeffie... that's our daughter you're talking about."

Jeffie gave Victor one long look, and he slunk off, silently reprimanded. "Victor is in complete denial. Come on, I'll introduce you."

Luna Tic was tall, stately, and glamorous in a gold lamé sheath that hugged her curves. A necklace of Swarovski crystals was draped around her neck, and matching earrings dangled and spun. She clung to her betrothed, Dougie Vey. The middle-aged, short, pudgy, balding man sported a cigar stub in his mouth, which he rolled around with his tongue.

Jeffie hooked her arm through Lila Mae's and they sauntered across the room to her daughter.

"Honey, why don't you introduce your beau to your cousin?" Jeffie asked.

"Lila Mae!" Luna squealed. She hugged Lila Mae and air-kissed her cheeks.

Luna smiled coyly. "Dougie, this is my cousin, Lila Mae Alcott."

Dougie gave Lila Mae the once-over as he stuck out his hand. "Dougie Vey. Nice to meet you."

"Charmed, I'm sure," Lila Mae said. "I understand you're from Vegas?"

Again, Dougie sized up Lila Mae. "Managed a casino."

"Oh, did you retire?" Lila Mae asked.

"Yeah. I'm tired of the business and wanted a fresh start."

At that moment, Madge, Rick, Teddy, and Tilly made an appearance.

"Oh, there's my big sister and her family," Lila Mae said. "If you'll excuse me?" She scooted away from her cousins and Dougie Vey to greet Madge.

Madge's eyesight was spot on. She glanced in the direction of Jeffie, Luna, and the portly man. "Is that…"

"Sshhh!" Lila Mae scolded. "Keep your voice down. I swear you must be getting deaf to talk so loud, Madge!"

Madge cringed. "Has she gone completely bonkers? Look at his belly! And he's bald! Luna could have any man. Why did she choose him?"

"Give it one good guess," Lila Mae said with saccharine sweetness.

Teddy rubbed his fingers together on his right hand.

"See? Even Teddy knows Luna's a money-grubbing floozy," Lila Mae said. "I wish Amelia and Carmichael were here to see this!"

Chewie came through the front door and looked around for

Bernie. He discovered him sitting on the sofa with Bambi and Trevor. He headed in their direction.

"Where is Amelia and Carmichael?" Madge asked.

"At the house. Amelia won't let Chiquita out of her sight," Lila Mae said. "And Chiquita may be husband-hunting."

Madge looked at her sister with a smirk forming. "Who's she got her eye on?"

"Jingo."

"I can't imagine Jingo interested in a maid," Madge said. "He has several degrees."

Lila Mae balked. "Honestly, Madge! He's a man. Chiquita is one hot chick, and she's a fantastic cook, just like her cousin."

The next wave of the family arrived: Dorothea with Henry steering the twin stroller. Walter and Zoe were next. Jeffie and Victor swarmed down on them. Jeffie fawned over the twins.

"Look at those precious babies!" Jeffie said. "Dorothea, I think they're going to look just like you."

Walter and Zoe hugged Jeffie, then Walter and Victor shook hands. Walter scanned the room and stopped at Luna and her man. "That doesn't look good," Walter said as he nodded toward Dougie Vey.

"Why don't we just give you a retainer now," Jeffie said, depressed.

Lila Mae shook her head. "It's another nightmare brewing. Anyone up for a pool on how long this takes, or what day it will happen on?"

The door opened again, and Chance entered. He saw Lila Mae among the guests and headed over to her. He pecked her lightly on the lips, then acknowledged the rest of the group.

"Hi, Madge." He could see that Madge's dander was up. Chance silently looked at Lila Mae, wanting the scoop.

Lila Mae took hold of Chance's arm and turned him ever so slightly so he faced her young cousin. Chance spotted Luna's beau, and his mental detective antennae were alerted.

"That man looks suspicious. I know if Uncle Tito were here, he'd have this guy's history via the psychic network," Chance said.

"I'm pretty sure if Joseph were here, he'd be burning sage!" Lila Mae said.

No sooner had she spoken than Joseph entered the house. He hurried up to Dorothea and the babies and nudged Dorothea's hands off the stroller. "Go mingle," he said.

Dorothea joined her sisters and immediately tuned into their moods. "What's going on?"

"I'm pretty sure this is the worst of Victor and Jeffie's embarrassments," Madge said. "I don't know what's wrong with that girl, but time's running out for her."

Dorothea followed her sister's stare. She audibly gasped. Henry clamped his hand over his mouth.

"He's got to be in his sixties, don't you think?" Henry asked.

"I know Jeffie must have cried rivers last night," Lila Mae said. "I can't believe Luna would take up with someone like him."

Walter shook his head. "I can't see this ending well."

"Do you think Victor and Jeffie would mind if I did a background check?" Chance asked.

"Don't you have to have a reason to do that?" Lila Mae asked.

"Looks like reason enough to me," Henry said, nodding in Dougie Vey's direction.

"I second that," Walter said.

Everyone watched as Luna and Dougie Vey chatted with Tilly and Teddy.

"How's Teddy's speech therapy coming along," Lila Mae asked Madge.

"He's managing a few words, but he still clings to his paper and pen."

They watched as Teddy scribbled notes and passed them to Luna and Dougie Vey. There seemed to be a deep conversation going back and forth with all the pieces of paper being passed by Teddy.

Suddenly Teddy looked toward Chance and waved. He scribbled another note and passed it to Luna. Then he guided Tilly toward Lila Mae and the group. He widened his eyes dramatically.

"What were you talking about with that man?" Madge hissed. She did her best to keep her voice down.

"They were talking about the casino and why that man decided to quit his job," Tilly said. She leaned in and whispered. "I don't like him one bit. He's as crooked as a snake."

CHAPTER FOUR

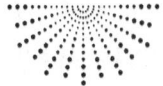

*L*ila Mae placed her handbag on the kitchen desk. She was lost in thought for a moment, but snapped out of it and filled the electric teakettle. Chance entered the house with Louie on his heels. He approached Lila Mae at the counter and put his arms around her.

"I love you," he said.

"I love you too," she said with a sigh.

Chance turned her around and raised her chin. "Don't worry. It will sort itself out. There's nothing anyone can do about Luna. She's a total misfit." He kissed her forehead.

"Grab the cups," she said. She went into the butler's pantry and retrieved a box with tea choices.

Chance looked over the choices. "Where's that cinnamon tea I like?"

Lila Mae grabbed a packet and held it out to him. She chose chamomile for herself and dropped her tea bag into the cup.

Chance pulled several scraps of paper out of his jacket pocket and studied them.

"What's that all about?" Lila Mae asked, glancing at the notes.

"Teddy wants me to call him. He gave me these notes from his conversation with Luna's beau," Chance said.

Lila Mae read over Chance's shoulder. "Huh. Looks like they were having a rather deep conversation."

"Being a former lawyer, Teddy saw several implications and his bells were clanging."

The water boiled, and Lila Mae poured. Chance grabbed the cups and brought them to the table. He pulled his cell phone out of his pocket and pulled up Teddy's number, and called him via speakerphone. A mechanical voice answered.

"Hello," the voice reverberated.

"Hi, Teddy, it's Chance.

"Hey Chance. Did you have a chance to look at my notes?" Teddy asked.

"If I'm reading this correctly, Dougie left the casino rather abruptly."

"He skirted around the subject when I asked if he had retired." Teddy said. The mechanical voice had a slight echo. "There's something fishy about his walking away from that job. Managers are typically paid very well, and they get bonuses."

Lila Mae sat quietly across the table from Chance.

"I'm going to do some low-key looking into this," Chance said.

"Let me know what you discover," Teddy said. "To change the subject slightly, Tilly and I are moving in together."

Chance and Lila Mae controlled their verbal surprise. Her mouth dropped open.

"I'm glad you two are taking the leap. You're good for each other. What did Madge say about you leaving the nest?" Chance asked.

Lila Mae swatted Chance.

"She was a little upset at first, but Carmichael calmed her down. Tilly and I spend a lot of time together, so neither Madge nor Suzanne see us by ourselves. We're always together."

"Where are you going to move to?" Lila Mae piped in.

"Oh, hi Lila Mae. We've got our eyes on a townhouse on Kirby Drive. It's within walking distance to Whole Foods, Trader Joe's and all the places we go to."

"You could walk to the movie theater on Richmond," Lila Mae said. "When do you think you're going to buy the townhouse?"

Teddy hesitated a moment. "Don't squeal on us, but I bought it last month."

Chance and Lila Mae had a jaw-dropping moment. "Do I hear wedding bells?" Chance asked.

"No, not yet. I want to be able to speak properly, and Tilly wants to finish her first year of college."

"That's smart," Lila Mae said. "Your secret is safe with us. When do you think you'll move in?"

"We're furniture shopping right now. That takes a while. We also want to swap out the refrigerator. We don't like the traditional side-by-side models. There's no room. We want the entire top to be a refrigerator and the bottom a freezer. But we may get a 100% refrigerator and a separate upright freezer."

"I know what you mean," Lila Mae said. "I like the French door split models myself."

"We're going to dinner with Chewie and Gina, so I'd better go," Teddy said.

"Have a good time," Chance and Lila Mae echoed. They stared at each other for a moment.

"Who would have thought Tilly would turn herself around one-hundred-eighty degrees?" Lila Mae said.

Chance shook his head. "More like a three-sixty-five spin if you ask me. In the past several months there's been so many screw-ups and changes for that girl it's hard to digest."

"Maybe there's still hope for Jeffie and Victor's little gold digger!" Lila Mae jested.

* * *

CHEWIE PARKED the dark chocolate Bentley in Hamilton's Steak House private parking lot on Main Street. Out of habit, he opened the back door where Teddy and Tilly sat, then jaunted around to the passenger side and helped Gina out.

The girls were dressed to perfection. Gina wore a purple, blue, and gray above-the-knee spaghetti-strap dress that hugged her curves. She carried a purple bolero sweater to stave off the freezing air conditioning, which was typical of Houston restaurants.

Tilly was glamorous in a beige, gold, and brown above her knees fitted dress. She braved the reputation of the restaurant in her sleeveless dress, knowing the maître d' would provide something if she was freezing.

Chewie and Teddy wore dress slacks, short-sleeved shirts, and casual jackets. Hamilton's didn't require a tie, although both men owned an assortment of business attire. They partnered up with their girlfriends and held hands as they walked away from the Bentley.

The demolition of the two blocks, which once held old shopping centers and an ancient apartment complex adjacent to Hamilton's, recently occurred to allow for more condominiums, townhouses, and apartments along the Red Line, Houston's downtown rail.

The razed lots were in the deplorable post-demo condition before construction, not entirely cleaned up, and was a magnet for gang-related activities and the denizens of that culture.

As the foursome walked to the steak house, several macho male gang members hooted and howled at the girls. Gina clenched Chewie's hand and practically dragged him away. The Asian-American's temper was steaming at the catcalls and lewd remarks.

Teddy placed his arm around Tilly's waist in a protective gesture.

"Don't stop!" Tilly said. "Don't look at them. It just fuels their ability to intimidate."

They picked up their pace and entered the steak house. The maître d' smiled at this familiar foursome. Before he could express his greeting, Chewie stepped forward.

"You have to do something about those thugs in the lot next to your parking lot."

The maître d' shook his head. "I'm sorry you had to experience a bit of discomfort. There will be police protection tonight. They typically get here by dusk." He snapped his fingers, and a waitstaff hurried over. "Show our guests to Table fourteen-A."

Teddy knew that table fourteen-A was in a quiet location with views of the Red Line. They had been seated at this table on several occasions and considered it *their table*. He slipped the maître d' a ten-dollar bill, pulled out his phone and typed. His mechanical voice said, "Thank you."

The maître d' appeared surprised. "Is that an app that helps you talk?"

Teddy typed. "Yes," the voice echoed. "There's a few bugs, but now I don't have to pass notes all the time."

The waiter escorted the group through the restaurant to their table. He presented menus and took their beverage orders and hurried away.

"I'm having my usual," Chewie said.

Gina wiggled her mouth as she studied the pages of the menu. Having made her decision, she closed the menu and smiled.

"What are you having?" Chewie asked.

"You'll hear soon enough," she teased.

Teddy typed. "I'm having the New York strip steak."

"Isn't that your usual?" Chewie asked.

"I guess it is," Teddy said.

Everyone waited on Tilly. "Okay. I'm ready," she said.

The waiter returned with their drinks. Vodka and tonic with a healthy shot of lime juice for Chewie, Merlot for Gina, Toohey's Old, an Australian beer, for Teddy, and a lime flavored sparkling water for Tilly. As was customary, they raised their glasses.

"Salut!" they said with gusto.

Each took a sip then turned their attention to the waiter. He was familiar with them and liked their toasts.

"Everyone ready to order?" he asked.

* * *

As CHEWIE PACKED AWAY the last bite of his ribeye, he noticed the others staring at him. "What? I don't scarf down my food like the three of you. I savor it and aid my digestion by eating slowly."

"You're always last," Gina said. "I can tell you love your ribeye's."

"I don't know where you put it all," Tilly said. "That baked potato was huge."

Teddy just smiled.

Everyone watched as the Red Line shot down the track, whistle blowing. The waiter returned with a dessert tray. "Can I tempt you with a molten brownie, caramel custard, coconut cake, or a slice of blueberry pie?"

"Let's split some custard," Gina said to Chewie.

"Okay," he said. He knew that really meant he would get a couple of bites and she would devour the majority.

The waiter turned his attention to Tilly and Teddy.

"I know you want that coconut cake," Tilly said.

Teddy gave the thumbs up sign.

The waiter whisked the dessert tray away and another wait staff removed their dinner plates. A third wait staff served coffee.

"We found our living room furniture," Tilly said, excited.

"I love furniture shopping," Gina said. "What did you get?"

"Teddy wanted a red leather sofa, but I told him it's better to have a neutral color like black or dark brown so we can accessorize with colors," Tilly said. "I think after a year or two we would get sick of a red sofa."

Teddy typed. "It makes sense. Plus, with a traditional color we can change out pillows and throws for different color combinations."

"Did you get recliners?" Chewie asked.

"I want one of those heated massage recliners," Tilly said. She dug out her phone and thumbed through pictures and showed Gina and Chewie her choice. "This doesn't have those huge ugly slots for your legs. I hate those."

"Oh! I like that. I can't wait to try it out," Gina said. "Hurry up and get moved in so we can come over."

After everyone had their fill and sipped the last of their coffee, the head waiter returned with two payment wallets and presented them to the men. They completed their cash transactions and exited the restaurant.

"Do you want to take the train downtown and walk off the calories?" Gina asked.

"I don't want to leave the Bentley here," Chewie said, taking in the deplorable lot.

Suddenly, six ghetto-dressed, tattooed and pierced thugs were close behind them. Chewie pulled the fob out of his pocket and clicked it open.

"Get in the car," he told the others.

The girls rushed to the car and climbed inside. Gina clicked the locking mechanism. She and Tilly looked frightened. Gina got out her phone and texted someone.

Chewie and Teddy stood their ground.

"Got you a real nice ride," one guy said. "Bet you have a wallet full of cash."

"Tell those purty gurls they don't have to be afraid of me," another said. He stuck his studded tongue out and waggled it suggestively.

"Come on, man. Give up the keys," one of them said.

Chewie held his hand out and waved them forward. "If you think you can get past me, give it a try. Hope you have good insurance."

Passersby on the sidewalk slowed and watched the drama unfold. A woman held her cell phone out and shot a video sequence.

Chewie and Teddy stood side-by-side. As the gang approached, surrounding them, they rearranged themselves until they were back-to-back. One of the guys rushed Chewie. Unknown to him, he was walking into the personal space of a Shaolin Kung Fu master. Chewie's air ballet and quick moves dispatched the guy so quickly the others hesitated.

One gave Teddy the benefit of a doubt and struck out at him. Being a welterweight boxer during college, Teddy was no slouch in the protection department. Although it had been a couple of decades since he was in the ring, he stepped up in form.

Teddy had a longer reach than his opponent, plus organized sports prepared you better for street attacks. The unlucky gang member heard his nose crack as Teddy's fist smashed him lightning fast.

Chewie and Teddy were now surrounded by a heap of bleeding, bleating and broken gang members when a police car pulled up and parked followed by a Lexus. The officer was on his radio calling for backup to cart the gang members away.

Chance swaggered toward Chewie and Teddy. "Gina should have known you'd take these punks down."

"I think I broke this one's arm," Chewie said.

"This guy has a broken nose," Teddy said, pointing.

The officer looked at the battered and bruised group on the ground then turned his attention to Chewie and Teddy. "Glad you were prepared to defend yourself. We've had numerous complaints about these scumbags. Thanks to you, they will be out of commission for a while."

Gina and Tilly got out of the car and approached Chance and the others. Gina looked Chewie over. "You've got blood on your jacket!"

"Not mine." Chewie smiled and kissed her.

* * *

BAMBI WAS TAKING a much-needed break while Trevor napped. She sprawled on the sofa and turned the TV on. She brought up YouTube videos and focused on Houston. She yawned as she scrolled through the previews.

Suddenly, she sprung to a sitting position and clicked on a familiar face. The action started. Her lips parted in surprise as she watched Chewie lay out the grungy thugs, along with Teddy boxing his way out of his situation.

She scrambled for her phone, half hidden in the sofa cushions and fumbled through her recent conversations and pressed Call Back.

"Lila Mae! Pull up YouTube Houston! Hurry!"

Bambi looked for the identifier number and rattled it off to Lila Mae.

* * *

LILA MAE, Amelia, and Chiquita watched the action on the flat-screen TV in the living room, enthralled. Chiquita squealed as Chewie leaped through the air and smashed one of the thugs with his foot. No sooner had his feet touched the ground, he swung around in a graceful dance and connected an open palm to one of the gang members' faces. It was over within moments. The sidewalk was littered with broken, bleeding, groaning bodies.

"That's our protector!" Lila Mae all but shouted. "I'm so glad Chewie is part of our family!"

Amelia smiled slyly. "The action in the Goose bar was better, though."

Lila Mae elbowed Amelia gently as they shared a giggle. Chiquita looked askance at the women.

"Oh, all right. You deserve to see this show," Amelia said. She grabbed the controller and pulled up Chewie's debut on YouTube.

Chiquita watched, awe-stuck, mouth hanging open. She let loose a string of words in Spanish.

"English, Chiquita!" Amelia said.

"This guy's incredible! You'd never guess in a million years that he's a walking weapon!"

Louie barked and scratched on the kitchen door.

"Oops," Lila Mae said as she headed into the kitchen to let Louie in. She opened the door, and he bounced through the doorway. He stopped, looked up at Lila Mae, and whined.

"What's wrong, Louie?"

He whined again. Lila Mae scooped him up in her arms to comfort him. "What's the matter, little boy? Did Scooter snub you?"

"Who's Scooter?" Chiquita asked.

"He's the neighbor's cat," Amelia said. "Scooter and Louie have a strange relationship. One minute they're friends, the next they're fighting, and Louie does not come out the winner."

"Ooohhh," Chiquita said as she scratched the top of Louie's head. "Maybe you need a nicer friend, Louie."

"I keep telling him Scooter is not his friend, but he won't listen," Lila Mae said. "Even Uncle Tito has tried to get it through to him, but we can't do anything about it."

The house phone rang loudly.

Amelia jumped. "Why's that ringer so loud?" She scrutinized Chiquita suspiciously. She grabbed the phone and glanced at the Caller ID. "It's Bambi."

"Alcott residence. Amelia, head chef and friend to Lila Mae, speaking," she said. She ended with a giggle. "Yeah, she's here. Hold on." Amelia passed the phone to Lila Mae.

"Thanks for calling about Chewie! That was something else," Lila Mae said. She listened, her face lighting up. "Oh, that sounds like wonderful fun. Let's do it! You've got the entire list, right? Send out a preliminary note with a couple of dates that work for Jewel and Alvin. I can't wait!"

Lila Mae disconnected the call. "We're going to have a family night at the bowling alley!"

Amelia became thoughtful. "We should make a list so we don't forget anyone."

Lila Mae grabbed a yellow tablet and a pen. "Good idea. We should invite Pecos and Dolly."

Chiquita's face lit up. "Don't forget to invite Jingo!"

CHAPTER FIVE

*T*here were no available parking spaces in the Chaline Bowl parking lot. A car circled the lot and finally gave up and parked on the street. Susie manned the front desk and greeted people. Jewel walked the floor in customer service mode.

Jewel's walkie-talkie squawked. "Jewel, I've got a serious jam on lane nine," Alvin said.

Jewel pressed the button on her device. "Okay. I'll move them over to eleven until you can clear it."

"K."

She hurried in the direction of lane nine, but was almost knocked down by two boys running wildly. Jewel pulled out a whistle and blew it at the boys. "Stop running, or you will have to leave!"

The boys slowed to a fast walk. She tweeted her whistle once more. They looked over their shoulders. Jewel shook her head sternly. The boy's scowled, but they slowed to a walk. She watched with approval then hurried over to the jammed lane.

"Hi, folks. Would you mind if I moved you over to lane

eleven while the jam is being reset?" Jewel said. "I'll give you a free game for your troubles."

There were no complaints as the foursome gathered their food, drinks and belongings and followed Jewel. She sat at the console and programed in their free game.

"There you go. Thanks for being understanding," she said.

She hurried on her way and spotted her boss. "Hi, boss. Are you and the family having a good time?"

Bambi patted Jewel on the back. "We're having a blast. How's it going?"

Jewel reported the jam that Alvin was tending to, and explained that Mr. Nettie had the flu.

"Oh, that poor man!" Bambi said. "He's quite old, so I hope he'll be okay."

"Yeah, he's getting up there, but he'll pull through," Jewel said. "I'm walking the floor until he returns."

"Well, I'd better get back to the folks," Bambi said.

The Alcotts and their extended family members took up multiple lanes. Joseph's guides and angels were riding on his shoulder. Every ball he released was a strike. His team comprised Chance, Pecos Ektadoro, Cissy, Zoe, and Madge. His teammates were pretty decent bowlers. Pecos swore he had never bowled before, but he took to the lane like he was born with the ball in his hand.

Bambi had decided that couples had to split up to make it more interesting. Rick, Walter, Tilly, Lila Mae, Jingo, and Henry made up a team, and Teddy, Dolly Sanchez, Amelia, Dorothea, and Victor made up another team.

Carmichael, Luna, Bambi, Chewie, and Chiquita made up a team. And Jeffie, Gina, Dougie, Suzanne, and Lawrence made the last team. Gray watched from his wheelchair on the sidelines since his broken femur was still on the mend.

Jingo and Chiquita spent every spare moment either staring at each other, completely smitten, or chatting while waiting their turns. Jingo had fairly good bowling skills, but Chiquita couldn't focus on the game.

Madge almost knocked herself out with her ball, but when she released it, she typically made strikes. Everyone stood back when Dorothea was up for a turn. Dorothea was totally uncoordinated.

Every second or third ball she released ended up in someone else's lane. Bambi tried her best to correct Dorothea's wild swing by having her change her stance every two or three boards on the floor, but it was hopeless.

"Don't worry, Dorothea, we can come during off-hours and I'll give you lessons," Bambi said.

"Just stand back so I don't kill you," Dorothea said.

Luna and Dougie Vey ate pizza with Gray. Dougie chugged his fourth beer. His voice grew louder with each red cup.

"We should try to get a casino here in Houston. Plenty of land. Got the population," Dougie said.

"They won't allow it," Gray said. "Why didn't you stay in Vegas if you long for a casino?"

"Don't long for one, just thinking of the money," Dougie said. "Make someone rich."

The family games ended with Joseph's team the winners.

"Okay everyone, head over to my house," Bambi announced.

Everyone turned in their shoes at the shoe counter and headed out the door.

DOUGIE AND LUNA drove through River Oaks. He inadvertently turned on Del Monte.

"You were supposed to turn on Olympia," Luna said tactfully.

They cruised past Lila Mae's house. Kimberly and Judson Munson were strolling down the sidewalk.

"Did you see that?" Dougie hollered.

"What?" Luna said.

"Those people!" He made a U-turn and drove slowly. Dougie held his phone up and snapped a picture.

"What's so interesting about them?" Luna said. "Slow down. Take the next left."

"I know someone who's looking for them," Dougie said with a glint in his eyes.

He turned left, and they found Bambi's house just as Pecos and Dolly arrived. They followed the stream of bowlers up the driveway to the front door. Pecos was about to ring the bell but Charlemagne opened the door holding a piece of paper and a roll of tape.

"I was just going to hang up a sign for people to come inside instead of waiting for someone to answer the door," she said. "Won't you come in?"

She looked beyond the group.

"He's not here," Pecos said.

"Oh," Charlemagne said, disappointed. She had hoped to see Uncle Tito again.

They all went inside the house. Charlemagne pointed for everyone to go to the great room.

CHAPTER SIX

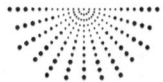

*L*ouie sat and stared out of the bottom window in the French door. He gave a couple of little *ruffs* at Scooter who taunted him from his perch atop the fence. Suddenly, Louie jumped to his feet and barked so ferociously he bounced back a few steps. Louie raced through the house barking. He jumped against the French doors in the living room, but could not see his friend.

He rushed back to the kitchen door and searched the fence line. His friend was gone.

LILA MAE, Amelia and Chiquita munched on sandwiches and sipped water. Chiquita picked up a chip and looked it over.

"I've never seen these before," she said. She took a bite of a whitish-colored chip with brown specks. "Oh, these are so good!"

"Those are taro chips," Amelia said.

A loud knock sounded on the kitchen door. All three women turned their heads toward the door.

"Who in the world could that be?" Lila Mae said.

Louie ran to the door, barking all the way. Amelia got up and glanced that way. "Oh, no. I wonder what they're doing here," she said.

Lila Mae dabbed her mouth with a napkin. "Who is it?"

"The Munsons."

"You're serious?" Lila Mae stood and marched to the door with Amelia and Chiquita on her heels, and opened it. Louie dashed outside.

"Kimberly, Judson. What brings you to my doorstep?"

Kimberly's expression was filled with venom as she stared at Lila Mae. "Where is he?"

Lila Mae and Amelia shared a questioning look. "Please explain your cryptic question," Lila Mae said.

Judson cleared his throat. "Scooter is missing."

Amelia flung her arms wide. "He's not here."

"Why would you even think he would be in my house?" Lila Mae asked.

"The scratching incident," Kimberly snarled.

"And you think I would have taken him in after that huge fight?" Lila Mae asked. Her tone suggested she thought her neighbors were idiots.

They all stepped outside into the sun. Louie came over to Lila Mae and sat down.

"When was the last time you saw him?" Lila Mae asked.

The Munson's conferred by making eye contact with each other. "Yesterday afternoon."

"He's most likely around the neighborhood somewhere," Amelia said. "It's not like he's on a leash."

Louie jumped to his feet with a *ruff*. He took off across the side lawn, barking like a lunatic. Everyone moved in his direction. They watched as Louie stopped in the middle of the backyard, head raised to the sky, barking nonstop.

A hawk swooped in and grabbed a squirrel. Louie started

barking until the hawk was out of sight. Louie returned to the group. He whined pitifully.

"Oh, no!" Lila Mae said. "I think Louie's trying to tell us what happened to Scooter."

Kimberly sniffed in abject disgust.

"We're sorry to have disturbed you," Judson said. With that, he ushered Kimberly down the sidewalk by the elbow.

"Those are terrible people," Chiquita hissed.

"And you haven't even been around them that long," Amelia said. "What a piece of work those two are."

"Poor Scooter. Louie is going to be very lonely," Lila Mae said.

They walked back to the house and silently ate their sandwiches.

CHAPTER SEVEN

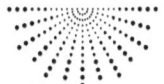

*C*hewie knocked on Dorothea's kitchen door. Joseph rushed to the door. "Hey, cuz. Come in. I'll be ready in a minute."

Chewie took in the sight before him: Joseph's white chef jacket was stained beyond any modern washing miracle product. "Look at you! You're a mess!"

"The babies are a handful," Joseph said as he rushed out of the room.

Dorothea entered the room. "Hi, Chewie. Where are you and Joseph going?"

"We're all going out to dinner and a movie," Chewie said. He took in Dorothea's bedraggled appearance. "You okay?"

Dorothea plopped onto a barstool. "Even with full-time staff, the girls run me ragged."

"You probably need a spa day," Chewie suggested.

"That would be so wonderful, but what I'd really like is one undisturbed night's sleep. Henry gets up and helps when he hears the girls cry, but even with the live-in Nanny, it's full-time work," Dorothea said.

Chewie swallowed hard. He was definitely out of his element.

Joseph rushed into the room, all spit-shined in a polo shirt, khaki pants and soft loafers. "Ready!"

"You look so nice," Dorothea said.

"Yeah, no baby burp," Joseph said.

* * *

CHEWIE AND JOSEPH stopped at the host stand at Vietopia in the Kroger shopping center at Westpark and Buffalo Speedway while Gina slipped around the corner. She popped back to the front.

"They're here," Gina announced. She turned to the hostess. "Our friends are here."

Chewie and Joseph followed Gina around the corner to a large, round table where Teddy, Tilly and a gorgeous blond man sat. Joseph looked from the blond man then over to his cousin, silently questioning Chewie.

Chewie blushed, shrugged and nudged Joseph forward. "This is Eirik. This is my cousin Joseph I told you about."

Eirik stood. Joseph's eyes followed the tall, muscular Norseman to a standing position. He towered a good five inches over Joseph. They shook hands, but did not release them.

"How nice to meet you, uh," Joseph said, stumbling to say the name correctly. He noticed a dimple in Eirik's right cheek and smiled.

"The pleasure's all mine," Eirik said with a hint of an accent. "I'm Norwegian. A lot of people think my name is Eric, which in a sense it is, but it is pronounced Ay-rik."

"Ay-rik," Joseph said, feeling out the strange name. He and Eirik released the handshake and stared at each other, highly interested in what they saw.

Gina took the helm and the group seated. She strategically

seated Joseph and Eirik across from each other. "Have you been waiting very long?"

"We. Just. Arrived," Teddy managed to say.

"Oh, wow!" Joseph said. "Your voice is coming back!"

"Congratulations!" Gina said.

"The therapist has made a big difference," Tilly said. Her face radiated happiness.

"Still. Sore," Teddy said. He pointed to his throat. "Vocal. Cords."

The waiter came and took their drink order.

"Are you drinking that throat tea I suggested?" Joseph asked.

Teddy made a face.

"I know it tastes terrible. Add honey or jelly, or something else. It will help your vocal cords!" Joseph admonished.

Eirik stared at Teddy for a moment. "Did you have a stroke?"

Teddy shook his head.

"He suffered from PTSD after this big case he worked on and went into a coma," Tilly explained. "There's no physical reason for his inability to talk." She rubbed Teddy's shoulders and pecked him on the cheek.

"Have you tried hypnosis?" Eirik asked.

Teddy slowly shook his head, staring at Eirik, his interest piqued.

"I will cure you," Eirik said with an air of confidence.

Everyone gawked openly at the big blond man. Joseph nudged his cousin. Chewie shrugged.

"Have you done this before?" Tilly asked.

"Doctors send trauma patients to me all the time," Eirik said with pride. "Ninety-five percent success rate. Look at my website." He dug into a pocket and handed out business cards.

Eirik swung his eyes over to Joseph. "Chewie told me that you use old-world Chinese methods for many things."

Joseph tittered. "That is correct. I protect the family from psychic attacks and many other things."

Eirik smiled. He winked at Joseph. A flaming red blush crept up Joseph's face to his ears. He tittered.

* * *

MADGE WORKED her way down an aisle in Whole Foods with her cart brimming with neatly wrapped packages of seafood and meat, and bags of veggies and fruit. A man and woman charged down the aisle with their cart toward Madge, bike helmets in the child seat area. They stopped at the coffee and perused the shelves, grabbed a container and continued on their way.

"Harrumph," Madge muttered. She continued down the aisle and approached the checkout stand. The biking couple was at the next checkout line behind someone. Madge pulled her own bags out of the bottom of the cart and handed them to the clerk. She completed her purchase and wheeled the cart out to her nougat Bentley with the red interior.

Two loud rumbles close by broke her out of her reverie of the moment. She turned toward the offending noise, a full scowl on her face. She watched as the biker woman backed her neon purple three-wheeled motorcycle out of her parking space, followed by her partner. They zoomed out of the parking lot and disappeared down Kirby Drive.

Madge closed her mouth. She stared after the twosome, lost in fantasy. After a moment, she gathered her wits, got in the car and headed home. She pulled into the driveway and tooted the horn. Carmichael emerged from the colossal house and stood at the trunk. Madge popped the trunk and got out of the car.

"I've got to run an errand, but wanted to get groceries home because it's so hot," she said.

"No problem," Carmichael said. "What's up?"

Madge plastered a haughty expression on her face. "Nothing, why?"

Carmichael shrugged. "See you later." He grabbed the bags

and headed to the house. He unloaded the bags onto the kitchen counter, then pulled out his phone. Carmichael texted rapidly:

Madge is acting weird.

A ding sounded.

What do you mean? Sick? Did she have a stroke? Should you call 9-1-1? Amelia texted back.

No, you know... weird. She brought back groceries, but took off again. She had this look on her face.

The phone dinged again.

Did she say where she was going?

Carmichael looked frustrated at the phone. He held the phone to his ear. After one ring, Amelia answered.

"No, she didn't say where she was going. Said she had to run an errand, but it's something sneaky—I just know it!"

"Well, you can never tell with Madge," Amelia said. "I'll ask Lila Mae when she gets home."

"Let me know," Carmichael said.

* * *

AMELIA DRUMMED her fingers on the counter. She shook her head—thoughts of Madge in past escapades tickling her brain, the best being the shooting range with Teddy. She looked out the French doors and shook her head yet again. Chiquita and Jingo were focused on each other. Chiquita tipped her heel in the air, listening to him. Jingo fidgeted. "Uh oh. I know a husband hunter when I see one."

Louie trotted up to Amelia and gave a little *ruff.* Lila Mae's chocolate Bentley pulled up the driveway. The garage door rolled up, and the car rolled forward.

"Your mama's home," Amelia said.

Louie whined and stood on his hind legs and pawed the lower glass pane. Amelia opened the door. Louie darted past her as she stepped outside.

Lila Mae popped the trunk and got out of the car. She retrieved her dry cleaning from the back seat. Amelia met her at the trunk, reached in and grabbed a Whole Foods paper sack.

"Your sister is up to something," Amelia said.

Lila Mae frowned. "Which one?"

"The one who does goofy things."

"What's Madge up to?" Lila Mae said.

Amelia pulled out her cell phone and brought up her conversation with Carmichael. Lila Mae read and used her thumb to scroll.

"Looks like we'll have to wait for the reveal," Lila Mae said. "There's no telling what's going on in that head of hers."

CHAPTER EIGHT

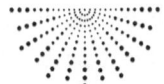

Madge's nougat Bentley pulled into the Team Mancuso Powersports dealership on the Southwest Freeway. She parked the car and got out, staring at all the colorful motorcycles. She went into the showroom and stopped in her tracks. A brand-new Can-Am Spyder RT Limited six-speed semi-automatic champagne metallic motorcycle was ten feet in front of her. She placed her hand on her chest.

A weary salesman approached Madge. "May I help you, ma'am?"

"What other colors does this come in, and do you give riding lessons?" She stammered out.

The salesman gave her a look-over and snapped a brochure out of a stand and flipped it open with flourish. "Here you go."

Madge looked over the color chart. "What if I want a color that isn't on the chart?"

"Special order, but that adds to the cost and adds about six weeks to the delivery," he said. "If that's not a problem, I can get the paperwork started for you."

Madge dipped into her purse and pulled out her checkbook.

"How much do you want to put down?" the salesman asked as he steered Madge to a small room.

"I'll pay in full," Madge declared.

The salesman smiled like a clown, his commission dangling in front of him. He showed her to a chair and went around to the other side of the desk and logged into the computer. "I'll need your driver's license and insurance card."

Madge dug her license and insurance card out of her wallet and slid them across the table surface.

"You'll have to arrange for motorcycle insurance prior to delivery," he told her.

"That's no problem," she said. Madge dipped into her purse again and pulled out a paint sample. "This is the color I'd like." She slid the paint sample across to the salesman.

He looked at the neon-aqua paint. "Hhmm. Let me check with my manager to see if the body shop…."

"The factory should be able to match this," Madge said in a steely voice.

The salesman stood, sample in hand, and excused himself. "I'll be back in a moment."

Madge studied the brochure. She read every panel. The salesman and his manager strode into the office. The manager held out his hand.

"Otto Schmidt, Mrs. Abercrombie," he said. They shook hands. "I wanted to see if you had a second color choice in case the factory…"

"I want that color," Madge said. She drilled him with a haughty look, letting him know there was no room for negotiation.

The manager smiled widely, looked at his associate, and said he would be back in a jiffy. The salesman sat at the desk and started typing Madge's information into the computer. "I've never done a special order before, so my manager will have to help me with some of the details."

His cell phone rang. He looked at the caller ID and answered. "Yes, sir. I'll get out of the file and you can take over."

He turned to Madge. "My manager's going to fill in the particulars, then he'll be here in a few minutes."

Madge perused the motorcycle paraphernalia on the walls along with ads from oil companies, parts, gear, and clothing. As she gawked at different posters for leather jackets, boots, and headgear, the manager bounded into the office with paperwork.

"Okay, Mrs. Abercrombie, I talked to the factory and there's no problem. They can do an aqua metallic that will sparkle in the sunlight and moonlight!"

Madge beamed a huge smile. "Wonderful!"

"There's an additional cost of twenty-two hundred dollars," he added.

"Is that all? I thought it would be a lot more," Madge said.

"The total comes to thirty-eight thousand, six-hundred forty-six dollars and ninety-five cents," Otto said.

Madge clicked her pen and wrote the check.

* * *

BERNIE WAS SNOOZING on the sofa in his private suite at Lake Sides Assisted Living Center. His cellphone buzzed and wobbled on the coffee table. He snorted, sputtered, woke up and looked around for the disturbance to his nap. Bernie noticed his phone moving in a circle as the buzzing continued. He reached out and grabbed it.

"Hello?" he said with a sleep-voice. He listened as the caller talked nonstop. "Slow down, Herman." Bernie frowned. "Did you have any idea this was coming at you?"

Bernie grunted in disbelief. "Okay. I'll be there in an hour."

He disconnected the call and fumed silently. He clicked on a name in his contacts. After two rings, the call connected. "Chewie, I've got an emergency meeting in an hour." He disconnected the call and clicked on another name in his contacts list.

"Madge, you need to drop everything and head to the factory. We've got an emergency. Be there in an hour. I'll call your sisters and Bambi." He didn't give her a chance to make an excuse. He hung up on her.

After Bernie made his calls, he headed to his bedroom and changed his shirt. The elevator bell dinged, and Chewie stepped into the living room.

"I'll be right out," Bernie hollered.

Chewie sat in one of the side chairs and checked his messages. He answered texts from Gina and Teddy. He read a message from Carmichael about a problem he was having with his computer and told him he would check it out as soon as possible.

Bernie came out of the bedroom, dressed in a suit.

"You look nice. Where to?" Chewie asked.

Bernie shuffled over to him. "We have a situation at the factory."

Chewie took a long look at Bernie. "Do I need to kick someone's butt?"

"Not likely, but it appears the workers are a bit disgruntled and may walk off the job, and there's a big order that has to be prepared and shipped. The girls and Bambi are going to meet us there."

Chewie grabbed the walker that was leaning against the wall and presented it to Bernie.

"Must you?" Bernie asked with a snarl.

"Why fight it?" Chewie asked. "This thing keeps you from falling. Do you want to break a hip like Mr. Miller in three-B?"

"Bud was snockered. He couldn't have seen that step down at that restaurant if he had Hubble lenses for glasses. And it was dark in there."

"Don't make excuses for him. If either of you had taken your walkers, they would have seated your party in a different location," Chewie said.

Bernie fumed—he couldn't stand it when Chewie was right, which was most of the time. He grabbed the hated walker and made his way to the elevator with Chewie at his elbow.

* * *

As Chewie drove, Bernie sat in the back seat working on his phone. "Gina, is Walter busy?" He listened and waited for several minutes.

"Walter? I'm heading over to the factory. Herman David just called. Seems there may be a strike or something brewing. Do we have worker's agreements? Okay, good. I'll see you there."

Ten minutes later, Chewie pulled into the half-empty parking lot for the old red brick five-story building and parked the Bentley amid the Chevys, Fords, Toyotas, and Hondas. Before Chewie opened his door, a woman rapped on his window.

"What's your business here?" she asked, all huffy.

Chewie carefully opened the door, which pushed the woman aside as he stepped out of the car. "That's none of your business, ma'am."

"It IS my business when someone rich pulls up in their big ole car when I can barely feed my kids on the salary I make," she said.

Bernie opened his door. Chewie sprang over to assist him out of the car, then closed the door and popped the trunk. He pulled out the walker, and for once, Bernie did not curse the contraption.

"What do you mean you don't earn enough to feed your kids?" Bernie demanded.

"Five-hundred twenty-three dollars a week before taxes. Do the math," the woman said. "I've got two kids. They don't get any extras, just necessities. I've been a loyal employee for fifteen years, and this is all I get for it?"

Bernie looked her over. "I'm here to talk to the manager and find out what's going on. What's your name?"

"Pearl Hicks."

"I remember you," Bernie said. "You were married to Elgin. He died five years ago—I'm sorry for your loss."

The woman stared hard at Bernie, trying to place him. She cleared her throat loudly and moved aside. Chewie maneuvered around the woman, and he and Bernie went to the front door and entered the building.

The reception desk was vacant. Bernie looked around quizzically. "There's supposed to be someone here at all times to greet visitors."

"The parking lot was almost empty," Chewie said.

Bernie pulled his cellphone out and called a number. "Herman? I'm in the lobby. There's no one at the reception desk. What's going on?" He listened for a moment. "Okay, Chewie and I are on our way up."

He pocketed his phone, grabbed his walker and trudged off toward the old elevator with Chewie at his side. "Punch the fifth-floor button."

The elevator door opened, and they entered and rode up to the executive suites.

CHAPTER NINE

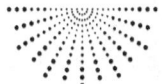

$\mathcal{H}$erman David stood when he heard the elevator ding the arrival of his employer. He attempted to tidy his desk, but there were so many stacks it was a futile effort.

Bernie's walker made a clomp-clomp sound as he and Chewie walked down the short hallway and entered Herman's office. They looked around at the chaos in Herman's office. Bernie's hackles rose.

"What the heck is going on here?" Bernie asked in a huff of exasperation.

Herman fidgeted. While he was younger, taller, and bulkier than his employer, he was intimidated by the aged billionaire. "There's just so much to do and it's hard to keep track of everything."

Bernie sat in front of the desk. Chewie stood behind his chair. Bernie turned to him. "Sit." He then focused on Herman. "Sit."

Chewie took the chair beside Bernie and gave Herman the once-over, clearly showing his disdain for the man. Herman all but fell into his chair, his head flitting from Bernie to Chewie.

"First up, where is everyone? Where's the receptionist? Where's your secretary? Where's the HR lady?"

Chewie leaned in to Bernie. "Admin."

Bernie stared at Chewie.

"New title. Get with it," Chewie whispered.

"Whatever—where is she?" Bernie asked.

"Oh…well… she quit several months ago," Herman sputtered.

Bernie looked askance at Herman. "Why did she quit, and why didn't you hire someone else?"

Herman grabbed a crumpled paper napkin from one of the piles on his desk and dabbed his forehead. "She was having problems at home, so she thought it best to quit and take care of herself."

"And the receptionist, and the HR lady?" Bernie asked.

"They just moved on," Herman said. He was sweating bullets.

Chewie leaned in to Bernie. "May I speak with you in private?"

Bernie squinted, thought for a moment, and turned to the manager. "Herman, why don't you go outside and direct the girls when they arrive. Bambi's never been here before and won't know where to park or where to go once she arrives. She'll be in a yellow car."

"Sure. Sure," Herman said. He bolted out of his chair and out the door of the office. The elevator dinged as the doors opened.

Chewie put a finger to his lips, got up, and stealthily walked out of the office. He checked the office to the right, then the office to the left. Satisfied that the manager had indeed taken the elevator down to the lobby, he returned to the office, closing the door behind him.

"I wanted to get him out of here," Chewie said. He walked to the desk, sat down in Herman's chair in front of the computer and clacked on the keyboard for several moments. "I'm locking him out of the entire system until we know what's going on.

Nothing he said makes much sense, and I suspect he's been stealing from you."

"I bet you're right. There's something not right, and it looks like a huge mess. When the girls get here, we'll determine what needs to be done," Bernie said.

Chewie clacked away, looking at the computer system and the structure of programs, files, then accounts and logins. "We need to see the books, payroll and the bank accounts. I think this guy has embezzled from the company. I suggest you fire him, but don't let him pack up even his personal belongings. Tell him we will have them delivered to him at the address we have on file for him."

Bernie thought for a moment. "I can't just fire him without knowing the problems."

Chewie thought of a solution. "Then give him a paid vacation. He's locked out of the system, but not out of the building. He could still come in and trash things, shred paper files, and destroy important documentation. How long has he worked here?"

Bernie tapped his fingers. "If I'm not mistaken, about ten years. He replaced Bill Sanders, who had retired. Call Gina. Ask her to get that locksmith out here immediately. I want every door that has a lock to be re-keyed. He'll have to go from one end of the property to the other to make sure every single door, no matter if it's a bathroom or what, is re-keyed. Let's get each floor re-keyed with the same key for the entire floor. When we have everything under control, we can re-key each office with its separate keys."

Chewie got out his phone.

The elevator dinged. Chewie got up and opened the office door. He motioned the girls and Walter inside. He stepped outside the door and called Gina and reiterated the instructions.

* * *

AMELIA TURNED a thoughtful face to Chiquita. "I think something is brewing at the factory, and we should prepare a meal for the troops. Let's go to Pete's and get something for the crowd. Then I'll text everyone and let them know the menu."

Chiquita removed her apron and hung it on a hook inside the butler's pantry. "Okay. What do you think is going on?"

Amelia shrugged. "I don't know, but when Bernie calls an emergency meeting, it IS an emergency."

They grabbed their purses and left the house.

* * *

VICTOR WAS SEEING patients every twelve minutes, moving from exam room to exam room. He was currently busy with Mrs. Fulham when a commotion sounded in the hallway. He recognized Nurse Eva's strong German voice, which escalated into a shouting match.

"Excuse me for a minute, Mrs. Fulham, I'd better see what's going on," Victor said.

He stripped off his non-latex gloves, dumped them in the hazardous waste receptacle, and stepped out into the hallway. Two big, burly men were barely held at bay by Nurse Eva.

"What's going on here?" Victor asked.

One of the brutes shoved Nurse Eva out of the way and barreled up to Victor. "Where are they?" he demanded.

Victor looked at the man questioningly. "Where's who?"

"Dougie Vey and your daughter," the creep said.

"This is an OB-GYN office—you know, for women who are pregnant," Victor explained. "They certainly aren't here."

The second man came forward. "Don't get smart with us. You either tell us where they are, or we trash the place." To demonstrate, he clobbered a rolling cart that contained portable monitoring equipment. The equipment went flying and landed on the carpet.

Victor watched in shock. "That's thousands of dollars of equipment! Are you two crazy?"

The two men approached an open exam room. They went inside and commenced to swipe everything from the counters to the floor and bashing equipment. Glass and metal crashing to the floor was loud.

"Call nine-one-one," he shouted to Nurse Eva. He shooed her out of the hallway into the reception area. "Okay! Please stop," he said to the thugs.

"You gonna tell us where they are, or do we demonstrate a little more?"

"They're at the San Luis resort down at Galveston," Victor said.

One of the brutes grabbed Victor by his white coat and lifted him off the floor. "You're positive about that? If we was to waste a trip, we'll burn your house down."

"That's where they are," Victor gasped out.

Sirens sounded in the distance, approaching fast. The two thugs looked at each other and headed toward the red exit sign. Chance and two policemen rushed through the door from the reception area. Two more cops came through the door at the exit, blocking the thugs' escape.

One of the thugs reached inside his jacket. Chance had his gun out in a split second. "Hands where I can see them."

Both thugs reluctantly raised their hands.

"Cuff them," Chance said.

The police handcuffed the thugs and led them outside.

Chance approached Victor. "Are you okay?"

Nurse Eva rushed to Victor and looked him over. "I'm glad they didn't hurt you!"

Victor sat in the chair beside the weight scale. "It could have been a lot worse. Nurse Eva, take pictures of all the damage for the insurance company, then call the building maintenance and see if they can help clean this up."

"What happened? I take it this was a visit from Dougie Vey's Las Vegas friends?" Chance asked.

"They kept asking where Dougie and Luna were. I told them the first thing that popped into my head—the San Luis. I sure as hell didn't want them at my house. They said they'd burn it to the ground!" Victor said.

"Let me see what information I can get out of them so we know what we're dealing with. Call Jeffie and warn her. Maybe get security teams at the house and office just to be on the safe side," Chance said.

"Good idea. I'll have Jeffie make the arrangements," Victor said.

Chance patted him on the back, then left.

* * *

Madge rushed into the manager's office, followed by her sisters and Walter. Her feet were clad with sparkly flip-flops and her toes were separated by purple pedicure wedges while neon emerald green polish dried.

"What is this all about?" she thundered. "I had to leave my mani-pedi appointment!"

Bernie's demeanor changed as he stared down his eldest daughter. "I'm sorry to interrupt such a crucial event with this trivial business."

The elevator dinged again, and Bambi stepped out and joined the meeting.

"Let's move to the conference room," Bernie said. "Where's Herman?"

"Was that the man who showed me where to park?" Bambi asked.

"Most likely," Chewie said.

"He left," Bambi said.

Chewie and Bernie gave each other the thumbs-up sign.

"This place is a mess," Lila Mae said, shocked as she looked around the manager's office.

Every surface was covered with stacks of paperwork, file folders, and unopened mail. Piles of paper sat on the floor around the perimeter of the office.

"Chewie locked him out of the system until we know what we're dealing with," Bernie explained.

"Good thinking," Walter said.

They moved to the conference room, and Walter set his briefcase on the dark cherry-wood table. He unlocked the case and pulled out several thick manila folders and set those on the table. Everyone sat.

"It looks like we have all been remiss in our duties," Walter said. "While we have received monthly reports and statements, from the looks of Herman's office, I'd say we were deceived into thinking everything was running smoothly."

"Do you mean no one ever came up here to check the inner workings?" Bambi asked, surprised.

Bernie huffed in exasperation. "Appears we gave the fox the keys to the chicken coop."

"Was that lady... Pearl outside when you came in?" Chewie asked.

"Yes, she about knocked me down," Dorothea said in a snippy voice.

"Why don't I ask her to sit at the front desk and wait for the locksmith?" Chewie suggested.

"Good idea," Walter said.

Chewey took off to find Pearl.

Bernie took charge and explained the conversation with Herman David. Walter flipped open a folder that contained HR information and ran his finger down the list through several pages.

"There's nothing here about those people being terminated, quitting or anything." His fingers drummed on the table. "We're

65

going to need Chewie to get into that system and find the records."

Chewie returned to the office. "Pearl is at the front desk. She's perked up a little—I told her big changes were on the way."

"That's good. Who knows what's been going on," Bernie said. "Someone is going to have to go through Herman's office and categorize all those stacks of paper. In addition to that, we're going to have to check all the other offices and see if there's unfinished business."

Walter made notes on a legal pad. "We should also hunt for a hidden set of books. Since we don't know what has been going on, there's a good possibility there are two sets of books. Chewie, I'll have Lawrence Thompson, my computer guru, hook up with you. Between the two of you, we might get this sorted out in a short period of time."

Walter pulled out his phone and sent a text.

Gina, please have Lawrence drop everything. Tell him to come to the factory ASAP. We're on the fifth floor.

"Okay. We should be seeing Lawrence in a little while," Walter said.

"That man is a computer genius," Lila Mae said. She remembered Lawrence uncovering deep secrets several months ago.

The elevator dinged. Pearl stuck her head into the conference room. "That locksmith is here. Do you still want me to stay at the front desk?"

Bernie patted the empty chair near him. "Come in for a minute, Pearl. We need to know what's been going on around here." He turned to Chewie. "Why don't you get the locksmith started?"

Chewie left the room.

Pearl appeared uneasy as she walked to the chair and sat down. She looked around the table and let out a nervous breath.

"You told me how much you made here at the factory," Bernie started. "When was the last time you got a raise?"

Pearl thought for a moment. "Four years ago, I think."

Walter jotted a note. "Did you have a performance review?"

Pearl shook her head.

"How come you weren't working in the factory when we got here?" Bernie asked.

"There's only a few people working today. Mr. David told the rest of us that orders were very low and there was going to be a layoff," Pearl said. "But I know that's not true because Corina said she saw a fax from one of our clients for an order for hundreds of products."

All heads swung from person to person around the table, and a lot of nodding began.

Chewie returned to the conference room and sat down.

"When was the last time you saw the secr...err...admin, or the HR lady?" Bernie asked.

"There's not been anyone up here on the fifth floor except for Mr. David in a long time," Pearl said. "We've got a skeleton crew in the factory and most of the lines are shut down."

"This is worse than we thought!" Madge bellowed. "Should we have that man apprehended? Freeze his bank account?"

"Have to have probable cause before we can go after him," Walter said.

The elevator dinged. Lawrence sauntered toward the voices and knocked on the open doorway. He waved to everyone.

Walter stood. "Thank God you're here, Lawrence. This is Chewie. The two of you need to get into this system—dig deep and find out what's going on. Chewie can explain."

Chewie stood, shook Lawrence's hand, and they walked out of the conference room.

Lila Mae looked thoughtful. "Madge, didn't Teddy defend a client who was accused of embezzling?"

Madge stared into space. "I sort of remember that. Let me text him."

"Have him come join us," Walter said. "The more experienced hands on deck, the sooner we can get things rolling." He turned to Pearl. "Why don't you go down to the floor and tell the folks what we're doing and that we will be down later."

Pearl looked relieved as she rushed out of the conference room.

Silence shrouded the room. Lila Mae's phone chirped an incoming message.

"Can we save the company?" Bambi asked.

Bernie patted her hand. "Everything will be okay. It may take some hands on by everyone in this room, but my legacy isn't going belly-up anytime soon."

"Amelia and Chiquita are preparing dinner for everyone. They just sent out a text, so check your phones and text Amelia back," Lila Mae said.

Everyone fiddled with their cell phones checking texts.

CHAPTER TEN

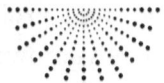

A black Cadillac Seville with Las Vegas plates was parked in front of Valobra Master Jewelers on Westheimer in Highland Village. The store's thick, etched door opened and Luna was escorted out of the store on Dougie Vey's arm. Her sundress' crisscrossed straps delicately held the dress on her tanned shoulders, while a dipped front displayed abundant cleavage. Luna held her manicured hand out in front of her admiring the new sparkly bauble on her finger.

"Oh, Dougie! It's so beautiful! I love diamonds!" she gushed.

"They look beautiful on you, Luna," Dougie said. He leaned in and smooched her shoulder.

Luna dug into her purse and pulled her phone out and thumbed the screen. "Oh, no! Daddy had some trouble at the office today, honey. Two guys were looking for you and they tore up a bunch of his equipment." Luna turned to Dougie, alarmed.

"What do you mean, hot cheeks? Who was looking for me?" Dougie asked, suspicious.

"I'd better call him and find out what this is all about," Luna said as she pressed the call button. "Daddy? Are you all right? What happened?" She listened, gasped, and stared Dougie down. "I don't know who those men were. Hold on, let me ask Dougie."

Dougie waved at her to try to get her to end the call. He gave up as she shoved the phone at him, squinting with a threatening expression. He grabbed the phone.

"Victor? I hear you had some problems? What happened?" Dougie listened, his face not giving away emotions at all. "I have no idea who would do such a thing! And you're sure they were asking about me? Oh, and Luna too? Huh. I don't have a clue." He listened for a few minutes more and grunted. He passed the phone back to Luna.

"I will, Daddy. You too." She ended the call. Luna turned to Dougie. "Why would someone want to hurt my father? What's going on, Dougie?"

"Peaches, I have no idea what that was about. Must be a misunderstanding," he said.

* * *

Lila Mae, Dorothea, Bambi, and Madge each grabbed a stack of papers from Herman's desk and brought them to the conference room. Bernie and Walter left to go down to the factory to talk to the workers. The elevator dinged, and Teddy strode into the conference room.

He took in the table covered with stacks of paper. He pulled out his phone and a stylus and typed. "What do we have?" a mechanical voice asked.

They each, in turn, explained the problem. Lila Mae told Teddy where all the stacks of paper came from. Teddy went into high gear.

"Each of you take one stack of papers and sort them out into different categories. When you're finished with the stacks, combine your piles of the same categories. Someone show me where Herman David's office is so I can look around," Teddy said through his phone.

Bambi walked Teddy over to the manager's office. "This is it. You should have seen it—all that paperwork in the conference room was in here, all over the place." She grabbed another stack in a corner on the floor and left Teddy to his own devices.

"Here's an order from Saudi!" Madge said. She glared at the sheet of paper. "How do we know this has been filled and shipped?"

"We'll get it all sorted out, Madge," Lila Mae said, forever the peacekeeper.

Dorothea got all excited. She jumped up and down, waving a piece of paper. "Here's an order from Ireland!" She fanned herself. "Oh, I hope these chocolates have been shipped. This is for a special event." She looked at the calendar on her phone. "It's next week!"

"Wouldn't there be shipping manifests?" Bambi asked. "We could check the shipping department and see if these have been sent."

Lila Mae waved her hands in a downward motion. "Let's all calm down. We need to get through these stacks of paper to see if there are more orders and what the rest of this is all about. We can't stop and gab about everything we discover! We'll never get finished."

"Lila Mae's right," Madge said. "Let's stick to business. We'll each make our own stacks and grab another pile and go through all of this mess."

About ten minutes later, Teddy joined them in the conference room and rolled up his sleeves. He grabbed a stack and started his own sorting piles.

* * *

CHEWIE AND LAWRENCE sat at different desks in another room. They had taken the computer equipment out of the manager's office and set up in the old HR office.

"Okay! I found all the login accounts with passwords," Lawrence said. "If we come across something that's locked, we should be able to crack it open."

Chewie had removed his Kato jacket and rolled up his sleeves. "The human resources lady hadn't logged in for five months. But the good news is that she has a very organized folder and file scheme." He clacked away on the keyboard.

Lawrence perused dozens of open windows on the monitor. He flitted from one window to the next. "Here's shipping and receiving. And here's the incoming and outgoing fax files. Do you know if there's a copy room here? I'm wondering if the copy machine is hooked up to the network—I'd assume it would be, but that's another thing we have to check out."

"I'm not sure. Want me to go take a look around?" Chewie asked.

"Sure. I'll see what else I can find that would be immediately useful," Lawrence said.

Chewie pushed his chair away from the desk and left the room. He wandered down the hallway and discovered the copy and supply room. The full-service copier was networked. There were several sheets of paper in the receiving tray. He grabbed those and perused the contents: orders. He left the copier room and entered the conference room.

"Here's a couple of orders," he stated.

Dorothea approached him and grabbed the orders. "Oh my God! These are due Tuesday!" She fanned herself with the paper.

"Put them in this pile," Teddy said via his phone.

Chewie returned to the copy room and checked all the cords on the machine. Everything seemed to be in order. He went through the copier menu and found the log. It was password-protected. He grabbed his phone and texted Lawrence, who texted him the password.

Chewie pulled up the history files. Luckily, this was the type of system that copied jobs and stored them. He printed a summary of the copy and print jobs, then the incoming and outgoing faxes. The summary alone was one-hundred twenty-five pages, showing the date, number of pages, and the first couple of lines of what was copied, printed, or faxed. This would make it easier to see which entries needed to be printed. He grabbed the summaries and returned to the HR office.

"I'm going to check each floor. Be right back," he said.

Lawrence grabbed the stack of pages and plunked them down in front of him on the desk. He ran his finger slowly down the summary.

"What the...?" Lawrence grabbed a yellow highlighter and slid it across an entry, then continued scanning the page, high-lighting items of interest.

Twenty minutes later, Chewie returned with four other summaries. "Third and fourth floor copiers haven't been used in months. The second floor has a decent amount of usage. First floor has some interesting stuff."

BY FIVE O'CLOCK everyone was dragging. The conference room table sported neat stacks down the middle of the table. The piles the girls and Teddy sorted through had shrunk considerably. There were stacks along the wall on the floor with a labeled top sheet.

The girls looked haggard. Teddy seemed to be in his element. Dorothea sported a band-aid on her finger from a paper cut. Lila Mae rubbed her eyes. Bambi adjusted her bra, and Madge scratched her butt.

"We need to gather the troops and go eat," Lila Mae said. "I'm about out of energy."

"Good idea," Madge said.

Teddy pressed keys on his phone. The mechanical voice announced: "A good day's work."

The girls stood, grabbed their purses and rounded up Chewie and Lawrence. Teddy slipped on his jacket and met them in the hallway. The elevator dinged, and Walter and Bernie stepped out on the fifth floor.

"You read our minds," Walter said. "Let's call it a day, and we can resume work tomorrow.

"Everyone text Amelia and let her know you're on the way," Lila Mae said.

* * *

THE DINING TABLE was packed with people and piled with food. Amelia had added the two spare leaves to the table to make enough room for everyone.

"This roast is scrumptious, Amelia!" Lila Mae said. "I'm ravenous!" There was an empty chair beside her.

Chiquita was quiet, watching everyone around the table. She picked at her food, trying to keep track of one conversation to the next.

"Where's Chance?" Chewie asked.

"He's on his way," Amelia said. "He was going to swing by and pick up Gina."

Lawrence snickered. "The entire office will be here."

"Where's Zoe?" Madge asked.

"She's over at Suzanne's," Walter said. "And I know Tilly has a class tonight."

"This sweet potato and pecan casserole is to die for," Lawrence said. "My fiancé will kill me if I don't get the recipe." He winked at Amelia.

"Sure, no problem," Amelia said.

The kitchen door opened, and two sets of distinct footsteps could be heard approaching the dining room. Chance and Gina joined the group.

"Oh, this smells marvelous!" Gina said. "I brought Chance up to speed on the drive over."

"So how did things go?" Chance asked as he sat beside Lila Mae.

"You wouldn't believe it unless you saw it," Lila Mae said. "That manager must have had a nervous breakdown, or something."

"*Or something*," Teddy typed. "Just from what I saw, there's probable cause justifying his being picked up for embezzlement."

"There's a huge stack of orders," Bambi said. "We don't know if they've been filled or not."

"We have to find out if the Ireland order has shipped! They have a special event next week!" Dorothea practically had a meltdown. "We'll never be able to live it down if their order doesn't arrive on time, and there's that order due next Tuesday that Chewie found on the copier."

"We've got the shipping and receiving folders. Hopefully procedures were followed," Chewie said.

"How'd your day go?" Carmichael asked Chance.

Chance dabbed his lips with his linen napkin. "Police were called to Victor's office."

The girls, Bernie and Walter, stopped eating. "What happened?" Walter asked.

"Looks like thugs from Las Vegas showed up looking for that Dougie Vey character," Chance said.

"Oh, no! They didn't hurt him, did they?" Lila Mae asked.

"Luckily, they left him alone, but made a mess of the equipment," Chance said. "He's going to have a huge insurance claim."

"Luna is like a walking black cloud," Madge said. "No matter what she touches, it goes up in the tornado."

"I imagine they're having an interesting time over at their house," Dorothea said. "Poor Jeffie!"

CHAPTER ELEVEN

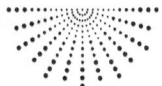

*L*ila Mae was propped comfortably against pillows at the headboard lost in thought, her paperback mystery novel forgotten in her lap. The bathroom door opened and steam billowed out as Chance came into the bedroom wrapped in his robe.

"What's on your mind? You look like you're contemplating something," he said.

She swung her head to look at his side of the bed as he adjusted the covers and pillows, and climbed in. "Oh, just thinking a million things of no consequence."

A tray holding two on-the-rocks glasses was on the bed. Chance grabbed his and guzzled. "Ah. Kahlua and cream. You can't go wrong with that."

Lila Mae picked up her glass and sipped. "It helps, after the day we had today."

"I can't believe the mess you walked into," Chance said.

"Both Walter and Teddy said there's probable cause to have the manager arrested. We now have to finish sorting all the stacks of paper from his office. Chance, you would not believe it."

She grabbed her phone and thumbed through pictures. "Look at his office before we cleared it out to the conference room." She handed him her phone.

"Good God! What the hell was he doing?" Chance took another slug from his glass.

"We're not quite sure. His admin and the HR lady quit months ago. I'm not sure about the line workers. Daddy and Walter will most likely fill us in tomorrow. They spent hours with the factory workers who were on-site today, but who knows about the ones who were downsized." Lila Mae shook her head.

The silence was broken when an outside disturbance in the neighborhood sounded. Louie jumped up out of a dead sleep in his dog bed and let out a *ruff* while he determined the source. He ran to the window and hopped onto a round, padded hassock and looked out the window. He barked up a storm.

Chance and Lila Mae got out of bed and joined Louie at the window.

"Shush, Louie," Chance said. Louie continued to bark. Chance tapped him on the shoulder. "Shush!"

Louie grumbled, but quieted down, ears perked.

"What's going on?" Lila Mae asked, craning her neck. "Can you tell where it's coming from?"

Chance listened for a moment. "I think the Munsons are having a fight."

"Huh. Just them, or is someone over there bothering them?"

"Hard to tell. No outside lights on," Chance observed. "If it doesn't settle down in the next few minutes, I'll call it in."

* * *

DOUGIE VEY HANDED the valet his ticket at Eddie V's Prime Seafood on Kirby Drive. Luna appeared content after the sumptuous meal at the high-end restaurant. She knew there was no way Dougie could conceivably fasten his jacket without the buttons exploding, if he could even close the sizable gap between buttons and buttonholes.

After several minutes, the Caddy was brought around, and Dougie and Luna were on their way. Dougie steered the car out of the parking lot onto Kipling. A large, black SUV tapped his rear bumper.

"What the hell?" Dougie yelled.

Luna clutched the door in terror as the bumper was tapped harder. "What's going on? That's not an accident! Someone's doing this deliberately!"

Dougie made the turn onto Kirby and sped up. The SUV screeched around the corner and slid in back of the Caddy. The SUV kept bumping the Caddy more and more forcefully. Finally, Dougie pulled into the retail shopping center where Bed Bath & Beyond was located. The parking lot was empty at ten p.m. The SUV skidded to a halt behind the Caddy, blocking any escape.

"Stay in the car," he barked at Luna.

"Should we call the police?" Luna asked, panic-stricken.

"No! Let me find out what this is all about!" Dougie hollered.

He hoisted himself out of the car and turned to face the two thugs who had visited Victor. Dougie recognized Pee Wee and Blackjack. Pee Wee grabbed Dougie and threw him against the Caddy.

"We're here to collect the Boss' money," Pee Wee said.

Dougie was sweating buckets. "I don't know what you're talking about."

Pee Wee hauled off and punched Dougie in the gut. Dougie doubled over and spewed his half of the three-hundred fifty-nine-dollar meal, which resembled his steak and lobster tartare.

"That help you remember?" Pee Wee asked.

Blackjack went to the passenger side of the Caddy, yanked the door open and pulled Luna out of the car. She screamed up

DAWN GREENFIELD IRELAND

a storm until Blackjack clamped his beefy hand over her mouth. She continued to scream into his hand, imploring Dougie with her fearful expression.

"Tell you what," Pee Wee said. "We'll hold on to this insurance until you remember things more clearly." He jerked his head toward the SUV.

Blackjack dragged Luna across the pavement and tossed her into the back seat of the SUV. "You make one more sound, and I'll cut your tongue out," he warned her. "You understand?"

She was too scared to speak. He slapped handcuffs on her and handcuffed her to the seatbelt fastener between the back seats, then he shut the door. He stood by the passenger door while Pee Wee finished up business with Dougie Vey.

"You've got twenty-four hours to get your memory working again," Pee Wee said. "If the boss doesn't have his money by the next business day after that, we'll start disassembling your little cupcake and delivering her in boxes."

Pee Wee sauntered back to the SUV. He and Blackjack got in, and they screeched out of the parking lot. Dougie collapsed against the Caddy. After a moment, he shuffled around the car and shut the passenger door. He tried to stand fully upright, but failed. He held tight to his stomach as he slid into the driver's seat. Dougie rested his head against the steering wheel.

* * *

CHEWIE UNLOCKED the doors of the Alcott Chocolate factory with the new keys on the keyring—all labeled and easily identifiable. Bernie stood to the side, grasping his walker. Pearl approached him.

"You still want me at the front desk, Mr. Alcott?" She asked tremulously.

"Yes, Pearl. If you can keep track of anyone coming and going, that would be a great help," Bernie said. "If Herman

80

David shows up, turn him away. Call upstairs if there're any problems whatsoever."

"Call the cops," Chewie said. "He needs to be arrested, anyway."

"I promise I'll do a good job, Mr. Alcott," Pearl said. "That snake better not show his face around here!"

Chewie got the doors unlocked and went inside looking for the light switches. Bernie and Pearl followed him in as more cars arrived in the parking lot. Pearl moved around Chewie and threw the light switches on.

"They're sort of hidden," she explained as she showed them the bank of switches too far from the doors.

Pearl settled into a chair at the curved reception center with the high counter. "I'll make a sign-in sheet."

"Good idea. You can add us to the sheet," Bernie said. "This is Chewie." He spelled the name for her. "We'll be upstairs in the conference room if you need us. There's a phone in there. Do you have the number?"

Pearl perused a telephone list taped under the counter, out of sight from guests. "Yeah, here it is, fifth-floor conference room."

"Okay. Looks like we're all set then," Bernie said. He clomped over to the elevator with Chewie at his side.

* * *

LILA MAE SET two bags on the welcome mat outside the front door of the building while she opened the door and held it with her hip. She grabbed the bag's handles and made it inside. Pearl was on her feet, ready for business.

"May I help you?" Pearl said. She viewed Lila Mae with suspicion.

"Are you Pearl?" Lila Mae asked. "I'm Lila Mae Alcott."

"Oh, hi, Ms. Alcott," Pearl said. "You need help?"

"No, I think I've got it."

"I'll add your name to the sign-in sheet," Pearl said, taking care of business.

"Thanks," Lila Mae said. "The others will be here soon." She headed over to the elevator and put one bag down and hit the button. The elevator dinged, and she stepped inside.

When she arrived on the fifth floor, the aroma of coffee greeted her. She went into the break room and put the bags on the counter. Lila Mae unloaded several boxes of kolaches and pastries. She opened cabinets and found small paper plates, napkins, and forks.

"Come and get it!" Lila Mae yelled out. She piled several pastries on a small plate, grabbed a napkin and fork and headed to the elevator.

Chewie and Bernie perused the plate of goodies.

"I'm bringing these down to Pearl. Be right back," Lila Mae said.

"I love those things," Bernie said.

"I called late last night and placed an order so they'd be ready this morning," Lila Mae said. "They sell out pretty fast."

"Good thinking," Chewie said. "I love the ones with cheese."

* * *

THE TEAM SAT around the conference table, consumed with their tasks. Dorothea checked the orders against the shipping documents that Lawrence had found and printed. She had two stacks: delivered orders and unknown if even produced.

Madge took the unknown orders to determine if they were being created, or if they required custom molds.

Bambi sorted through invoices, trying to determine whether payment had been received—or even if the invoices had been mailed.

Lila Mae opened envelopes from utility companies,

vendors, and other unknown sources. Walter had suggested she staple the envelope to the contents so they could make sure the address was on file if it wasn't on the bill or other literature.

Walter, Bernie and Teddy were in the manager's vacant office trying to make sense of the human resources nightmare, bank accounts, benefits and other legal matters. Walter had called Bob Marx, the floor manager, to take a complete inventory of supplies and to report back when he and his team were finished.

Lawrence wandered in. "I've uncovered the accounts payable and receivables, and the payroll files. They're a complete mess."

Teddy typed on his phone. "We should see who worked in those capacities and get them in here, that is, if they are available."

"Bernie, have you found those people on the list of employees?" Walter asked.

Bernie shuffled through several pages and pulled out a sheet of paper. "Here you go. You calling them, Walter?"

The elevator dinged and Henry came into the office. "Thought I'd come in and lend a hand."

"How'd it go at court yesterday?" Walter asked.

"A win-win. The Beaumonts are finally divorced. She took him for one point two million, and he happily wrote the check to get rid of her."

Dorothea rushed into the office, flapping a piece of paper in front of her. "The Ireland order hasn't been shipped! Their event is next week! We'll have to overnight it to Ireland! What are we going to do?"

Walter picked up the conference room phone and called downstairs. "Bob? Walter here. Do you know anything about this custom order for an event in Ireland?" He listened. "I'll bring it down and you look it over and let us know if this requires a custom mold."

Walter stood and headed to the elevator. "Be right back, Dorothea."

* * *

EMILY LEWIS, Sheetal Gupta, Bodie Williams and Alice Kensington sat in the conference room on the first floor. Their grim faces told a story of their work history. Henry and Teddy entered the room; they scanned the unhappy faces before them.

"We're glad you could come in at such short notice," Teddy typed. "My name is Teddy Abercrombie, and this is Henry Divine. We are attorneys for Alcott Industries and the Alcott Chocolate Company, and we are trying to sort through the mess left by the former manager."

Henry jumped in. "Uh, Teddy has frozen vocal cords, that's why he talks through his phone."

Teddy gave a thumbs-up. The group introduced themselves one-by-one, along with their former title in the company and why they left. A two-hour discussion ended with the happy faces of the reinstated employees, along with a plan of action.

"Emily, we'll have you back in your office in a jiffy. We were using it as one of our war rooms," Teddy typed.

"Your time may be better spent with Walter Branson and Mr. Alcott," Henry said. "They will want to talk with all of you to explain further what is, or actually wasn't, going on with each of your areas."

They headed to the elevator and rode up to the fifth floor.

"Why don't we gather in the break room?" Henry said. "Help yourselves to coffee and pastries while I round everyone up."

Teddy entered the HR office where Walter and Bernie thumbed through pages and pages of printouts. "We've got Emily Lewis—the HR lady, Sheetal Gupta—the payroll lady, Bodie Williams, payables, and Alice Kensington, receivables back on board. They're in the break room. Jody Meyer, the manager's former admin, said if we ever called her again she'd sue."

Bernie shook his head. "I can't believe this man practically ran my company into the ground! He's damaged our reputation with this mess!"

* * *

DOUGIE VEY STUMBLED out of a motel room in Berino, New Mexico, twenty-six miles from El Paso, TX. He made it to his car and got in. Still not recovered from the punch to his gut, he was hunched over the wheel. He backed out of the parking space in front of his motel door and wound his way onto I-10, headed toward Houston. He was deeply guilt-ridden for slinking off into the night and leaving Luna in a precarious position, which would only end badly. With any luck, he would be back at the Tic's house before ten o'clock that night. He dreaded the confrontation with the doctor and his wife.

* * *

LUNA WRAPPED herself in a chenille bedspread to keep warm in the hotel room. Her bedraggled state matched her mental condition, as she was half fried from the hostage experience. From listening to the conversations of her kidnappers, she had pieced together that Dougie siphoned about ten million bucks over his career as manager of the casino.

She didn't quite understand how a business would not miss the money sooner, but she didn't understand how businesses worked, never having had a nine-to-five job. Her singing gigs were not in the same category as a person who worked for a company on salary.

Luna glanced at the enormous diamond on her hand and made a little *huff* sound. She now knew where the money came from for all the clothes and jewelry, and the meals at fancy restaurants. Closing her eyes, Luna mentally inventoried her life to date. She realized she was running into a huge life deficit, and thought of everything she had put her parents through over the years, and all the money she had cost them. She teared up. Luna silently vowed to get her act together and pay her parents back for every single stupidity they bailed her out of—one situation after another.

*　*　*

CHIQUITA AND JINGO were having an animated conversation in the driveway at Lila Mae's Del Monte house. Amelia spied on them through the French door window. She shook her head. Louie trotted across the kitchen floor, and Amelia smiled slyly.

"Louie, I'm counting on you to get Chiquita back in here," she said.

Louie gave a little *ruff* and hopped in front of the door in anticipation of fulfilling his new job requirement. Amelia let him outside and watched as he raced over to the two lovebirds. She scooted away from the door so she wouldn't be caught spying. Louie bee-lined to Jingo and Chiquita. He hopped against Jingo's legs, waiting for attention. Jingo bent down and picked up Louie, and patted him.

Amelia watched as Chiquita waved at Jingo and scooted back to the house. Amelia rushed to the butler's pantry and disappeared before Chiquita opened the French doors and came inside. She stuck her head around the corner as the door closed.

"Oh, there you are," Amelia said innocently.

Chiquita clasped her hands together by her heart. "Guess what?"

Amelia faked cluelessness. "What? Tell me!"

Chiquita radiated with infatuation. "Jingo asked me to dinner next week!"

* * *

AMELIA AND CHIQUITA piled into Amelia's Volvo station wagon and headed over to Madge's house. As they rolled up the driveway and parked at Madge's front door. Chiquita gawked at the ostentatious behemoth of a house.

"Wow, she's richer than Lila Mae," she said as she craned her head, taking in the house and grounds.

Amelia shook her head. "Same money, different lifestyles. Lila Mae doesn't feel the need to flaunt her wealth. She got rid of her big house a long time ago."

They got out of the car and headed to the front door. Carmichael swung the door open and smooched Amelia on the lips.

"Hi, hon. Hi, Chiquita. Let's get the assembly line going so we can deliver lunch," he said. "I've got five different breads and rolls, an assortment of lunch meats, tuna, hard-boiled eggs, small bags of chips, pickles, a big salad bowl, and I baked cookies and brownies."

"Wow, you've thought of everything!" Amelia said. "Should we make the sandwiches, or let them pick and choose what they want? Some people want mayo or mustard; some don't want anything—what should we do?"

Carmichael tapped his lips in thought. "Yeah, maybe just deliver this stuff and let them have at it."

"Did you ask anyone if they had salad dressing, mayo and mustard at the factory?" Chiquita asked. "No point in bringing all those bottles if they don't need them."

"Good idea," Amelia said. She pulled out her phone and texted Lila Mae. Carmichael and Chiquita read over Amelia's shoulder.

A few minutes later she received a text back.

We've got all of that in the refrigerator.

Amelia texted back: Check the expiration dates.

Lila Mae texted: Need mayo. That's all. Bring regular-sized paper plates. We only have small plates.

Amelia texted back: We'll be there shortly.

Carmichael went into the butler's pantry and grabbed an unopened package of high-quality dinner paper plates. He returned all condiments to the refrigerator, except for the Trader Joe's mayo. They loaded the bounty into boxes and bags and headed to the front door. They packed the back of Amelia's station wagon and drove to the factory.

* * *

PEARL HELD the door open as lunch arrived.

"Give us a few minutes and come up and put a plate together," Carmichael said.

"I can't leave the front undefended," Pearl said.

Amelia blanched at Pearl's word choice. "We'll send someone down to guard the place."

Pearl hit the elevator door for them, then pressed the button for the fifth floor. The doors closed, and she headed back to the desk.

About forty minutes later, Bambi came downstairs to relieve Pearl. "Everything's in the breakroom. Go help yourself. There's a lot to choose from."

"Okay, thanks. Make sure that anyone who comes in signs the sign-in sheet," Pearl said. "Don't let anyone wander around."

"I'll make sure everything is carried out according to your instructions," Bambi said. She rounded the corner of the reception counter and sat at the desk while Pearl took the elevator to the fifth floor.

Ten minutes later, the front door opened, and Herman David entered. He looked around, then approached the desk. Bambi was on her feet in an instant.

"May I help you?" She said in her best professional voice.

Herman was nervous. "Yeah, I need to get something I left behind in my office."

"Sign in, please." Bambi pushed the clipboard with an attached pen on a string in front of him. "Let me call upstairs to have someone escort you."

She glanced at the phone list and called the conference room where she last saw all three attorneys and Bernie, along with the Alcott sisters. She grabbed the clipboard. "I have Mr. David here. He said he forgot something in his office?" She squeaked out.

She hung up and turned her attention to the former manager. "Someone will be right down. Would you like to take a seat?"

Herman drummed his fingers on the countertop. He kept glancing at the door.

The elevator dinged and Walter emerged. He did not hold his hand out in greeting. "I understand you forgot something upstairs?"

Herman desperately tried to hide his nervousness. "Yes, I'll only be a minute."

"What is it that you forgot and where is it?" Walter asked.

Herman's forehead was moist. "Oh, just a personal item. My late wife bought me a leather computer pouch that I used to carry a novel to read at lunch. It means a lot to me."

"I don't remember seeing anything like that. Come on up and we'll see if it's still there," Walter said. The men entered the elevator.

The front desk phone rang as the elevator door closed. Bambi answered it. "Yes?" She listened. "I'll keep vigilant. Walter is bringing him upstairs right now."

* * *

WALTER AND HERMAN stepped out of the elevator and walked to the former manager's office. Herman perused his former office. All the paperwork was missing. The former manager immediately walked over to the bookcases and cabinets that lined the wall and opened a cabinet door. He got down on his knees and felt around and pulled out the black bag.

"Here it is," he said. He turned to leave, but his passage was blocked by Teddy, Lawrence, and Chewie. Lawrence's height and bulk alone would make anyone nervous, but the already anxious former manager gripped the bag to his chest.

"Let's see what you've got there," Walter said. He stuck his hand out.

Herman opened the bag and pulled out a paperback. "Just my book. This is my personal property."

"You no longer work here. Everything in this office belongs to Alcott Industries and Alcott Chocolates," Walter said. He wiggled his fingers in a *hand it over* wave. Herman shoved the book back into the bag and reluctantly handed the bag over. Walter pulled the novel out, handed it to Chewie, then dug into the bag.

Chewie fanned the book upside down. Several sheets of folded paper fell to the floor. Teddy retrieved the pages and perused them while Chewie continued to fan the book. Walter pulled a black thumb drive out of the bag that was all but hidden in the recesses.

"What do we have here?" Walter said as he held up the thumb drive. He handed it over to Lawrence, who turned on his heel and hurried from the room.

Herman was gushing water from every pore in his body.

Walter taunted him. "Don't worry, Lawrence has a master's degree in forensic accounting and criminology. He's not only fast, but thorough."

There was a moment where Walter thought for sure Herman would pass out, but the man managed to stay upright.

Lawrence returned to the office. He held up the thumb drive. "Everything we need to prosecute."

The elevator dinged, and two cops preceded Chance. They entered the office. The cops looked everyone over. One looked at Walter.

"Herman David?"

Walter presented Herman with a nod.

The cop turned him around and handcuffed him.

"Miranda him and take him downtown," Chance said.

"Please, will someone go to my house and get my duck and take care of him!" Herman said. "He can't fly and needs to be looked after. He's in the backyard, and his name's Quack."

The cops walked Herman out the door while reciting the Miranda Act. Pearl rode down the elevator and relieved Bambi as Herman was removed from the building and placed in the police car.

Chance and Walter exchanged looks. "Quack?" Chance asked. "Do I need a search warrant to get the duck?"

"There are four witnesses, me included, to back you up," Walter said as he nodded to Teddy, Chewie and Lawrence. "What are you going to do with him?"

Chance shrugged. "I'll ask Lila Mae. She'll know what to do and who to contact."

* * *

CHANCE'S LEXUS PULLED into Lila Mae's driveway. He texted Amelia to let her know he was there. "Okay, Quack. You're at your new home."

The mallard quacked up a storm from the back seat. He obviously did not appreciate the free ride, or being cooped up in a cardboard box. Amelia, Chiquita, and Louie came outside, curious about their new charge. Chance got out of the car, opened the back door and retrieved the box.

"Let's go in the backyard and I'll let him out. I hope he doesn't figure out Louie's dog door, or he'll be in the front yard in no time," Chance said.

"So, this was that scumbag manager's duck?" Amelia asked.

"Yeah, at least I can say he isn't a total loser," Chance said. "He was really worried about the duck and begged someone to take care of him."

"Who has a duck for a pet?" Chiquita asked. "Don't they poop all over the place?"

"I'm pretty sure he's an outside pet," Amelia said, mentally questioning Chiquita's common sense.

They stopped near the reconstructed stream and bridge, and Chance set the box on the ground. Louie was all over the box, sniffing up a storm while Quack quacked nonstop.

"Okay, Louie," Chance said. "You better be nice to Quack. He's your new yard-mate."

Chance started to open the box, and the duck's iridescent green head popped through the top. He quacked a long *quaaaaaccckkkkk*, followed by a stream of quacks, obviously telling his side of the story about being shoved in a box and hauled away from his former home.

"Oh, he's a beautiful drake!" Amelia said.

"What's a drake?" Chiquita asked.

"A boy duck," Amelia explained.

"He sure is pretty," Chiquita said. "I love that green!"

Quack hopped out of the box, fluttered his wings and waddled toward the stream. Louie ran alongside the duck and mouthed Quack's neck.

Quack hauled off and bit Louie on the rump. They had a standoff. Louie gave a little *ruff* and Quack quacked. An agreement was reached. They both continued to the water.

"I think they'll be okay," Chance said.

Amelia's phone dinged a message from Lila Mae.

Do not feed the duck bread, popcorn, chocolate, onion, garlic, avocado or citrus fruit. Jingo will have to build a house for the duck.

"No bread or popcorn?" Amelia looked questioningly at the text. "We always brought bread and popcorn to the duck pond at the zoo."

"Guess you'll have to do a lot of Googling," Chance said.

CHAPTER TWELVE

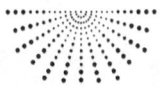

*W*alter called a meeting with Henry, Teddy, Bernie, and Emily Lewis, the HR lady. Everyone was sipping coffee around the desk Walter took over in a vacant office.

"I think we're ready to get the show on the road again. I suggest a company meeting to brief all employees, current and past, about what happened, what the future has in store for everyone in the company, and to see who wants to come onboard again."

He shuffled through some pages on his desk. "I suggest after the meeting, we divide the attendees among all of us and have one-on-one meetings. We will go over their current status, discuss their last performance review, their last raise, and offer a cost-of-living increase."

Everyone was silent as they digested what Walter had said.

"Let's do it," Bernie said.

"I'll have Gina type up a letter on corporate stationery, and we'll get them in the mail for a meeting next week," Walter said.

"What if we don't have current information on some of them?" Emily asked.

"We can only hope that if they moved, they have either changed their address with the post office, or someone in the company knows them to tell them about the meeting," Henry said.

Teddy typed on his phone. "I don't think there will be very many unreachable people. If they come forth after the meeting, we'll just bring them up to date and see if they want their old job back."

Walter tapped the desk. "Okay. I'll forward the employee list to Gina, and she can get that going. Anything else we need to discuss?"

"We have the inventory from the floor manager," Henry said. "We're down to bare bones as far as supplies go."

"What about all those orders the girls found?" Bernie asked. "Have they been confirmed as shipped?"

Teddy typed.

Emily stood. "I'm going to let you men discuss the manufacturing end."

"Okay, Emily. Thanks for coming on board," Bernie said.

Emily stood, took her coffee cup and notepad, and left the room.

"We don't seem to have a sales force, or anyone in-house to manage the orders before they are sent down to the floor manager for production," Teddy typed.

Walter stood. "Let me ask Emily if there was such a person on staff."

"Walter, hold on a second," Bernie said. "We need to hire a new manager, an admin, and maybe this person for sales, unless we promote from within."

* * *

DOUGIE AND LUNA looked like two sad sacks sitting across from each other at the International House of Pancakes.

"I really messed up, Luna," he said. "I'm really sorry you had to go through that with those creeps."

Luna's mouth was in a tight line, and her face scrunched in a *I'm not happy* glare. "Those thugs ruined a lot of equipment at my father's office, Dougie. Can you imagine what those expectant mothers went through when those guys were wrecking the place?" She fiddled with the ring on her finger.

"Look, the money's gone. We're going to have to get jobs," Dougie said. "I can't replace your dad's equipment. I'm dead broke after these pancakes."

Luna slid the ring off her finger. "You'd better hawk this then."

* * *

TEDDY SAT in a leather lounge chair in Eirik's office. The environment was conducive to a soothing atmosphere and Feng Shuied to the hilt for the best results for the client's wellbeing, and for Eirik's prosperity.

"Just relax. I want you to breathe in deeply and out again, three times," Eirik instructed.

Teddy followed instructions, breathing deeply in and out.

"Okay, now, let's see what your vocal cords are capable of, okay?"

"K," Teddy said.

"I want you to say, hello, Eirik, how are you today."

Teddy gave it a try. The words came out all crackly and rough, fading into a cough.

"Okay, that gives me something to work with. I'm going to hypnotize you now. Do you have to go to the restroom, blow your nose, or anything?"

Teddy typed. "I'm good to go."

* * *

AT THE END of their session, Teddy blinked alert.

"How do you feel?" Eirik asked.

Teddy typed. "Refreshed."

"New rule, Teddy," Eirik said. "No more using your phone for your voice or writing notes unless your vocal cords are strained. You are using the phone and notes as a crutch."

Teddy balked. He reached for his phone, stopped and stared at it.

"Okay," he said in a raspy voice. It sounded like *uh cuh*.

Eirik stood. Teddy followed suit.

"How about returning in one week?" Eirik asked. "I'd like to check your progress. You may need a few tweaks."

Teddy cleared his throat. "I'll put you in my calendar," which sounded like *oll phat ewe n my caw.len.duhr*. He cleared his throat again.

"Tell everyone they are to help you, not cheat," Eirik said.

Teddy grumbled and shook his head. Then he gave the thumbs-up sign and left the office.

* * *

LUNA AND DOUGIE sat across from Victor and Jeffie in the den.

"This is all my fault," Dougie confessed. "I did some things I'm not proud of, and those things followed me here and hurt you. I promise to pay you back for all the damage that the insurance doesn't cover."

"We're going to start looking for jobs," Luna explained. "I wish I had followed your advice and gone to college after high school."

Jeffie stared at her daughter hard, not believing what she heard. "It's never too late to get an education. You could work during the day and go to school online for many basic courses, or take classes at night."

"You need to go online and check for jobs. Do either of you qualify for unemployment?" Victor asked.

Luna and Dougie looked at each other. "I have no idea, but that's a thought!" Dougie said.

"You can apply online," Victor said.

* * *

LILA MAE, Dorothea, Madge, and Jeffie settled on Lila Mae's living room furniture with a full view of the backyard, while sipping tea.

"Oh, look! You have a duck in your backyard," Jeffie said.

"That's Quack, the former manager's duck," Dorothea said. "He can't fly."

"Was that jerk arrested?" Jeffie asked.

"Yes, we're rid of him!" Madge bellowed.

Lila Mae cringed. "Madge, what is going on with your loud voice? Are you going deaf?"

Madge winced. "I just get excited and don't know my own power."

Lila Mae eyeballed her sister. She knew that was a discussion for later.

"So, tell us about what happened with Luna and Dougie," Dorothea said.

Jeffie shook her head. "I can only pray to God and all the saints that my daughter sees the light. Dougie came clean about the mess he caused and promised to pay Victor what the insurance didn't cover."

Lila Mae and her sisters were startled by the news. "Huh," Lila Mae said. "Who would have thought?"

"And that's not the best part," Jeffie said with a devilish look. "They're both job hunting, and Luna is contemplating college!"

Dorothea had a moment. "Lila Mae, maybe Dougie would be a good fit for the manager's job. He did manage a casino."

Lila Mae and Madge considered their sister's suggestion.

"He's an embezzler," Madge said. "We might as well hand him the bank account numbers."

"While that's true, if everyone understands his complete background going forward, his experience even with that transgression would be helpful to prevent embezzlement in the future," Lila Mae said. "Does that make sense?"

Dorothea, Jeffie and Madge nodded.

"Jeffie, tell Dougie to go to the factory tomorrow. And, you know what? They need a receptionist for the lobby. Maybe Luna would be a good fit," Madge said.

* * *

THE CADDY PULLED up and parked in the Alcott Chocolates parking lot at nine a.m. sharp. Luna and Dougie, dressed in conservative business attire, walked into the lobby, and Pearl greeted them.

"May I help you?" Pearl asked. She did not have a greeter's voice; instead, she sounded like she was conducting an inquisition, and the end result was burning at the stake.

"We're here to see Walter," Luna said. "I'm Luna Tic and this is Dougie Vey. Walter is expecting us."

Pearl scrutinized them while pointing to the sign-in sheet. "Sign in." She picked up the phone and called upstairs.

"Walter? It's Pearl. There's two people to see you. A lunatic and Mr. Vey."

She listened. "That's what she said."

She listened some more. "Oh!" Pearl blushed beet-red. She hung up the phone.

Pearl faced the visitors. "You can go up to the fifth floor. Walter will meet you at the elevator."

Dougie and Luna walked to the elevator and rode up to the fifth floor. Walter approached them.

"Good to see you again," he said. They all shook hands. "Luna, you will be meeting with Mrs. Lewis, our HR representative." They walked to Emily's office, and Walter made the introductions and shut the door behind him.

"Dougie, we're going to the conference room."

They walked the short distance and were greeted by Bernie, Teddy, Henry, Lawrence, and Chewie. Walter made the introductions and everyone sat.

"I realize this is not your typical interview, but with your background, Dougie, which is questionable, at best, and the dire situation we are faced with here, we thought we should talk with you," Walter said.

They had an intense round-table discussion. As a former embezzler, Dougie laid out what, and how, Herman David may have gone about stealing from the company, and how and where he had squirreled away the money.

Then they went on to discuss the state of chaos, the manager had left the company in when he was arrested. They further questioned Dougie in depth about how he conducted business in his role at the casino. Since Lawrence had already contacted investigators in Vegas to gather intel, everyone around the table already knew everything there was to know about Dougie's job.

Aside from the little indiscretion of his embezzlement, Dougie had been a highly prized casino manager who ran a tight ship. He had been respected by his superiors and employees alike, which was quite rare.

After nearly two hours, Bernie nodded to Walter, satisfied that Dougie was the right person for the job. Walter laid the company cards on the table for the position, and Dougie accepted the role.

"We're putting our trust in you, Dougie," Bernie said. "Just understand that if you should fall off the proverbial wagon of honesty, you will have to go so deep underground to protect yourself from the holy terrors my daughters and Bambi can be, not to mention Chewie and Teddy. Your life would be in grave danger."

Henry leaned forward. "That's strictly off the record and no one here will ever recall that being said to you."

Dougie indicated his clear understanding. Walter escorted Dougie to Emily's office to finalize the deal. He returned to the conference room and shut the door.

"Well?" he said.

There was nodding around the table.

"I think he will be an asset to the company," Henry said.

"I agree," Teddy said. It sounded like *Ahh gree.*

"His record is impressive," Chewie said. "Everyone liked him, and he got the job done efficiently. All we can do is give him a chance to prove himself."

"What Chewie said. My people were very thorough, as you saw from the report. He's lucky to be alive, so that says a lot," Lawrence said.

Bernie stood. "I'm starving! Come on, Chewie. Let's go to Lila Mae's. Amelia always has something good on hand."

* * *

THE DAY of the big company meeting finally arrived. The second floor, where the automatic lines had been shut down months ago, was the only place that could hold that size of group, so the absence of the ramblings of machinery did not make it noisy. Fifteen rows of four chairs at eight-foot tables were down two aisles, and additional folding chairs leaned against a wall. A stapled packet of papers was at each position on the tables, along with a pen and scratch pad.

A podium stood on a temporary stage, with a microphone. Two tables with three chairs each and name tents were on each side of the podium. In the back of the room, near the door where people would enter, coffee and pitchers of water were waiting. Chewie double-checked the sound system and microphone.

Luna manned the reception desk on the first floor, and instead of using a sign-in sheet, Gina had included a form with each letter sent. Current and former employees were required to print their name, job title, address, phone and email address. Luna collected the forms as people arrived, and she sent everyone to the second floor. She handed anyone who had forgotten their form a clipboard and a pen so they could fill out the required information.

There was a tense moment when a disgruntled woman slammed her form down on the counter and glared at Luna. When she disappeared in the elevator, Luna called upstairs to Walter. "This really angry woman is on her way up."

She listened to Walter, grabbed the form and read off the name: Jody Meyer.

"Okay, thanks," Walter said. He rushed over to Emily and informed her that the former admin did, indeed, show up.

They watched Jody enter the room, help herself to water, and take a seat in the fifth row on the right aisle. She grabbed the forms in front of her and glowered as she flipped through the pages.

"I'd better warn the team she might cause a disturbance," Emily said. She went out the side door and down the hall to find Bernie and the others.

Soon, the tables were filled, and some of the chairs had been set up in back of the rows for unexpected people. They were handed clipboards with the stapled pages attached. A thrum of conversations buzzed across the factory floor. The Alcott sisters and Bambi sat to the side near the head tables.

Walter stood at the microphone and tapped it. Everyone focused on the stage, Walter, and the people at the tables. The room became quiet.

"Welcome everyone. We appreciate you coming to this

emergency meeting for the Alcott Chocolate Factory. My name is Walter Branson and I'm the corporate attorney for all Alcott Holdings. With us today is the founder of Alcott Industries and Alcott Chocolates, Bernard Alcott; Emily Lewis, director of human resources; Dougie Vey, the new manager of Alcott Chocolates; Henry Divine, contractual attorney for Alcott Industries; and Teddy Abercrombie, another contractual attorney for Alcott Industries."

The place was so quiet you could hear the whup-whup of the large ceiling fans overhead, scattered throughout the floor.

"I'll confess that I didn't expect everyone would show up, considering how the company had been managed. After we discovered the state of chaos, the former manager was arrested and now awaits trial. No one came forward to contact us over the last several months to tell us what was going on. I can only impress on each and every one of you that it is your right to go above your supervisor if you know for a fact that something is wrong and not being addressed."

Walter looked over the attentive faces. "And let me be clear about this. I'm not talking petty jealousies, he-said, she-said, and finger-pointing over trivial things. I mean serious business. Bad practices. Dangerous situations. OSHA problems. Bullying. Sexual harassment. Your first option is to go to your direct supervisor. If that doesn't get any action, or if your problem is with that person, you can either take your complaint to HR or the company manager. Always know you have options to report a grievance."

Walter took a breather. "I'd like to turn the meeting over to our founder, Bernie Alcott." Walter stepped over to the vacant chair and sat.

Chewie came forward and helped pull Bernie's chair back, and to get him steady on his feet and over to the podium.

Bernie gripped the sides of the podium to steady himself. He looked across the factory floor at all the faces looking expectantly at him.

"Over the years, I've had the opportunity to meet many of you right here in this building, or at company picnics and other wonderful events. I've met husbands, wives, children, grandchildren, boyfriends and girlfriends. I've attended weddings, funerals, and even a couple of baby showers. It seems that something happened to our company culture and one man practically destroyed what has taken me years to build, with your devotion and help."

Bernie squinted and adopted a dead-serious expression. "That will never happen again. This team will guarantee that. I promise you. Even if I drop dead next Tuesday at two, this business will continue to run and prosper, and our employees will be valued and rewarded for their contributions."

Bambi leaned into Lila Mae and whispered. "Wow! Bernie is a wonderful speaker. I almost want to work here!"

Dorothea leaned toward Bambi. "Our father cherishes this business and these people. It must have been a terrible blow to him when everything hit the fan."

Madge glowered at her sisters and Bambi. "Sshhh!"

Bernie had just finished introducing Dougie Vey when the sisters and Bambi quieted down.

"Good morning. My name is Douglas Vey, but everyone calls me Dougie. I'm new to this city, this industry, and this company, but I'm not new to this position. I have spent the past decade managing one of the wealthiest casinos in Las Vegas, and I was responsible for nine thousand people."

The sisters and Bambi picked their jaws off the floor as they looked at each other.

"It's unfortunate what happened here, but this isn't the first company to experience near collapse, and I can guarantee it won't be the last. However, I want to stress to each and every one of you that I run a tight ship, and I won't tolerate any funny business. If you perform your responsibilities with pride and go home each day with the feeling of satisfaction that you contributed your very best, and had a good time with your coworkers, then that's an achieved milestone in your career, and you can be proud."

Dougie paused for a moment.

"I look forward to getting to know each of you—and I will get to know you, you can count on that. I knew each of my former employees by their first name—all nine thousand of them, so I'm pretty sure I will really get to know all of you!"

There was a smattering of laughter from the attendees.

"You each have a packet of forms before you. If you had left, or had been downsized, and you would like your job back, or to be considered for another position, fill in the paperwork. If you are still employed here and would like to be considered for a different position, fill out the information and check the appropriate boxes. After everyone has finished with the paperwork, please come up to one of these tables, look for the letter of your last name to determine whom you will talk to. There are refreshments in the break room. Please be patient."

Dougie stepped back and returned to his chair. Henry shook his hand. "That was a great speech."

"I've talked to a lot of employees in my life. You treat them well and they will reward you with loyalty and hard, conscientious work," Dougie said.

CHAPTER THIRTEEN

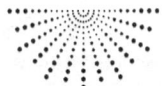

$\mathscr{L}$ ila Mae and Amelia sat on cushioned white rattan chairs at the table in the outdoors loggia room, sipping mango iced tea. Both women had lined tablets and a pen in front of them. The ceiling fans paddled at warp speed and did little to chase the heat and humidity away.

"Where's Chiquita?" Lila Mae asked.

"Probably sexting with Jingo," Amelia snickered.

"Sexting?" Lila Mae asked in concern. "Good Lord!"

"Yeah, since they went to dinner the other night it's been a nonstop love fest," Amelia said, giggling.

Lila Mae thought for a moment. "Well, they DO make a nice-looking couple."

Amelia scowled. "Yeah, but I don't think Uncle Tito sent her here to find a husband."

Louie ran over to the loggia, and Quack ran with flapping wings as fast as his legs would carry him.

"Sorry, Louie. I'm empty handed right now. We're going to talk with Uncle Tito in a few minutes," Lila Mae said. "Amelia doesn't have anything either, so don't think there's a free handout at the table."

Louie glanced from Lila Mae to Amelia, his little tongue sticking out a bit. His face wore a questioning expression. Lila Mae immediately thought of the old commercial that ran for ages on TV, *Where's the Beef?* She chuckled.

She patted him and scratched him behind the ears. Quack quacked and nudged Louie out of the way. Lila Mae ran her hand over his head. He flapped his wings in appreciation.

The French door opened, and Chiquita stepped outside and slid into a chair. Her face was all aglow.

"How's Jingo?" Lila Mae asked.

Chiquita grimaced slightly. "He had to bring one of the big mowers to the repair shop."

Amelia frowned. "Those are fairly new. Remember when he upgraded his equipment, Lila Mae?"

Lila Mae shook her head. "Things aren't what they used to be. These days products are manufactured to be replaced, and it's a shame. I remember the old refrigerator we had growing up. I can't recall the brand, but this was before automatic defrosting freezers. That thing lasted for decades! My mother loved that refrigerator."

"Yeah, my mother refuses to give up her old refrigerator," Amelia said. "It's so small, and you have to defrost the freezer compartment every month, otherwise you've got what looks like several inches of packed ice and snow up there."

"He won't have to pay anything—it's under warranty," Chiquita said.

"That may be so, but that piece of equipment is out of commission and he'll either have to rent something so he gets through the work on his schedule, or come up with another solution," Amelia said.

Lila Mae's iPad announced an incoming call, and Uncle Tito appeared on the screen when FaceTime chimed in. She angled the iPad so they could all see and be seen.

"Hello, Uncle Tito!" they all chorused.

"Where's my iced tea?" he grumbled.

Amelia snickered as she raised her glass to the iPad screen. "Here. Take a sip. Mango flavored."

"You'd better have some left tomorrow," he muttered.

"I think mangos will be extinct by tomorrow," Amelia joked.

Chiquita let loose with a barrage of Spanish.

"English, Chiquita," Uncle Tito said. "It is rude to have a private conversation when you are with other people who don't speak the language. It excludes them."

She blushed. "Spanish is faster!" She turned to Amelia and Lila Mae and shrugged. "I just asked Uncle Tito if he could stop by my mother's place and bring a couple of my boxes with him."

Uncle Tito focused on Amelia. "Pecos is running the numbers for weddings—his, yours, and others."

Amelia blushed geranium-red.

"What in the world are you blushing for?" Lila Mae asked, giving Amelia the once-over.

"It's just embarrassing when people focus on my wedding when Carmichael and I haven't even talked about it," she said.

"There's a lot of upcoming changes for many people in the near future," Uncle Tito said. "Life-altering changes, but not in a threatening way. We'll talk about that when I get there."

The women stared at the iPad screen, each wearing their own expression of concern. Then they looked at each other, all silently questioning that statement.

"Will you be here for dinner?" Lila Mae asked. "If so, we'll put together a nice dinner party."

"Yeah. I'm leaving here in about an hour. I'll stop a couple of times for naps along the way," Uncle Tito said. "Chiquita, I'll call your mom and get your boxes. Anyone need anything from here?"

"Can you pick up a couple of bottles of that pure organic vanilla extract?" Amelia asked.

"Will do. I'll see you soon," Uncle Tito said, then signed off.

* * *

THE DINNER PARTY was moved from Lila Mae's to Madge's, utilizing her larger dining room table for the crowd. Chiquita set the table for over twenty guests. Carmichael spread a long table runner down the length of the sideboard table where hot bowls of food would be placed.

Amelia removed two succulent pork roasts from the large oven and set the roasting pans on the trivets to cool down. Joseph manned the stovetop, creating his mashed potatoes with caramelized onions. A pot of water with a steamer basket was standing ready for garden-fresh green beans from the farmers' market.

Carmichael returned to the kitchen with his floured cutting board and baking sheets. "We can start the green beans and rolls in about 15 minutes. The rolls will take 20 minutes to bake."

"The roasts have to rest for 30-40 minutes," Amelia said. "Then they have to go back in the oven at 475 degrees for 15-20 minutes. I can start making the gravy."

Amelia used two large roasting forks to move each roast to a large platter. Then she placed a roasting pan on a portable double-burner hot plate on the large kitchen island, turned two of the burners to medium-high, and added water and seasonings to the pan. She scraped the bottom of the pan, loosening the baked-on drippings.

Chiquita came into the kitchen and hovered near Amelia. "Here," Amelia said, thrusting the spoon at Chiquita. "Keep stirring and scraping. If it starts to boil, turn both burners to a simmer."

Amelia grabbed a small canning jar and a box of Arrowroot powder. She scooped in three tablespoons of arrowroot powder into the jar, added water, sealed the jar with the screw cap, and shook. She handed the jar to Chiquita.

"Pour this in and keep stirring until the gravy thickens," Amelia said.

After handing off the gravy mix, Amelia joined Joseph at the stove. "Need help?"

Joseph, in a chef jacket stained beyond ever getting clean, stirred his onions. They were a beautiful caramel brown. "Test the potatoes."

Amelia took the fork resting on a small plate and stuck it into one of the potatoes in the pot. "They're done." She grabbed potholders and the pan cover.

Carmichael nudged her out of the way. "Let me. This is heavy."

"Hot pan coming through!" Amelia announced as Carmichael walked the potato pan to the sink and drained the water.

The doorbell rang.

Carmichael became flustered.

"I'll go," Joseph said. He rushed out of the kitchen to the front door. He greeted Lila Mae. "Welcome! You're the first. Can you man the door? Madge is helping Dorothea with the twins."

"No problem." She shooed Joseph back into the kitchen. She set her purse on a chair and wandered into the kitchen. "Something smells good!"

The doorbell rang. Lila Mae made a beeline out of the kitchen and took up playing hostess.

* * *

PEOPLE MARCHED from the living room to the dining room where the feast awaited. Everyone was there except Uncle Tito. Bernie managed to be first in line. He speared two slices of pork roast, one large spoon of mashed potatoes, which he welled for gravy, and a serving of green beans. He lavished the entire plate in gravy and tottered to the table and sat.

The line comprised Dorothea and Henry, Madge and Rick, Teddy and Tilly, Chewie and Gina, Luna and Dougie, Victor and Jeffie, Walter and Zoe, Chiquita, Amelia and Carmichael, Bambi, Eirik and Chance.

Baskets of rolls and plates of sliced butter were on the table. Carmichael flitted all over the room.

"Sit down, Carmichael!" Madge said. "People know where everything is if they need something. You're wearing yourself thin."

The doorbell rang, the door opened, and footsteps marched to the dining room. Uncle Tito joined the diners. "Sorry I'm late. There was an accident on I-10 coming in. Let me go wash up."

Amelia stood and grabbed a plate, piling it with food. She set the plate at the only vacant place on the table. Uncle Tito joined the group, pulled out a chair, and sat down. He nudged Amelia. "Thanks for looking out for me. These people look hungry!"

Lila Mae made the introductions. "Uncle Tito, this is Dougie Vey, Luna, and Eirik. You remember my cousin Jeffie and her husband Victor?"

"Sure do." Uncle Tito stared at Tilly. "I'm not sure we've been introduced."

"You remember Tilly, don't you?" Dorothea asked. "She's Suzanne's daughter."

Uncle Tito's face lit up in a smile. "Of course. You've changed your look drastically. I didn't recognize you."

Tilly blushed. "I was quite a mess the last time I saw you, but that's all behind me now." She leaned into Teddy, her expression filled with love. "Teddy and I just moved in together."

"I'm glad things worked out," Uncle Tito said. He swung his focus to Luna. "And what about you?"

Luna turned beet red. She grew up hearing stories about

Uncle Tito and she knew he had info on her through not only his personal psychic hotline but also her cousins as well. She squirmed ever so slightly in her chair.

"Let ancient history stay buried in the past," Luna said, touchy.

Walter stepped in to defend Luna. "Luna's the receptionist at the chocolate factory, Uncle Tito, and she's doing a great job."

Luna glowed at Walter's comment. "And Dougie's the manager now."

Uncle Tito gave Dougie Vey the once-over. Suddenly, Uncle Tito zoned out.

Dougie reached his hand out, but didn't touch. "Are you okay?"

Madge elbowed Dougie. "Sshhh! He's getting a message for you."

"A message?" Dougie asked, skeptical.

"Just be quiet. We'll discuss it later," Luna whispered.

"Beware of a gift coming your way. If you accept the gift, you seal your fate," Uncle Tito said in a sing-song voice. He came out of his trance, rolled his shoulders, and looked across the table to Dougie. "Did I give you a message?"

Dougie stared at Uncle Tito, unnerved. "Yeah, but I'm not sure what it means."

"Sometimes you have to wait until the situation is aligned with your astrological houses," Uncle Tito said. "Just keep the message tucked away in your head."

Uncle Tito rubbed his hands together. "So, Pecos has run the numbers. We're supposed to get together Saturday and I'll report back."

Dougie looked around the table. "Horses or dogs?"

Everyone around the table chuckled—that was exactly what they had all thought before they knew Pecos.

"Wedding dates," Lila Mae explained. "Pecos is a numerologist."

* * *

LILA MAE PLUNKED her purse on the kitchen desk. She loved the long summer nights. Eight-thirty and it was still light outside. Chance came inside, followed by Louie. He sauntered up to Lila Mae and wrapped his arms around her. They smooched.

"I'm going to get my slippers on," Lila Mae said.

"Do I have any clean casual clothes here?" Chance asked.

"Yes, you do. I think you should bring more; you spend more time here than you do at the condo," she said.

Chance tsk-tsked as they went upstairs. Lila Mae kicked her shoes off while Chance ducked into the closet.

"Kahlua and cream?" she asked.

"Sounds great," Chance called out from the closet.

There was a rattle of bakeware downstairs. "Sounds like Amelia and Chiquita are back."

Lila Mae went downstairs. Amelia was putting the roasting pan away.

"That was a wonderful dinner. I loved your roast pork. Did you bring leftovers?"

"You bet. I love Joseph's mashed potatoes."

Chiquita came inside with two large, stacked, covered glass bowls and a gallon zipper bag filled with rolls.

"Who made those rolls?" Lila Mae asked.

"Carmichael. He's the king of rolls," Amelia joked. "I've got to see the recipe to make sure, but I think he adds cream of tartar."

Chance came downstairs without his jacket and shoes. He looked around the kitchen counter, the table, and the island. No drink. He went into the butler's pantry and gathered supplies.

"Sorry," Lila Mae said.

"It's okay," Chance said. "I don't expect to be waited on." He held the bottle of Kahlua up to Amelia and Chiquita.

"Nope. I've got to get home. Carmichael's probably waiting for me," Amelia said.

"Thanks, but I'm beat," Chiquita said. She left the house and walked to the garage apartment.

"I'll see you tomorrow morning," Amelia said as she headed to the door.

"Have a good night," Chance said.

"Go put your feet up," Lila Mae said.

* * *

AMELIA STEERED the Volvo down Lila Mae's driveway and stopped at the sidewalk. She looked for oncoming traffic to the left, then turned to the right. The hair stood up on her arms as she stared at a huge lump on the sidewalk, about twenty feet from the driveway. She opened her car door, unbuckled her seatbelt, and got out. She walked around the car and down the sidewalk with trepidation, and stopped a few feet away—from the body of a dead woman.

She turned and ran back to the Volvo, jumped in and threw the car in reverse. Amelia came within inches of bashing into Chance's Lexus. She threw the car into park, jumped out and rushed to the kitchen door, slightly hyperventilating. The door was locked. She banged on the door. Chance rushed to the door. He took one look at Amelia's face and led her inside to the kitchen table.

"What happened?" he asked.

Lila Mae was on her feet and around the table. "Were you in a wreck? We didn't hear a crash."

Amelia's mouth opened and closed, but no words came out. She pointed to the right, then managed one word. "Dead!"

Chance was out the door in his stocking feet. He ran down the driveway and turned to the right.

CHAPTER FOURTEEN

lashing police lights lit up the night at the end of the driveway on Del Monte. News trucks lined the street, all media vying for the breaking story of a murder in River Oaks. The media were rabid, wanting to know who the victim was. Lila Mae's parking area was packed with Alcott family members' cars. The family and extended family members were banned from the end of the driveway to not distract the police activities.

Frank and Stacy with HPDs crime scene unit were at the site with their cases of bags, bottles, collectors and tools, as was Chance who had donned his jacket and shoes again. The sidewalk was lit with powerful portable lights.

Stacy processed the body, going over the entire back surface, collecting what she could to help identify the murderer. She snapped pictures with the Nikon camera, examined the woman's fingers and her shoes, snapping more pictures. Stacy retrieved a spray bottle of Fluorescein from her kit and sprayed the sidewalk surrounding the victim.

She placed a sheet of white plastic beside the body.

"Chance, give me a hand, will you?" Stacy asked.

Stacy and Chance rolled the woman onto her back.

Chance stared at the familiar face. Without a word, he turned and walked up the driveway and waved the family into the house.

They gathered around the kitchen island. Amelia was still shell-shocked. Chiquita blew her nose from crying so hard. Madge just looked mad as usual. Dorothea wore her hands out with frayed nerves. Lila Mae nursed a headache. Bambi sniffled —she was way too familiar with murder.

Everyone waited on Chance. He glanced from Amelia to Lila Mae, a strange look on his face. He drew a breath. "The victim is Kimberly Munson."

"My neighbor?" Lila Mae all but screeched. She and Amelia looked at each other, shocked.

"Is that the awful woman who looks down her nose at you?" Madge bellowed.

"Why would anyone want to kill her?" Amelia asked, staring straight at Chance. "Honestly, we know she's a piece of work, rude, mean and nasty, but is that enough for someone to kill her?"

"Sometimes it only takes one incident for someone to dive off that deep end and commit murder. And if it was some irritant that occurred on a regular basis, the person snaps," Chance said.

"But we never heard any shooting," Lila Mae said.

"Not even anything like a car backfiring," Chiquita said.

"She was shot in the back, then in the back of the head," Chance said. "Most likely used a silencer."

The women all exchanged glances with each other.

"That sounds like a mob hit," Madge said. She clutched the front of her shirt.

"Just wanted to give you a heads-up," Chance said. "I've got to pay a visit to her husband."

* * *

CHANCE RETURNED TO THE SCENE. His eyes swept the area, then he focused on the ground as he walked down the sidewalk. He discovered a partial footprint less than a foot from the body. It looked as if the killer had stepped in blood.

"Frank, over here," Chance said.

"What'd you find?" Stacy asked.

"A good footprint," Frank said. He snapped a picture of it with the second Nikon camera. Then he sprayed it with Fluorescein to see if the whole bottom of the shoe would show. Sure enough, a ghost of the rest of the footprint appeared. "Let's see if I can trace where it came from."

Frank yelled at an officer. "Grab one of the hand-held lights for me, will you?"

The officer trotted over with the light and shone it toward the ground.

Frank slowly walked away from the body, following the trail of blood, the officer walking a couple of steps ahead of him. Frank discovered the first sign of the attack on the woman. A broken tooth and a dime-sized spot of blood at approximately one hundred feet from the body. Someone had clobbered her from behind, toying with her. He snapped a picture, drew a circle around the tooth, and another circle around the blood, then bagged the tooth.

Moving closer toward the body, approximately ten feet away, he found more blood. This was where she was shot in the back, he figured, but it didn't kill her. She crawled to her final resting place on the sidewalk where a bullet to the back of the head, execution style, ended her life.

Frank returned to the farthest point where he had bagged the tooth. He held a spray bottle of the chemical in one hand, and the officer held the powerful light. Frank sprayed a wide path as he walked down the sidewalk.

"Chance, I've got a footprint going away from the body," Frank called out. He set the bottle down and snapped a picture. The footprint glowed a good print.

Chance hurried to where Frank and the police officer stood. Frank sprayed the area again so Chance could see the evidence.

"Let's see if we can find more," Chance said. The three of them moved down the sidewalk.

Frank sprayed the chemical; the officer held the light, and Chance kept his eyes glued to the ground. They discovered a couple more prints, took pictures, and kept going. A print showed up in the Munson's driveway in the direction of the house and garage.

* * *

CHANCE RANG THE DOORBELL. He knew Manuela would have left hours ago, but there were lights on downstairs so he expected Judson was at home. He glanced at his watch: ten thirty. Many people watched the ten o'clock news, weather, sports, and financial spotlights before bedtime, so he didn't think this was too late.

He heard footsteps approach the door, a pause, and the door being unlocked. When the door finally opened, Judson Munson wore a surprised expression. "Detective Walker, what in the world are you doing here?" Then he noticed the flashing police car lights and the activity down the sidewalk. "Was there an accident at Lila Mae's?"

* * *

JUDSON MUNSON SAT on his black and white checked sofa with the red pillows, in a state of shock, an almost empty on-the-rocks glass in his hand.

Chance sat across from him, observing every nuance. His phone was on his knee, and he audio-recorded the interview.

"What time did Kimberly leave this evening?"

Judson thought for a moment. "I'm pretty sure her Republic of Texas dinner meeting was for six o'clock, so she would have left before I got home from the office. Say, five-thirty."

"Was this a monthly meeting?" Chance asked.

"Yes. Kimberly is... was... has been the president for the past three years," Judson said.

"Where did the meeting take place?" Chance asked.

"I don't know," Judson said. Then he perked up. "I'll bet it's on her desk calendar. Let me go get it." He left the room and turned to his right. He returned a few minutes later with a black appointment book opened to the current week. Judson showed the book to Chance. "She noted the meeting place and time."

Chance studied the calendar book. "I'll need to take this to the investigative team."

Judson flinched. "I should look at the next couple of weeks and see if there are people I should contact—cancel appointments and all that."

Chance flipped the page and saw several notations then flipped another page and saw some of the same notations, plus different agendas. "Why don't you take pictures of pages for the next several weeks?" He laid the book on the coffee table.

"Good idea," Judson said. He pulled his cellphone out of his pants pocket and, after maneuvering the book and phone to get the page aligned properly, he took pictures while Chance turned the pages. He sat down across from Chance, utterly lost.

Chance closed the book. "You didn't hear Kimberly's car pull into the garage when she returned home tonight?"

"No. The house is pretty well insulated, so we rarely hear outside noises," Judson said.

"So, you wouldn't know if someone followed her home?" Chance asked.

Judson shook his head. Chance stood.

"If I have any more questions, I'll give you a call." With that, Chance let himself out.

* * *

THE NEXT MORNING, Chance stood at the coffee bar in the HPD break room with his boss, Captain Mike Hennessy. Mike grabbed a sticky, gooey cruller out of a pastry box and took a bite. He and Chance grabbed their coffees and headed down the hall to the Captain's office.

They settled into chairs. Chance set his coffee on the desk. "I know he's lying about something, but I don't know what."

Mike sipped coffee. "Where's that thought coming from?"

"For one thing, I heard him approach the front door, so the place isn't as soundproof as he makes it out to be."

"Maybe he has hearing problems," Mike said. "For all we know, he may think the house is soundproof, but he's going deaf."

Chance nodded. "Johnson has Ronnie and Tom going door-to-door to see if anyone was walking a dog, or sitting on the patio with a drink and may have heard or noticed anything."

"Is there a walk-through door from the garage to the drive-way?" Mike asked.

"I'll go back out there this morning and take a closer look. I know Stacy planned to return and get a better look at the scene," Chance said. "And there's the footprint in his driveway."

* * *

CHANCE PULLED up in Lila Mae's driveway and headed to the kitchen door. Amelia whipped the door open.

"Who killed her?" Amelia blurted.

Chance held up his hands. "Too soon to tell."

"Let the man in the house," Lila Mae called out from the kitchen table.

Amelia blanched. "Oh! Sorry Chance. French Toast?"

"That would be great," he said as he bent to kiss Lila Mae on the forehead. "Would it be okay if Stacy parked in the driveway? She'll be here in about an hour."

"Sure," Lila Mae said. "How are things going?"

Chance went to the counter and prepared a cup of café mocha. "Slow. The guys are canvassing the neighborhood." He sat across from Lila Mae and took a swig from his cup. Amelia set a plate of French toast in front of him, along with a napkin and cutlery.

"We should make a casserole and bring it to Judson," Lila Mae said.

"What should we make? Scalloped potatoes and ham, a green bean casserole, macaroni and cheese, or my sweet potato casserole?" Amelia asked.

"Everyone likes mac and cheese. Just make enough for us too," Lila Mae said with a selfish laugh. She loved Amelia's four-cheese casserole. There never were enough leftovers.

* * *

LAWRENCE ROLLED across the floor in his office at Walter's law firm, his phone to his ear. Four monitors displayed the Alcott Chocolate Industries files. "Yeah, I see some ghosts of files and I'm trying to recover them. Shouldn't take me long." He ended the call and drilled his fingers across the keyboard in front of one of the monitors. A knock sounded on the doorframe. He spun around to see Agu and Madhub, two young contractual investigators who provided services to the firm. His face lit up.

"Hey, guys. Find anything for me?"

"Oh, we have some good news," Agu said in his melodious Nigerian voice.

"Yes, very good news," Madhub said. His English was accented only slightly from his Bangalore upbringing in the Silicon Valley of India.

Lawrence looked from Agu to Madhub, waiting.

"The Canary Islands!" Agu said. "This is a very sloppy embezzler."

"He bought a four-room furnished apartment for six-hundred ninety-one thousand, six-hundred fourteen dollars and eighty-seven cents ($691,614.87) on Tenerife Island, San Cristobal de La Laguna," Madhub said. "In a resort area."

Lawrence wondered if something was lost in translation. "Four bedrooms?"

They shook their heads. "No, only four rooms, and that's counting the bathroom," Madhub said. "According to the pictures, the views are magnificent."

"The good news is that we traced the money to two bank accounts: BBVA and La Caixa. You should be able to get the money back."

Lawrence's face lit up. "This is excellent news! I don't know what will happen with the apartment and the money that was used to purchase it, but all-in-all, this is great. Good job, boys. Let's go see Walter."

They left Lawrence's domain and walked back to Gina's command center. "Is Walter available?"

Gina noticed Madhub gripping his laptop. "Let me see what he's up to." She slid out of her chair and walked around the corner to Walter's office. She tapped on the door, then stuck her head inside to get a visual of the activity. Walter was going over some files on his desk.

"Hey, boss. Lawrence and the boys need to see you for a few minutes. They have a laptop, so maybe you should meet in the small conference room."

Walter looked up and smiled hugely. "I'm always interested

in what our experts have to say." He stood and walked to the door. He and Gina returned to the front of the office.

Lawrence, Agu and Madhub exchanged greetings with Walter in front of Gina's command center. "Let's go down here so you can present your show and tell."

They sat around the conference table as Madhub set up his MacBook Pro and connected to the large screen on the wall. Then they got down to business. Lawrence reiterated what Agu and Madhub told him, but let them go into specific details.

Madhub got the wireless connected and brought up the two banks where they traced the money to. Then he brought up the property that the manager had bought.

"Will you look at that view of the ocean!" Walter said. He looked over the property. "How much did you say he paid for this?"

"Just under seven-hundred thousand," Agu said.

"Kind of dumpy furnishings, if you ask me," Lawrence said.

"I agree. Do you think he went there and saw it in person, or bought it online?" Walter asked.

Madhub typed like scattershot and pulled up purchase agreements. "Looks like this was through an agent as an absentee purchase."

They all studied the documents Madhub had lined up on the screen.

"I'll have to turn this over to the big guys," Walter said. "I'm not sure about international real estate transactions. Gets trickier when we bring the embezzlement into the picture."

Madhub sent a zipped folder of files and the video of the property to Walter, Gina, and Lawrence.

"I just sent all of you a zipped folder, along with our invoice," Madhub said.

"I'll have Gina write you a check," Walter said. "Excellent work, boys."

Agu grinned. "This is why I like doing business with Alcott Industries. Interesting work and paid upon receipt!"

* * *

LILA MAE, Amelia and Chiquita stood at the end of the driveway watching Stacy as she worked the roped-off crime scene.

"Lila Mae, how much foot traffic comes down this sidewalk every day?" Stacy asked.

Lila Mae and Amelia huddled in thought. "We get people walking in workout clothes, but sometimes they walk in the street, people with baby carriages, little kids on their bikes with training wheels—it's hard to tell," Lila Mae said.

"Don't forget people like Manuela who walk to and from the bus stop," Amelia said. "Then there's service providers like Jingo. So, I guess we get moderate foot traffic. Why?"

Stacy looked down at the ground. "The murderer stepped in the blood. Frank traced those footsteps as far back as he could. We'll have to see if we can discover where they started, or where they returned to after the murder."

Lila Mae, Amelia, and Chiquita exchanged shocked looks.

"Do you think you can find him that easily?" Chiquita asked.

"Ha! There's nothing easy about finding a killer," Stacy said. "And sometimes clues aren't always on target."

* * *

STACY KNOCKED on the Munson's front door. After a few minutes, Manuela opened the door. Her eyes were red and puffy, and her nose leaked from an onslaught of crying. The maid's uniform was stretched to its limits—not a pretty sight when Manuela was barely five feet tall and weighed no less than one hundred sixty pounds. Stacy kept a straight face and tried hard to keep her focus on Manuela's face instead of her engorged body.

"May I help you?" Manuela sniveled.

Stacy presented her CSI badge. "I'm sorry to bother you, but I'm Stacy with the Crime Scene Unit for HPD. Would you be able to open the garage door for me? I need to see if Mrs. Munson's killer had access to the garage or her car."

Manuela sobbed at the mention of her late employer. She blew her nose into a wilted tissue. "I go push button."

"Thanks," Stacy said. She walked over to the garage, where her toolboxes waited. The garage door slid up the track. Stacy snapped on a pair of non-latex gloves, retrieved her powerful flashlight and her Nikon camera, and stepped over to the walk-in door and examined the doorknob and door frame. She discovered that either the doorknob had been recently wiped clean, or it had not been used.

Stacy snapped a picture of the doorknob, then attempted to open the door. It was locked. She walked inside the garage through the opened overhead door and found the light switch. She turned the lights on and approached the locked walk-in door. Stacy examined the doorknob with her powerful light and snapped a picture. The CSI expert turned the doorknob in an attempt to open the door, and the doorknob came off in her hand.

"Huh," Stacy said. She snapped pictures after she put the doorknob on the floor. "Maybe she darted out of the garage before the big door closed?"

She returned to the front door of the house and rang the doorbell. Manuela answered the door. "Hi Manuela. Is Mr. Munson home?"

"Si," Manuela said.

Stacy pulled a business card out of her pocket and handed it over. "Would you ask him if I could have a minute of his time?"

"Okay. I go get him," Manuela said. She shut the door, leaving Stacy outside.

The door opened a few minutes later, and Judson appraised Stacy. "May I help you?"

Stacy presented her badge and introduced herself. "Mr. Munson? Can you tell me how long the walk-in door has been non-functional?"

Judson stepped outside. "What do you mean?"

"Let me show you," Stacy said. She walked over to the garage and went inside, Judson on her heels.

She pointed to the broken doorknob on the ground. "As you can see, when I tried to open the door from the inside, the door-knob came off in my hand."

Judson was about to pick up the doorknob, but Stacy stopped him.

"Not a good idea to touch that just yet."

"Oh!" he said. "I see. It's part of the crime scene." He studied the doorknob and the door.

"I know I have never used this door—I typically use the mudroom door from the garage, over there." He pointed.

"What about your wife? Would she have pulled the car in the garage, closed it, and used that door to the outside?" Stacy asked.

"I can't imagine why she would do that. It's easier to come through the mudroom, especially if she had groceries, or dry cleaning, or shopping bags," Judson said.

Stacy grabbed her camera and took one last picture. "It was a thought," she told him. "I won't keep you, Mr. Munson. I'm sorry for your loss."

CHAPTER FIFTEEN

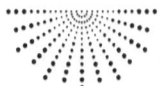

a brand spanking new Can-Am Spyder Rt Limited 6-Speed Semi-Automatic motorcycle, in a sparkling aqua metallic, zoomed down Kirby Drive.

The helmeted driver, dressed in leathers including a black fitted jacket with a gazillion zippers, to form-fitting pants, motorcycle boots, and gloves, was hunched forward, gripping the handlebars for all they were worth.

The bike slowed, turned on the directional light opposite the Abercrombie mansion, and darted across the traffic lanes into the driveway. It came to a halt by the impressive front door.

The rider revved the engine. The front door wrenched open and Carmichael stomped outside.

"Excuse me," Carmichael said, trying to be heard over the engine noise.

The rider turned off the motorcycle and stepped on the ground.

"Mrs. Abercrombie will not tolerate…"

The rider removed the helmet. Madge shook out her hair and smiled wildly at Carmichael. "What do you think of my new ride?"

Carmichael's mouth dropped open. "Madge? What the heck?"

Madge removed her gloves, unzipped her jacket and gazed at the machine with love. "I saw this couple at Whole Foods about six weeks ago. This woman just looked so confident on her motorcycle."

"Where did you learn how to drive a motorcycle?" Carmichael asked, still not completely over the shock.

"The dealer hooked me up with a trainer. It's not difficult, you know. If I can learn how to drive this, anyone can...well, maybe not Daddy, but you know what I mean. I'm challenged, but this was easy."

Carmichael caressed the aqua paint job. "I love this color. Is it custom?"

Madge smiled at the memory. "I had to assert myself to get what I wanted. The nitwit manager tried to talk down to me to get me to change my mind, but I gave him the paint chip and he called the factory."

Carmichael chuckled. "He didn't stand a chance against the Abercrombie death stare." His chuckle bloomed into a full, snorting belly laugh.

"Sometimes it pays off," Madge said, trying to be offended, but not succeeding. She knew full well how her moods swung.

"Don't spoil the fun," she said. "I'm going to ride it over to Lila Mae's tonight for dinner. And don't tell Rick! I'll have to ease him into the idea."

"That should be interesting," Carmichael said with a laugh and a snort.

Madge glared at him. "And Carmichael, do not text Amelia!" She grabbed her gear, and they went into the house.

* * *

MADGE WAITED until she was fashionably late to leave her house and get to her sister's place on Del Monte. She wanted to make sure she *made an entrance* so she could show off her beautiful *wheels*.

Carmichael had gone ahead in his Bumblebee, the name he gave his yellow-and-black Mini Cooper. Madge threatened him, short of torture and death, not to spill the secret of her new ride.

She checked her watch—a Shinola Moon Phase Bracelet watch called, *The Birdy*, and determined that everyone would be having cocktails right about now. Madge slipped into her riding gear, grabbed the keys and helmet and headed out the door.

JUST AS SHE THOUGHT, Lila Mae's parking area was packed with the clan's vehicles. Madge swung up the driveway and parked on the edge of the driveway near the kitchen entrance. She revved the engine for all it was worth, then tooted the horn to make sure everyone was aware a motorcycle had arrived.

The kitchen door opened and everyone piled out and swarmed the motorcycle, drinks in hand. With a dramatic flourish, Madge removed her helmet and fluffed her hair. Amelia's mouth almost unhinged.

"What do you think?" Madge asked the group, all staring at her and the motorcycle in disbelief.

"Are you out of your mind?" Dorothea bellowed, for once sounding like her older sister.

"No wonder you've been talking so loud!" Lila Mae exclaimed. "This explains everything. Are you prepared to go deaf?"

Amelia stroked the bike. "I love it!" Her glazed eyes met Carmichael's, which did not share her enthusiasm. He shook his head rapidly.

"It's almost as pretty as my truck," Uncle Tito said, grinning.

"Did you get your driver's license updated to include motorcycles?" Chance asked.

"The dealership helps with a lot of things like that," Madge said.

Henry stepped forward. "What'd Rick have to say?"

Madge cleared her throat. "Rick hasn't seen it yet."

Henry, Chance, Carmichael and Uncle Tito smiled.

"What?" Madge asked, glaring at the men. "He's going to love it! I hope he gets one so we can ride together."

"Are you going to join a club?" Amelia asked.

"I hadn't thought about it, but that might be fun. They go on rides all the time," Madge said.

Lila Mae gathered the group. "Come on, we've seen the show. You want a drink, Madge?"

Madge looked at Lila Mae's drink. "What is that you're having?"

"A tiramisu martini. You'll love it!" Lila Mae said.

* * *

GINA ANSWERED THE OFFICE PHONE, announcing the name of the firm and her name. She listened and jotted the caller's name on a notepad. "Oh!" she exclaimed in disbelief. "Mr. Branson is in court this morning. Give me your contact information and I'll have him call you as soon as he returns." She wrote furiously.

She hung up the phone and stared at her notes. The Miami attorney had given her just enough information prior to his contact details to start a file for Walter. She wondered how he would handle this new development.

Gina prepared a legal folder and placed it on the corner of her desk. She would hand it off to Walter the minute he stepped into the office. Her fingers itched to grab her phone and text

Chewie, but she would never violate the confidence of her position.

"Come on, Walter!" she said. Gina walked around her command center and went into the small kitchen. The office admin rummaged in the refrigerator and pulled out a yogurt cup, then grabbed a spoon from the silverware caddy on the counter. She was anti-plastic and had bought a set of silverware at Target. Gina and Chewie picked up interesting coffee cups and glasses when they went to garage sales and auctions. She was glad he was on board with her ban on plastic.

The front door opened and closed. Gina dashed to the front with her yogurt in hand. Walter removed his drenched raincoat and hat and hung them on the hooks. Gina had a special place for inclement weather clothing, with a mat on the floor to catch drips.

"Boss! I'm so glad you're back! How'd it go?" Gina asked.

"There will be no bail for Herman David!" Walter boomed with a smile.

"That's good. That snake would disappear into the grass," she said. Gina rounded her desk and grabbed the folder. "A call came in from Miami."

Walter thought about that single word: Miami. He waited for it.

"Nathan's dead," Gina blurted.

Walter sucked in his breath. "You haven't told anyone, have you?"

She interpreted that to mean: Lila Mae. "Heavens, no! That has to come from you, and I didn't know any of the details. You need to call this attorney, Mr. Merriweather, immediately!"

"Do me a favor, have Lawrence run a full background check on Nathan. I don't know how much information this attorney will provide. I want to know the status of his finances, marital standing, community significance, whether he's had any criminal exploits, even a traffic ticket—the whole nine yards," Walter said.

Walter went to his office while Gina went down the hallway, yogurt temporarily forgotten. She tapped on Lawrence's door.

"Enter!" Lawrence yelled out.

Gina opened the door and popped her head inside. "New project."

"More important than the ongoing factory business?" Lawrence asked.

Gina walked in and closed the door behind her. She wriggled her head while weighing the two projects. "Equal importance. Lila Mae's highly loathed ex-husband just kicked the proverbial bucket. Walter wants the full meal deal on him."

Lawrence rubbed his hands together in glee. "Nathan Daniel Delabarrera finally bought it? Oh, this will be my pleasure to dig up all the dirt on that Lothario."

He spun his chair over to a work station and the keyboard clattered as he pulled up a website, logged in then entered the details for a broad-spectrum search that not only included the entire United States, but all of North America and Europe. He discounted the urge to search other countries, just knowing basic facts about the man. He went about checking search boxes with a gleeful smile on his face.

"That ought to do it." He turned to Gina. "I'll report back as soon as I have everything."

Gina gave him a thumbs-up. She left to go find her now-warm yogurt.

* * *

LILA MAE HURRIED to answer the home phone at the kitchen desk. She set her café mocha on the desk, grabbed the handset and looked at Caller ID.

"Good morning," she said.

"Hi, Lila Mae. Walter wants to know if you could drop by sometime this morning," Gina said.

Lila Mae frowned. "What's going on, Gina?"

Amelia and Chiquita glanced at Lila Mae, trying to gauge her concern.

"There's something he needs to discuss with you," Gina said.

Lila Mae glanced at Amelia. She shrugged. "I could be there at ten. Is that okay? We're running late this morning and I haven't given up my robe and slippers yet." When the conversation ended, Lila Mae looked up at the ceiling. "Now what?"

"Is everything okay with your father?" Amelia asked.

"I'm pretty sure everyone's okay. Gina didn't sound like she was trying to hide any bad news," Lila Mae said, thoughtful.

"Maybe Walter wants some Feng Shui info for the big embezzlement case," Amelia offered.

Lila Mae shrugged. "We won't know until I go."

Amelia and Chiquita finished making breakfast tacos. Chiquita carried the platter to the table as keys clattered against the door and Chance came in.

"Am I too late?" Chance asked.

"Nope, right on time. We're the ones who are late," Lila Mae said.

Chance made a cup of café mocha and joined the women at the kitchen table. "Stacy and Frank may be around this morning."

"Did your guys ever find anyone who heard or saw anything?" Amelia asked.

"Nope. I find it remarkable that someone can get killed on a sidewalk, completely unnoticed, but if a socialite were to wear mismatched shoes out in public, everyone would be all over it," Chance said.

Lila Mae elbowed him. "Are you feeling a little jaded this morning?"

Chance thought for a moment as he ate his second breakfast taco. "I think I'm just tired."

"Well, you practically work seven days a week, Chance. Maybe it's time to retire," Lila Mae said.

He stared at her. "But what would I do? Collect stamps?"

"I don't know, but it is something you should start thinking about," Lila Mae said. She looked over at the kitchen clock. Not quite half-past eight.

"What are you doing today?" Chance asked her.

"Gina called. Walter wants to see me this morning."

"I wonder what that's about?" Chance asked.

"I have no idea," Lila Mae said. "I'll find out when I get there."

GINA SAT as quiet as a mouse, counting down until Walter delivered the big reveal. Pleasantries over, the news was conveyed to Lila Mae. Gina didn't even have to fill-in-the-blanks with a guess. The audible exclamation from Lila Mae over the news and details of her ex-husband poured forth.

"Five times? Bigamy? Twenty-five million dollars? Where did he amass that fortune? He spent money as if he had his own printing press!"

It quieted down until Walter presented the next big reveal.

"Are you serious? Why me?" Lila Mae shouted.

FORTY-FIVE MINUTES LATER, a somewhat calm Lila Mae and Walter emerged from his office, arms linked, and stopped in front of Gina's territory.

"I've got a lot to think about, Walter," Lila Mae said.

Walter patted her hand. "I know you do, and I know you will

come up with a plan. I have to hand it to Nathan, though. We won't have to go through probate due to the trust he set up."

"He must have known he was sick," Lila Mae said. "Otherwise, I'm sure he would have left a mess behind."

"I'm working with the Miami attorney to make the process go smoothly," Walter said.

Lila Mae looked at Gina. "Okay, you're free to start the brush fire. I'll bet it was hard keeping that secret."

Gina giggled. "You have no idea! Now that Nathan's gone, though, you can shed all those bad feelings you once harbored."

"He's still the president and CEO of WHOT," Lila Mae said with venom.

Gina and Walter appeared confused. "Never heard of it, and that wasn't listed in his assets, or in Lawrence's dossier on Nathan," Walter said.

Lila Mae smirked. "WHOT stands for the Worst Husband of All Time."

CHAPTER SIXTEEN

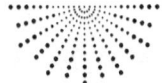

*L*ila Mae arrived home to four Bentleys, Chance's Lexus, and Uncle Tito's truck in front of her garage. She cringed, knowing Gina must have sent a group message.

Why would anyone think I needed comforting from that snake dying?

She sighed deeply, shut the car off, and went to the kitchen door to face the music of the inquisition. The door was opened from the inside, and Amelia engulfed her in a bear hug.

"It will be okay. You'll be able to process this," Amelia said.

Lila Mae separated herself from Amelia's clutches. "Have you gone bonkers, or something? He's finally dead and permanently out of my life!"

Everyone was in the living room. One of the first things she noticed was a couple of flower arrangements. She stared at the flowers as treacherous thoughts raced through her head.

Chance got up and put his arms around her, rocking her a bit. He whispered in her ear. "Behave."

She chuckled softly. He understood. They parted.

"I told you there would be life changes," Uncle Tito reminded her.

"I told you he's never wrong," Chiquita said.

Lila Mae sent a glare at Chiquita. She smirked at Uncle Tito. "Could have given me a heads-up on this particular change."

"What happened?" Madge asked in a mostly normal voice.

"Sit," Lila Mae demanded of the group. After everyone settled, she sucked in a huge breath. "Nathan Daniel Delabarrera, the worst ex-husband anyone could ever ask for, is dead. Evidently, he died while performing his stud services to one of the chosen Miami debutantes."

Dorothea's mouth dropped open. "Nathan was screwing a debutante? Was she ugly as sin, or did she have brain damage? He was an old man!"

Bambi cringed. "What a terrible man!"

"As you well know, Dorothea, Nathan could charm bees out of the hive," Lila Mae said.

"I'm going to hunt down the newspapers to read all the details," Madge thundered.

"You'd better share those with me," Amelia blurted. "I can't imagine a young woman taken in by the likes of him. What were her parents thinking of allowing her to even associate with that creep?"

"You all know how the upper crust of society works," Bernie said. "Look around River Oaks and the people who are in the society columns all the time. Some of the stupidest things I've ever read."

"Everyone has their own motives for their actions, or lack of," Chance said.

"Why did Walter need to see you?" Dorothea asked. "He could have told you that over the phone!"

"Wait for it," Uncle Tito told them.

Everyone glanced from Uncle Tito to Lila Mae. They held their breaths in the heavy silence.

Lila Mae took a moment to arrange her face, so she didn't look like the lunatic she felt like at the moment. "He left his entire estate to me."

"What?" Madge, Dorothea and Amelia shrieked in unison.

"Why would he do such a thing?" Amelia asked. "Was he trying to pay for his atonements?"

"After everything he put you through!" Madge blasted out. "Selling your beautiful Miami house to that... that stripper!"

"Porn star," Dorothea reminded her older sister. "Remember, we tried to watch one of her movies and you pulled the tape out of the VCR?"

"Look, Lila Mae, take what is given. That doesn't mean you have to keep whatever it is. You can always sell, donate, or gift his property," Bernie said. "It's not like you will ever need the money, if there's money involved."

Lila Mae waved them all to silence. "There's a lot I have to think about so I can direct Walter to do whatever it is I come up with. It's not going to be easy because I have all these emotions warring inside my head."

"You need comfort food," Amelia said. "Come on, Chiquita. This calls for macaroni and cheese."

* * *

LOUIE MADE little sleeping snorts as he slept in his bed in Lila Mae's office. She sat staring at the family tree spread across the monitor on her laptop. It was more of the whole clan, including extended family members, instead of a dedicated family tree like the type they had on Ancestry.com.

As Lila Mae perused the different legs of her relatives, she deduced that most of her relatives were wealthy, so she set them aside in her head. Next, she studied those near and dear people who were the backbone of daily life in the immediate family.

Her entire focus boiled down to four individuals: Amelia,

Joseph, Carmichael, and Chewie. She had excluded Bambi's Charlemagne, along with Chiquita because they were new to the family structure and would be provided for through other means if they stayed around.

Now that she had people lined up, she had to determine to what extent they would benefit from Nathan's estate. Lila Mae had Walter working on selling the Miami beachfront house. She figured it would take many months, if not years, to sell the mansion that was just over fifteen-thousand square feet. It had been built in 2009 by a popular builder who was known for top-quality craftsmanship.

The house was on a lushly landscaped lot with over two-hundred feet of beach frontage, two courtyards, an infinity pool, a dock, a summer kitchen, a waterfront-facing office, two generators, and a four-car garage. The main house had an elevator, twelve-foot ceilings, travertine and oak floors, mahogany doors/windows and Lutron lighting.

It was a gorgeous open floor plan with a living room, family room, and formal dining room. A huge selling feature was the fabulous eleven-hundred square foot kitchen with a coffee and tea bar, and access to a wine cellar. There were five bedrooms, a gym, and a library upstairs. The huge master suite with a seating area, wet bar, and room-sized closets was downstairs.

Walter was working with a Miami realtor to handle the listing and sale. Lila Mae was waiting to see how the house would be priced. She knew without a doubt it would exceed ten million dollars, but real estate wasn't her bailiwick.

She had spent a good twenty minutes looking at Miami Beach properties online and had to stop because it wasn't doing her any good. A realtor and an appraisal were the only options to move forward with selling the house.

After several unproductive minutes, where she felt like her head was spinning out of orbit, Lila Mae shut down the laptop and went downstairs. Amelia hovered around her.

"Are you really okay? Go sit down. I'll make tea," Amelia ushered Lila Mae to the kitchen table. "Chiquita, arrange some cookies on a plate!" Amelia commanded.

The two women jumped into high gear preparing tea and nibblers. Everyone settled at the table and sat quietly, looking at each other.

"I'm alright," Lila Mae said as she grabbed a dark chocolate-covered mint cookie. "It's been decades since Nathan and I were married, then divorced. Those first couple of years of hearing and reading about all of his carrying on were difficult to put up with, but after a while you become immune to the gossip."

"You weren't married that long, from what I heard," Chiquita said.

"Nine months," Lila Mae spat out. "That's how long it took him to show his true colors. But that was one stupid man. He could have gotten so much more if he had been a little sneakier. One of his biggest downfalls was his blabbermouth."

Amelia shook her head and grumbled to herself while stirring honey into her cinnamon tea. "Was he still married to someone when he died? Do you know any of the details?"

"Wife number five passed away last year. She was quite a few years older than him," Lila Mae said.

"The man had five wives?" Chiquita asked, somewhat shocked. She spewed out a string of Spanish while shaking her head.

"That's nothing," Lila Mae quipped. "Two of them were at the same time, and he was called out on bigamy charges."

Amelia scowled. "That scumbag. We know he'll definitely go down the slippery slope to hell. Good riddance."

Lila Mae stood. "Go home, Amelia. Chiquita, are you going out to dinner with Jingo tonight?"

Amelia stood. "Carmichael put a pot roast in the slow cooker this morning. It's going to be yummy."

Chiquita glanced at her watch. "Ay yi yi! I've got to get

ready!" She jumped up, grabbed her empty teacup, and dashed to the sink.

"Leave it," Amelia said. "Have fun tonight."

"You sure?" Chiquita asked. Amelia waved her away. "Thanks!"

* * *

CHANCE ROLLED up and parked in front of the garage at Lila Mae's at eleven forty-five. He let himself in at the kitchen door and hunted for Lila Mae.

"Anybody home?" He called out.

Louie trotted up to Chance from the living room. Chance bent and scratched the Tibetan Spaniel behind his ears and patted his head.

"Where's your mommy?" he asked. Chance headed toward the living room and looked out the French doors. Lila Mae was in the backyard with a quacking Quack.

Chance let himself and Louie outside. "It's pretty nice outside today. Must only be eighty-five or so with this little cool front."

"Hi, hon," Lila Mae said. They embraced and stood silently wrapped in each other for a few moments.

"I've got a hankering for naan. Want to go to Narin's?" Chance asked.

Lila Mae's face lit up. "Ooohh! Saag paneer! Rice pudding! Let's go!"

* * *

THEY WERE SEATED at a table for four, close to the buffet. The place was packed, and the line for the buffet was long. Chance and Lila Mae were five back from the plate stack and waited patiently.

They lucked out. Fresh pans of steaming food were being put in place. They finally had plates in hand and started the long process of making their choices. When they returned to their table, glasses of tea and a bread basket of fresh naan bread awaited them.

Chance grabbed a slice of naan and took a huge bite. He closed his eyes as he savored the taste of his favorite bread. "I love this stuff."

Lila Mae grabbed a slice of naan and tore off a piece. She dug into the saag paneer with her fork and spread it on the naan. She devoured the morsel. "I know what you mean. I can't live without Indian food."

Chance looked at her, lost in thought. "You got through the day yesterday. I take it everything is okay? You're okay?"

"Why in the world would Nathan leave me his entire estate?" she asked.

"Look at his track record. He knew that what he did was unforgivable. Maybe he thought you would forgive him," Chance said.

"It's not like I need the money, Chance. He could have left it to charities; a long-lost cousin or someone," Lila Mae said.

"What's the bottom line?" he asked.

"Not counting the house, which must be worth between ten and twenty million, the estate is twenty-five million dollars," she said as she bit into a Tandoori chicken leg. She delicately sucked her fingers prior to wiping them on her linen napkin.

She really didn't care if anyone else thought she was a slob. Chicken with a bone could be picked up, and she liked to lick the sauce off her fingers.

"Well, that's a tidy sum. I wonder who contributed to that number?" Chance asked.

"Four other wives and probably a couple of girlfriends," Lila Mae said. "I've been going over some plans in my head all morning. It's not like I need the money."

"I know you will put it to good use." Chance stood and surveyed the short line at the buffet. "Be right back. Want me to get you something?"

She shook her head. "I have to leave room for my rice pudding."

* * *

TWO LAPTOPS on Dolly Sanchez's kitchen table kept Pecos Ektadoro and Joseph Chung looking into details while Uncle Tito sipped coffee.

"For September, these are the days that the moon is not void of course," Joseph said. He rattled off a dozen numbers.

"What about October?" Pecos asked.

Joseph perused his chart. He listed seventeen numbers throughout the month.

Uncle Tito shut his eyes for a little while. He relaxed. "October twenty-first. It's a Saturday. It could be afternoon or evening."

"Okay, one down," Joseph said.

Dolly entered the room. "So, do you know when we're getting married?"

The three men announced the date together.

Dolly clasped her hands together. "Wonderful! Now I can make all the reservations and order the invitations!" She bent and kissed Pecos on the cheek, then hurried into the other room.

Pecos rubbed his hands together. "All right. Who's next?"

"Amelia and Carmichael," Uncle Tito said. "They need a lot of work. Those two scatterbrains have not planned ahead for their union. Actually, it's not Carmichael. He's raring to go, but Amelia won't make plans for some odd reason."

"They're solid, aren't they?" Joseph asked, showing a little fear.

146

"Oh, sure," Uncle Tito said. "I've got to sort this out. Maybe do a little session with the two of them."

"We'll find the best day for them and get them working on it," Pecos said.

"Check May next year," Uncle Tito said. "I'm sensing that would be a good month for them."

Joseph checked the moon phases for May and they chose May fourth, so as not to interfere with Mother's Day.

"Since Teddy and Tilly, and Gina and Chewie are best friends and go so many places together, do you think they would want a double wedding?" Joseph asked. "If so, we could focus on one day."

Uncle Tito repeated his inner process. Pecos ran their birth-dates in his program then explored the combinations several different ways.

"That was a good suggestion," Uncle Tito said. "Neither Gina or Chewie comes from money, and while Teddy is well off, he isn't wealthy. Tilly has the DuBoise money in back of her and I feel that Suzanne and Gray would be generous for a shared wedding day."

"June thirtieth would be the perfect day for them," Pecos said.

"I couldn't agree more," Joseph said.

"So, how are we going to get that ball rolling?" Uncle Tito asked. "This may take a little diplomacy with four mothers involved."

"There's only three mothers," Joseph said. "Teddy's mother passed away years ago."

"Madge will take that role," Uncle Tito said.

Joseph's acknowledged that; he became thoughtful. "I hope she allows the other mothers to have input. Madge can be a little overbearing at times."

"If we had chosen June twenty-third she may have steam-rolled everyone, but the thirtieth is a peaceful day so all plans leading up to that day should be balanced very well," Pecos said. He smiled his toothy grin.

Uncle Tito slapped his thigh and stood. "All right. We've got work to do! We need to get some people engaged!"

Joseph looked doubtful. "How are we going to go about doing that?"

"Psychic whispers," Uncle Tito and Pecos said at the same time.

Joseph covered his mouth with his hand and giggled.

*　*　*

TILLY, Teddy, Gina and Chewie sipped tea at a sidewalk café. Tilly doodled on a napkin. "I'm thinking of using my middle name instead of Tilly."

Teddy automatically reached for his phone, but Chewie snatched it away and waggled his finger at him. Teddy scowled.

"You know it's a challenge for me to talk still," he said directing his irritation to Chewie. His words came out as *Ewe no iks a chal lunge fer meep toot tawk still.*

"Look, you have to put more effort into it, like Eirik said. I know it's hard and you don't like what you hear in your ears, but it's the only way," Chewie said.

"You're a good friend," Tilly said to Chewie.

"So why do you want to change your name?" Gina asked.

Tilly looked at Gina across the table. "My name is associated with my horrible past. I was such a screw-up. I just want a clean break from all that."

"What do you want to be called?" Teddy asked. His words came out as *Wod dood ewe wonk toot beep culled.*

"Jolene," Tilly said.

"I don't know. I like Tilly," Teddy said. His words came out as *Ike dond node. Ike like Tildy.*

"I agree with Teddy," Gina said. "Don't get hung up on old perceptions."

Tilly hemmed and hawed, twisting her mouth while thinking it through. "Okay. I'll leave it alone for now."

A quiet moment passed. Chewie and Gina stared lovingly at each other. Teddy and Tilly clasped hands on the table.

Chewie seemed to have an epiphany. He glanced over at Teddy who appeared wide-eyed as a similar thought crossed his mind.

CHAPTER SEVENTEEN

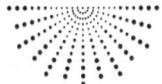

(W)alter beat Gina to the office—a rare occasion. He pulled out his keys and unlocked the door, flipped on the lights, and went into his office. He hung his Greek fisherman's cap on his weathered brass hat and coat rack and set his briefcase on the credenza. Walter heard the front door open.

"Morning," Gina called out. "The café downstairs was having a two-for-one on breakfast sandwiches. I snagged us each one."

She entered Walter's office and set a coffee and a sandwich on his desk.

Walter opened the wrapped breakfast sandwich. "I love croissant sandwiches. Thanks, Gina."

The office phone rang.

"Who in the world could be calling this early?" Walter said.

Gina grabbed the handset off Walter's desk. "Branson and Associates." She listened diligently and made notes on a blank sheet of paper. "May I put you on hold for a moment?" Gina pressed the hold button.

"It's the Miami realtor," she said.

Walter slipped into his chair. "Maybe they need more information."

Gina slipped out of the office to eat her breakfast and get settled. Walter picked up the receiver and pressed the button to answer the call.

"Branson here." He listened. "Two, you say?" He listened a bit more. "Email them over and I'll take a look at them." He ended the call, stood up, and left his office.

Gina was waiting on her computer to boot when Walter approached.

"We've got two contracts on the Miami house!" Walter announced.

Gina looked at her calendar. "It was just listed! Wow, that's wonderful!"

"Be on the lookout for the email. If you could print them out and put each in its own folder, I'll present them to Lila Mae. Won't she be surprised!"

Lawrence pushed through the door. He had an uncovered, tall paper coffee cup gripped by his teeth, an arm full of folders, his briefcase, and a small breakfast sack.

He deposited the file folders on the corner of Gina's command center, then grabbed the cup. "Good morning."

"What are all these?" Gina asked, nodding to the folders.

Lawrence patted the stack of folders. "These, my dear, are the hangman's knot for our buddy, Herman David. I've categorized them by offenses, if you will. We should make copies of these for Dougie. He's got a big mess to sort through, and these will shorten that process. He'll be able to see exactly what took place so he can rectify everything."

"Good job, Lawrence," Walter said. "I knew I kept you around here for a reason!"

"Ha!" Lawrence said. "I love the diversity of my projects, Walter."

* * *

THE GIRLS, including Bambi, sat at Madge's kitchen island counter eating eclairs and drinking iced tea while Carmichael hovered nearby.

Bambi licked her fingers, too gooey to use the lace-edged linen napkin on her lap, while Dorothea, all proper, ate her éclair with a fork and knife.

"For heaven's sake, Dorothea, pick it up!" Madge said, giving her youngest sister a look of disdain. "You'd think you never licked your fingers in your life, but I remember when you were not so proper."

Dorothea glared at Madge.

"Honestly, do you two always have to squabble?" Lila Mae asked. Her phone rang. She squealed as she hurriedly sucked on her fingers, grabbed her napkin, and finished the job.

"Will you answer that!" Madge bellowed.

"I'm trying!" Lila Mae said. She grabbed the phone with clean fingers and pressed the talk button just as the call went to voicemail. "Darn!" She noticed it was Walter, so she pressed Call Back and waited.

"Hi Gina, did you or Walter just call?" Lila Mae listened. "Oh! I can't believe we already have two offers!" She looked at her sisters and Bambi with surprise. "Are you serious? Tell Walter to take the best offer then. Okay. Let me know."

Lila Mae disconnected the call and turned to the girls. "This must be some house! Walter received two offers over the listing price!"

"Didn't he just have the house listed the other day?" Dorothea asked.

"What did it list for?" Carmichael asked. He grabbed the pitcher of tea and topped off the glasses on the counter.

"Twenty-five million, seven-hundred something," Lila Mae said.

Mouths dropped open.

"And these two people went over that amount?" Bambi squealed.

"Where's your laptop, Madge?" Dorothea asked. "Let's take a look at this house!"

Carmichael unhooked the kitchen laptop and brought it to the island. He slid it over to Lila Mae. "Here, you drive since you know the address."

"Do you have a mouse?" Lila Mae asked. "I don't like those touchpads."

Carmichael opened the kitchen desk drawer, retrieved a portable mouse and placed the tiny USB driver into the port on the computer for her. "Here you go."

Lila Mae navigated to the Internet, brought up the real estate website, found the house listing and clicked. They perused the fifty pictures with lots of ooohhhs and aaahhhs.

"Are you sure you want to sell this place?" Madge asked.

Lila Mae swung her head toward her older sister. "Seriously, Madge? This is a party estate. Are you going to don a bikini and have people traipsing through the place day and night?"

"It could be a family estate—you know, for when people want to get away and chill out at the ocean," Dorothea said.

"You two are out of your minds!" Lila Mae said. "I think the house and property are a little pricey to sit vacant until one of us wants to go to the beach. And, I don't know about you, but I'd like a much smaller beach house—something cozy where there's less focus on me."

Madge and Dorothea contemplated.

"I agree with Lila Mae. That big place is way too much house and property when you don't live there and don't know anyone to fill it up," Bambi said.

"I guess you're right," Madge said.

"Lila Mae is the sensible one," Dorothea said.

* * *

CHEWIE HAD a text conversation going on while he and Bernie waited for their meals at Houston's Restaurant on Westheimer.

"Who are you having a conversation with?" Bernie asked.

"Teddy. We're planning a surprise for our girls," Chewie said.

"What kind of surprise?" Bernie asked. "Are they going to enjoy it, or clobber you?"

"Top secret," Chewie said. "No one can know."

Bernie blew air out of his mouth. "Make sure you think this through."

"Don't worry, it's going to be great," Chewie said. He set his phone on the table, rubbed his hands together, and offered Bernie a big smile.

The server brought their meals. Roasted prime rib for Bernie, and a NY strip for Chewie.

"Did you hear that Joseph's mother and his grandmother are planning a trip to Houston to meet Eirik?" Chewie asked.

"Now that will be nerve-wracking. Poor Joseph," Bernie said.

"Poor Joseph? You mean poor Eirik!" Chewie said. "He's going to have Chinese coming at him in every way imaginable. I hope they don't freak him out to the point he breaks up with Joseph!"

"Oh! I hadn't thought about it from his point of view," Bernie said. "I can never understand his grandmother, and I can barely understand his mother when they are in town, but they are a loving family."

HAMILTON'S STEAK House was packed as usual as Teddy, Tilly, Gina and Chewie stood at the maître d' station. Teddy stared at the maître d' with an unspoken question. The man inclined his head ever so slightly, then winked. As the foursome were led off to their table, the conspirator gave the thumbs up to Chewie.

They were seated at their usual table and the familiar wait staff filled their water glasses, took their beverage orders, offered up the specials and disappeared with their meal orders. Within moments, their drinks arrived. Chewie excused himself to go to the restroom. Then Teddy followed suit. They returned to the table moments later.

Just as the conversation started, a string quartet approached and began playing an enchanting melody.

"Oh, this is nice. I wonder when Hamilton's started this?" Gina asked.

Teddy and Chewie grinned at each other. Gina and Tilly were oblivious until the men stood, went down on one knee each and pulled jewelers' boxes out of their pockets.

Gina screeched. Tilly gasped. Both said yes.

Gina plowed into Chewie, practically throwing him to the floor. She cried and hugged him, then stared at the beautiful ring on her finger.

Tilly managed to breathe as she stared at the ring on her finger. She stood, threw her arms around him and kissed Teddy into next week.

The patrons and staff erupted into applause. The quartet finished the song, then removed themselves from the room. Two staff members approached and handed over cell phones to the guys. Chewie and Teddy thanked them by giving each a twenty-dollar bill. They thumbed through their picture icons and produced the video and pictures.

They all watched the captured moments in rapture. Then Teddy and Chewie forwarded the video and photos to the girls and family members.

"A plan well followed," Teddy said.

"No wonder you looked a little nervous when we arrived," Gina said. She clunked Chewie's shoe with her own.

Teddy grabbed his glass and raised it.

"Salut!" the foursome said.

"We should have a double wedding!" Tilly suggested, excited.

Gina's mouth fell open. "Wouldn't that be fun!"

"We'll let you girls do all the planning. Just tell us when to show up," Chewie said.

Their meal arrived, and everyone dug in.

* * *

DOUGIE VEY and Bob Marx had several faxed orders laid out on a table on the second floor.

"These two require custom molds," Bob said. "The others are standard molds."

"How long would it take to have the mold created and get the order into production?" Dougie asked.

"We work with two different companies," Bob explained. "For small orders, we use custom candy molds. They have a great system and their turnaround is remarkable. We have the design drawn up and send the vector graphic file with the specs to them and they create silicone molds."

"Now, if it's a major production, something we are going to carry for ongoing orders, we use American Chocolate Mould Company. They are much more expensive, and their development takes four or five months. Their molding line could create around 48,000 pieces an hour," Bob said.

Dougie looked over the orders. "So, this one should go to Custom Candy Molds, and this one to the other company, right?"

Bob shrugged. "To meet the deadline, we'll have to have silicone molds made for this quick turnaround order, but we should invest in the molding line for their second order."

"Okay. I'll let you handle that. If you need anything, let me know," Dougie said. He walked down the center aisle and watched as the delectable creations whizzed down the line. He stopped and talked with workers for several minutes, then took the stairs to the ground floor.

Luna stapled several pages together fresh from the fax machine when Dougie approached.

"Hi, honey," she said. "Look, an order from Saudi for a herd of buffalo and a ranch! I love looking through the book with all the designs. They are amazing!

Dougie took a look at the fax. "I love this business. Should have found this job years ago."

"I love my job too," Luna said. "There's so much to learn. I like it when the tours come through. Everyone is so excited, and they get to sample the chocolates."

Dougie patted her on the shoulder. "This was good for both of us. Well, I'd better get upstairs. Still trying to get through the pile of files Lawrence dropped off."

Dougie walked to the elevator and stepped inside. He disembarked on the fifth floor and stopped by his admin's desk. Jody Meyer had returned to her former position after attending the emergency company meeting. When she was convinced that her former boss was behind bars, she accepted her role back.

"Hey, Jody," Dougie said. "How are you doing with that list I gave you?"

"Hi Boss," Jody said. "We don't have time to go over this right now, you have to get to your staff meeting."

Dougie glanced at his watch. "Be there in a minute." He rushed off in the direction of the men's restroom. A few minutes later, he walked down the hall to the conference room.

* * *

BERNIE AND WALTER sat at the round table in Bernie's suite at Lake Sides Assisted Living Center. Walter and Bernie each had paperwork in front of them.

"Dougie is doing a great job at the factory," Walter said.

"It makes sense that he could get that place turned around. He has an impressive background," Bernie said.

"Lawrence is working with several agencies to recover the siphoned money," Walter explained.

Bernie started talking, but Walter held up a hand. "Because the money isn't terrorist-related, no one is taking any action. And those banks keep their customers private. They will fight tooth and nail to keep the money in their banks."

"What! There's no way I'm going to sit back and let that thief have access to the money once he is out of prison!" Bernie roared.

"I know. Lawrence is trying to work some angles, but it isn't going to be a quick fix. The real estate is another matter. It may take several months to come to an agreement with the original owner. What a mess. I feel sorry for the guy because it puts him in a bind—he already bought another piece of property with the proceeds from the sale."

"That's not good," Bernie said. "Will he try to sue us?"

"There's no telling. It all depends on whether anyone suggests taking legal action," Walter said. "I think we are the most litigious country on the planet, so we will have to see. I don't mind offering a *pain and suffering* settlement, but if this guy sues, he's not going to get millions. The bottom line is for us to get all ties released from the property so we don't have any responsibilities."

Bernie let out a little huff. "I can't believe I allowed this to happen to my company."

"No point in beating ourselves up. It was a very expensive lesson. Now we have audits in place, along with cameras on each floor," Walter said. "It will never happen again."

They sat in silence for a moment. "What about this business with Nathan?" Bernie asked. "What's going on with that?"

"You're going to have to talk to Lila Mae about that," Walter said. "That's her business and a separate legal matter, you know that."

"Maybe I'll have Chewie take me over to her house," Bernie said.

* * *

CHEWIE PARKED the Bentley in Lila Mae's parking area in front of the garage. He and Bernie made their way to the kitchen door. Bernie tapped on the glass and looked for Amelia, or Chiquita.

"Where in the world are they?" he grumbled.

"Ring the doorbell," Chewie said. He reached around Bernie and pressed the button.

Amelia and Chiquita came running into the kitchen. Amelia got to the door first and unlocked it. Bernie pushed inside.

"Sorry, we were looking at wedding venues," Amelia said. "We saw your engagement video and pictures. That must have been something! Congratulations!"

"Yeah, Teddy and I planned everything down to handing our phones over to the waiters. So, have you and Carmichael set a date then?" Chewie asked, excited.

"Not yet. We got Dolly and Pecos's invitation and were checking out the chapel and one thing led to another," she explained.

"Where's my daughter?" Bernie asked.

"Oh, she's right in the middle of all this wedding stuff," Chiquita said. "We're in the dining room. Come join us."

Bernie clomped along with the walker. Lila Mae was in front of one laptop on the dining room table. Amelia and Chiquita had two chairs in front of the kitchen laptop on the table.

"Hi, Daddy. Want to see where Pecos and Dolly are getting married?" Lila Mae asked.

"What for? I'll be there so I'll see it then," Bernie said.

Lila Mae stared at her father. "Well, you're in a mood."

"Let's go somewhere and talk," Bernie said.

"This must be something if we need a private talk," Lila Mae said.

Amelia looked from Lila Mae to Bernie to Chewie, searching for signs from someone that would give her a clue. Bernie looked as if he had something on his mind. Chewie's face showed a question mark—he didn't know what this was about. Lila Mae studied Bernie.

"Okay. Why don't we go to the small study?" Lila Mae suggested. "Do you want some iced tea and cookies?"

"What kind of cookies?" Bernie asked.

"Chocolate chip with pecans," Amelia said.

"Did you make them?" Bernie asked.

"Of course," Amelia said.

"Then yes," Bernie said with a smile. "I never turn down anything you've cooked or baked!"

Amelia turned to Chewie.

"Count me in!" He sat in front of the laptop Lila Mae vacated and looked at the screen. "Oh, that's pretty."

* * *

BERNIE AND LILA MAE sat in the small study in the front of the house that was rarely used. Empty glasses and plates sat on the table. Bernie wiped his mouth with his napkin and placed it on the table.

"This was a good planning session, Lila Mae. You have a very good mind for business, and I like the way you thought out all scenarios and came up with the best choices," Bernie said.

"Your suggestion of the private label and use of the factory facilities is something I hadn't thought of," Lila Mae said. "That third floor would be an ideal space to set up. I want to put this plan into action as soon as possible."

"Have Walter work out all your details, then we can move forward," Bernie said.

CHAPTER EIGHTEEN

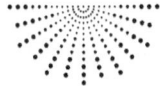

*D*ougie Vey stepped off the elevator and approached Jody's desk. "Anything new?"

"Yes! Some guy named Big Nose Sam called while you were meeting with Bob," Jody said as she handed him the message. "What a ridiculous name!"

Dougie paled. He gripped the pink piece of paper, then snapped back into reality. "Yeah, he's from Vegas. They all use stupid names there. Thinks it makes them sound important."

Dougie hurried into his office and shut the door. He leaned against the door and studied the ceiling for a moment. He went around his desk and sat in his chair, and stared at the message. Reluctantly, he picked up the handset on his desk phone and placed the call.

A booming voice announced his presence. "Sam."

Dougie swallowed. "This is Dougie Vey returning your call."

"Dougie. Good to hear from you. How's Houston?" Big Nose Sam asked.

"Great," Dougie said. He knew the boss already had all the intel on him and was aware he was at the chocolate factory, so there was no point in trying to hide or deny anything that came up in the call.

"That picture and info you sent has bought you a hundred percent reprieve, Dougie," Big Nose Sam said.

Dougie exhaled in relief. "I'm happy to hear that. Glad I could help."

"Are you and Luna getting married?" Big Nose Sam asked.

Dougie's face lit up at that question. "We haven't made any concrete plans yet, but we have discussed the possibility." He wanted to ask why, but knew that could open a dangerous path of discussions.

"Since you've got a legit job there, I thought I'd return some of that money for a nice wedding present," Big Nose Sam said.

Thoughts dashed across Dougie's face. He grimaced. "That's awfully thoughtful of you, boss, but I couldn't accept a money gift. I've got a brand-new life here and I like it a lot. When we do decide to set a date, I'll send you an invite and you can send a toaster or something."

He cringed. The boss would be insulted by his suggestion of a toaster, but Dougie knew he couldn't get roped into the glamour of big bucks. Those types of gifts kept a noose around your neck.

"A toaster? Ha! I'll buy you an entire kitchen, Dougie. You just let me know when," Big Nose Sam said. "I gotta go. Roger's bugging me."

"Okay, boss. Take care."

And the phone line disconnected. Dougie hung up the handset and wiped his forehead with the back of his hand. He was sweating bullets. He prayed this would be the last time he ever heard from Big Nose Sam.

* * *

STACY AND FRANK stood before a wall of photos from the sidewalk murder. The illuminated footsteps vanished midway down the sidewalk, then one appeared, turning into the Munson's driveway. There could have been a car parked in the driveway if the killer had followed the woman home.

"This killer knew what he was doing. His trail is pretty well hidden after this point," Stacy said, pointing to the driveway picture.

"Kimberly Munson was one strong woman to keep going after being shot in the back," Frank said.

"She was running for her life." Stacy stared at the wall for a moment longer. "I feel as if I'm missing something. It's right here in front of me, but I can't pull it out of this."

"She must have seen the murderer as she pulled into the garage, and it must have been someone she recognized. I think she ducked out the garage door while it was lowering so she could talk to that person," Frank said.

"That seems likely," Stacy said. "Unless she went into the house and came out through the front door."

"No hair, fibers or any other trace elements that did not belong to her specifically," Frank said. "

"Well, we've got nylon-filled hollow-point bullets. He wanted to maximize the damage on impact," Stacy said.

They continued to study the photos. "Huh," Stacy said. "Look at what we have here."

She pointed to the photo from the garage, where she took a shot of the doorknob on the ground when Judson Munson had been standing beside her.

"If I'm not mistaken, the shape of Mr. Munson's shoes looks awfully similar to the footprints we have that the killer gifted us," she said.

Frank pulled one of the pictures of the bloody footprint and stuck it up next to the photo Stacy pointed out. "Yeah, we need to get into Munson's closet."

"Let me call Chance," Stacy said. She pulled her phone out of her pocket and thumbed through phone numbers.

* * *

CHANCE STOOD before the wall of photos. "Too much of a coincidence. I'm glad you took that shot in the garage. Let's get a search warrant and get over there."

"Judge Windsor's been in a good mood lately; maybe she'd sign off without much of a fuss," Stacy said.

Two hours later, Stacy, Frank, Chance, and a uniformed cop were at the Munson's front door. When Manuela answered the door, she screamed, held up her hands, and started jabbering in Spanish.

"Can anyone interpret that?" He asked.

"My Spanish is too iffy," Frank said.

"Okay, I need to use an unorthodox method," Chance said. He called Lila Mae. "Hon, would it be okay if Chiquita came next door to translate for Manuela. She's upset and reverted to Spanish." He listened, then disconnected the call. "Help is on the way."

The clack, clack of Chiquita's high heels rushed down the sidewalk. Chiquita and Amelia, who wore sensible slides, rounded the sidewalk to the front door, huffing with excitement and a little exertion from their fast trip.

"I'm here for moral support," Amelia said. "Manuela doesn't know Chiquita, but she knows me."

Chance looked at Chiquita. "Okay, Chiquita, this is official police business. When I ask Manuela a question, I want you to ask it in Spanish, and you have to interpret every single word she says in answer. Do you understand?"

"Yes. I'm glad to help you. First, let me introduce myself to her and tell her that I work next door so she's okay, okay?" Chiquita asked.

"Sure, I understand. That would be helpful to calm her down," Chance said.

Chiquita turned to Manuela and spoke in Spanish.

"Manuela, mi nombre es Chiquita. Estoy trabajando con Amelia. Somos primos a través de tío Tito. La policía quiere que yo te traduzca para que te hagan preguntas. ¿Está bien?" (Manuela, my name is Chiquita. I'm working next door with Amelia. We're cousins through Uncle Tito. The police want me to translate for you so they can ask you questions. Is that okay?)

Manuela, completely distraught, looked from Chiquita to Amelia to Chance and his group. She started crying buckets. "¡Tengo papeles! ¡Por favor, no me lleves! ¡No hice nada!"

Chiquita translated for Chance. "I have papers! Please don't take me away! I didn't do anything!"

"Tell her this is not about her. It is about Mrs. Munson's murder," Chance said.

Chiquita translated into Spanish. "Dígale que no tiene que ver con ella. Es por el asesinato de la Señora Munson."

Manuela snapped alert. "Oh! Okay."

"Ask her if Mr. Munson is at home. Tell her we have a search warrant," Chance said.

"Manuela, la policía quiere saber si el Sr. Munson esta en casa. Tienen una orden de registrar la casa," Chiquita said.

"-No, el señor Munson se fue hace una hora. Puede estar en la funeraria. ¿Debería llamarlo?" Manuela replied.

Chiquita translated back to Chance. "No, Mr. Munson left about an hour ago. He may be at the funeral parlor. Should I call him?"

Chance shook his head. "It is not necessary to call him. We want to look at specific areas of the house. All doorways that lead into and out of the house, and Mr. Munson's closet where he keeps his shoes."

Chiquita translated to Manuela. "-No es necesario llamarle. Queremos ver áreas específicas de la casa. Todas las puertas que entran y salen de la casa, y el armario del señor Munson donde guarda sus zapatos."

"Okay," Manuela said. She let them into the house and showed them the door off the kitchen to the garage, the French doors to the backyard, and the French door from the master bedroom to the backyard.

"Frank, you check this doorway in the bedroom and I'll take a look at the shoes. Then we can check out the other doorways," Stacy said.

"Okay," Frank said. He rolled his cases just inside the bedroom door.

Chance turned to Manuela. "Where does Mr. Munson keep his shoes?"

Chiquita translated. "-¿Dónde guarda el señor Munson sus zapatos?"

Manuela entered the master bath and pointed to the closet on the right.

Chance showed her a picture of the shoes and asked if she recognized them.

Chiquita translated. "¿Reconoces estos zapatos?"

"-Sí -dijo Manuela-. "Tiene diez pares, todos de diferentes colores."

Chiquita translated. "Yes," Manuela said. "He has ten pairs, all in different colors."

Chance entered the closet with Stacy on his heels. They looked at the neatly displayed clothing and shoes. Chance counted. Eight pairs of shoes.

"Manuela, there are only eight pairs of shoes here. I'm sure Mr. Munson is wearing one pair. Do you know where the other pair is?" Chance asked.

Chiquita translated. "Manuela, sólo hay ocho pares de zapatos aquí. Estoy seguro de que el señor Munson lleva un par. ¿Sabes dónde está el otro par? "

"Están en la vestidor. Cuando salga del trabajo hoy se supone que los lleve al taller de reparaciones de calzados para que las suelas sean reemplazadas," Manuela said.

Chiquita translated. "They're in the mudroom. I'm supposed to take them to the shoe repairman and have the soles replaced when I leave work today."

"Show me," Chance said.

Chiquita translated. "Muéstrame."

They all took off to the mudroom, stepping around Frank who stayed at the bedroom door.

Manuela led them through the house to the kitchen and the mudroom beyond. A brown pair of shoes was on a small table near the door. She pointed to the shoes.

Stacy maneuvered around the group and set her case on the floor. She pulled out a pair of non-latex gloves and snapped them on. Then she pulled out her Fluorescein and sprayed it all over the shoes. She turned one shoe upside down and kept the other right side up.

The bottom of one shoe illuminated like Christmas lights, which showed it had been saturated with blood at some point.

"Ooo," Manuela said.

"Wow, look at that," Amelia said.

"What is that?" Chiquita asked.

"Blood," Amelia said.

Chance pulled out his phone and placed a call. "Mike, we need a full house search warrant. Stacy found blood on the bottom of Munson's shoe—it matches the shape and size of the footprint at the scene. We need to find the weapon." Chance listened to his boss, then ended the call.

"We continue what we set out to do. Johnson will bring the new search warrant out as soon as Judge Windsor signs off."

Manuela looked at Chiquita, wanting answers. "¿Qué esta pasando ahora?"

Chiquita translated to Chance. "What's going on now?"

"Tell her we found blood on the shoe, which makes Mr.

Munson a murder suspect. Chiquita, ask her if she knows if the Munsons have guns in the house."

Chiquita translated. "Dile a ella que encontramos sangre en el zapato -- que hace al Sr. Munson un sospechoso de asesinato. Chiquita, pregúntale si ella sabe si los Munsons tienen armas en la casa."

Manuela looked from Chiquita to Chance in open-mouthed surprise. She spewed out words. "Ella dice que nunca ha visto armas, pero el Señor Munson le dijo que él Pisó un animal muerto Ella trató de limpiar la sangre con blanqueador."

Chiquita translated. "She said she's never seen any guns, but Mr. Munson told her he stepped on a dead animal, and she tried to clean off the blood with bleach."

Manuela's lips quivered. She sniffled.

"Tell her she is not in any trouble at all, so not to worry," Chance said.

Chiquita translated. "Dile a ella que no se preocupe, no esta en problemas."

Manuela visibly relaxed. "Okay."

* * *

LILA MAE STOOD at the end of her driveway, looking down the street toward the Munson's house. She contemplated walking down there to wait for Amelia and Chiquita, but decided against it since they might be there a while, and she didn't want to interfere with Chance's investigation.

"Dang, I wish I knew what was going on down there!" Lila Mae said in frustration.

Just as she was about to turn back to her house, a familiar Mercedes drove past. The car paused at the Munson's driveway, then sped away and screeched around the corner.

Lila Mae pulled her phone out of her pocket and called Chance.

"Hey, I'm at the end of my driveway, and Judson just drove by on his way home. He took off fast when he saw the cars in his driveway," she said. She listened for a moment. "Love you."

A few minutes later, Amelia strode down the sidewalk, stepped into the road to avoid the police tape, then stepped back onto the sidewalk and joined Lila Mae at her driveway.

"Where's Chiquita?" Lila Mae asked, somewhat concerned.

"She may be there for a while. Manuela is pretty freaked out. One boss dead, the other one probably her murderer. She's practically forgotten how to speak English, so they may need Chiquita until they leave."

Lila Mae looked at Amelia, shocked. "You mean they think Judson killed his own wife?"

"Even though he was the better of the two, he's always been a scumbag snob, and now it looks like a murderer. That jerk stepped in his wife's blood and made Manuela clean his shoes. Told her he stepped on a dead animal! Can you believe it?" Amelia asked.

Lila Mae's mouth hung open. "Killed his own wife! Chance and I heard them fighting late one night."

"We know Chance, Stacy, and Frank will find out what happened. That guy can hide, but they'll find him." Amelia shook her head.

"At least Tilly's not a suspect this time!" Lila Mae said.

They chuckled, hooked their arms together and walked up to the house, and went inside.

CHAPTER NINETEEN

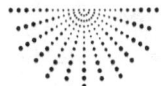

*L*ila Mae pulled open the door and stopped at the front desk where Luna worked.

"Hi Luna. My, but you have this set up wonderfully." They hugged.

Luna beamed. She hadn't heard praise from her older cousin since she was a young girl. "Thanks, Lila Mae. I'm so glad Walter and Bernie hired me. This is the best job ever! I've organized the orders coming in through the fax machines, and I confirm their receipt back to the sender. I also try to monitor the surveillance cameras as well. When I see something suspicious, I report back to Dougie."

Luna pushed the sign-in sheet toward Lila Mae. After Lila Mae signed in, Luna handed her a badge.

"Are these new?" Lila Mae asked. She noticed a basket on the counter with a sign that read: Drop your badge here when leaving.

"Yes, it's part of the new security process Lawrence and Dougie set up.

Lila Mae clipped the badge to her jacket. She glanced at her cousin. "You know what, Luna? I don't think I've ever seen you so happy."

Luna smiled widely. "That's because I don't think I've ever been this happy, even when I was singing at the big church. Nothing compares to this."

Lila Mae tapped the counter. "Before I forget, I'm expecting a team of workers to arrive at one o'clock. Would you send them up to the third floor for me?"

"Okay. I'll give each of them badges and will send them up. Do you know how many there'll be?"

"Four men and a truck. They'll be removing things from the third floor and taking them to the warehouse," Lila Mae said.

"Okay. I'll have them drive around back. They can park close to the freight elevator," Luna said.

"When this phase is finished, you'll see a lot more people for the redesign of the area," Lila Mae said.

"Gotcha covered," Luna said.

Lila Mae walked to the elevator and hit the button.

* * *

WALTER AND BERNIE sat at the conference table on the fifth floor. They were joined by Lawrence, Chewie and Teddy.

"Henry can't make it today, so it's just us," Walter said.

"Okay, let's jump in. What's the bottom line?" Bernie asked.

Lawrence passed sets of stapled pages around the table. "Unfortunately, the company is going to take a hit of four million dollars. I can't get the banks to release the money, and I can't get any of our government agencies to cooperate and take any action."

"So, what it boils down to is the guy is going to be rolling in money once he gets out of prison?" Bernie asked. He fumed silently.

Walter added to the misery. "I'm afraid I have more bad

news to deliver. The man who sold Herman the apartment is suing us for wrongful damage."

"You'd be better off letting him off the hook, releasing him from the property as soon as legally possible to cut his losses," Teddy said. His wording came out all garbled.

The men scrunched their faces trying to understand what Teddy said.

Teddy typed furiously and let the phone talk for him. He turned to Chewy and typed a message. "Don't you dare tell on me!"

Chewie wadded up a piece of copy paper and threw it across the table at Teddy.

"The bottom line is just under five million," Lawrence said. "You should be able to write that off as a loss. If you pursued the property, the lawsuit could cost you."

There was nodding around the table.

"The upside to this catastrophe is that every employee has had their photo taken and is wearing a badge, which is the only way they can get access to the building," Lawrence said.

"We have installed all the security cameras, but I believe we require more cameras outside, particularly near the freight elevator and the dumpsters," Lawrence said. "Chewie and I think it's too dark in those areas, so we are going to have lights with motion detectors installed as well."

There was nodding around the table.

"Good thought. Has the cleaning crew been badged? What do we know about them?" Teddy asked.

"We're going to have to delve into that further. Even though they don't work for us directly, since they are employed by a cleaning company, I want to make sure that everyone is a documented worker, and that no one that sets foot on these premises has a criminal record," Walter said.

"Let me look into that," Teddy said. He made notes on a notepad.

* * *

BERNIE AND CHEWIE walked to the area where small-volume special orders were created by hand. Several workers, dressed in white lab coats and wearing latex gloves, and white hats, filled custom molds.

"I think I'm going to have the girls come down here and learn how to do this. It's been twenty years since they've helped out with the chocolate orders, and we should have an emergency backup," Bernie said. "Bambi's never had the opportunity to make real chocolate."

"That's a good idea. Maybe we all should give it a try," Chewie said. "It doesn't look difficult at all."

Bernie smiled.

* * *

JOSEPH REMOVED HIS STAINED SMOCK. He perused a folded stack of them on the shelf in the butler's pantry. Not even one smock among the stack was like his former signature sparkling white smock he had been so proud of. Every single one was stained with baby burp. He shook his head.

"Time to place an order, and time for me to return to the kitchen and let the nanny do her job," he said as he slipped into a stained smock and left the closet.

Dorothea's head bobbed at the kitchen table. She was haggard from lack of sleep, and no amount of coffee was going to keep her alert. Joseph came into the kitchen and spotted his boss dozing over her coffee.

"Why don't you go take a nap?" he suggested. "The house is quiet; the babies are sleeping. You need to take advantage of these moments."

Her head snapped up. "Huh?"

Joseph came around behind her chair and massaged her shoulders. "Go lie down on the sofa while it's quiet."

"Good idea," she murmured. She got up and stumbled into the living room and collapsed on the sofa.

Joseph shook his head. Since Dorothea's pregnancy and the twin's births, everything had changed. No more dinner parties. His boss was a sleepwalker half the time. Joseph knew this would all change within a few more months when Haley and Camilla were a little older. He just hoped they would all make it through the baby gauntlet in one piece.

He went to the butler's pantry and sat at the desk. Joseph perused the current week on the calendar, then flipped the page. He picked up a pencil and wrote *dinner party* in the blank block for the following Tuesday. Then he thought about the menu. He decided on Chicken with Riesling as the main course, boiled new potatoes in a butter-parsley sauce, and green beans. It would take a lot of chicken and mushrooms.

Joseph ran to the bar and checked the stock of Cognac. He made a note to purchase another bottle of Baron Otard XO Gold Cognac. The current bottle was down to less than a cup. Then he ran down to the wine cellar and was almost giddy to see a case of Maximin Grunhauser Herrenberg Riesling Kabinett 2012, and two cases of Eroica Riesling 2012.

For the first time in months, Joseph felt alive. He raced up the stairs to the butler's pantry and clacked on the laptop, creating a list of people to invite. He was excited to present his plan to Dorothea. She needed a pick-me-up just as much as he did.

* * *

JUDSON MUNSON WAS on the run, afraid of what might be following him, and his brain was not functioning at its peak. He was about to drive the Mercedes to the valet station of the Hotel Contessa at the Riverwalk in San Antonio. At the last minute, he realized the error of that decision and stepped on the gas and kept going.

He could very well run into people he knew anywhere along the Riverwalk, which meant he would not be able to visit any of his favorite restaurants. His mind was a whirlwind of chaotic thoughts. It had been years—decades, in fact—since he had to think about staying under the radar.

The first thing that would have to go was the Mercedes, Judson thought. Changing the plate was an option, but he figured it would be better with a nondescript vehicle. He needed money and disposable credit, or gift cards. Judson knew he would still have time to drain at least one of his bank accounts, but he would have to move fast and get out of Texas.

Instead of finding a hotel, Judson pulled into a Chase bank parking lot. He checked the time. Thirty minutes before closing, so enough time to get what he needed. He figured he would have another six to twelve hours before they checked his banking records to see if he used his debit or credit cards. By then, he would be out of the state of Texas, and the police would have to guess which direction he took.

He was greeted by a young, male customer service employee.

"I need to withdraw forty-thousand dollars, "Judson said. "I'm headed to Amarillo to help Padre Martinez with the cleanup and restoration of the church from the fire."

"Oh! I hope no one was hurt," the young man said, concerned.

"Fortunately, the two meeting buildings that were destroyed were unoccupied at the time," Judson said.

After showing his driver's license, bank card, and checkbook for the account number, he had to assure the bank employee he was not under duress and being forced to withdraw the money. The young man headed directly to the manager's office to get approval for the uncommon transaction. Forty-grand in cash did seem odd; most people would get a cashier's check.

After thirteen nerve-wracking minutes that Judson forced himself to stay put in the chair, the employee returned to his desk with two Chase Bank money pouches. He unzipped the pouches and pulled out the cash from each. He separated the bills into denominations, then commenced to count them.

It took a few minutes to count forty-thousand dollars manually, clacking numbers into the computer. When everything added up correctly, the young man placed the money back into the pouches.

He printed the paperwork in duplicate and had Judson sign and initial what seemed like a thousand places. When everything was in order, the bank employee slid the two pouches across the desk to Judson. They stood, shook hands, and Judson had to wait for the door to be unlocked so he could exit the bank and be on his way.

Judson had to force himself to walk at a natural pace back to his car. Once inside, he locked the doors and threw back the passenger-side floor mat. There was a locked box built into the floor. He retrieved the key from his keyring and opened the box.

He picked up the Ruger and placed the two bags into the box. Having second thoughts, he pulled one of the bags out, unzipped it and retrieved about five hundred dollars in mixed bills. Then he tossed the pouch in the box, replaced the gun, locked the box and covered it over with the floor mat.

* * *

DOROTHEA WAS ABOUT to turn over on the couch, which would have tossed her to the floor. She groggily woke, sat up and got her bearings. She slipped into her sparkly slides and walked to the kitchen.

Joseph heard her approach and came out of the butler's pantry where he had been planning meals for the week.

"Did you have a good nap? You look refreshed," he said.

"It helped," Dorothea said. "I'm ready to try coffee now. I was too tired earlier."

Joseph sprang into action. "Café mocha, or plain coffee?"

Dorothea thought for a moment. "Café mocha."

She sat at the table, yawned widely, and rubbed her face. Gone were her Cleopatra eyes and flawless makeup. She could not remember when she had last sat before her makeup mirror. "Joseph, I need a change!"

Joseph brought the cup of café mocha to the table and a plate of nibbles. Dorothea picked up a plump date and bit into it. She finally got around to the cup and slurped Amelia's famous concoction, the entire family was hooked on.

Seeing her settle in and looking much more alert, Joseph presented his dinner party plan. "Yes, you do need a change! All you do is take care of babies. You don't do anything fun anymore!" He jumped up, grabbed the calendar and the menu, and returned to the table.

"Let's throw a dinner party! Next Tuesday is free, and I have drafted a sample menu." He slid the menu across the table to her.

"Oh, I love your chicken and Riesling. Instead of those potatoes, remember those baked potatoes you made last month?" Dorothea asked. She positively glowed, thinking of them. "They looked like lobster tails, and they were to die for!"

Joseph brightened. "You're right. They were good." He slid the paper back and made the change to the menu. "Would you want me to send texts to everyone, or do you want to do that?"

* * *

MADGE SAT at her kitchen island counter and snacked on tuna salad and crackers. She had just shoveled a forkful of tuna on a wheat cracker when her phone dinged. Then Carmichael's phone dinged. They looked at their phones.

"Oh, good. Dorothea is returning to the land of the living," Madge said as she read the text.

Carmichael tried to hold his sarcasm. "She did have twins, if you recollect."

"I seem to recall she has a couple of nannies," Madge snipped.

"They don't breastfeed the babies," Carmichael said.

Madge stared down Carmichael. "Look, Carmichael. Dorothea uses a breast pump like untold numbers of new mothers do. Those baby girls can wake up every hour and they'd still have milk. The night nanny can feed them."

"I realize that, but if they are both screaming at the same time, something's going to give," Carmichael said.

Madge capitulated somewhat. "I suppose. But she always adds drama to every single scenario in her life."

Carmichael shoved an overflowing cracker into his mouth and chewed. "Look who she followed. She never had a chance to express herself because you and Lila Mae were so far ahead of her, and so much more accomplished."

Madge thought about it. "We need to think about how we can make this a fun evening for her." She shoved another tuna-stacked cracker in her mouth. "I'm going out for a ride. There's a bike club I want to check out."

Carmichael balked slightly. "You're going to join a motor-cycle gang?"

"Not a gang. There's a club for middle-aged people, you know. It's not like I'm going to join Hells Angels," she thundered.

* * *

MADGE PULLED her Spyder into the parking area of a warehouse complex in Bellaire and parked among the dozen or more bikes. The sign over the door read: Old Goat Riders. She snickered as she removed her helmet and gloves, flipped her sunglasses up over her hair, and unzipped her leather jacket. Her boots looked a little goofy with her crop pants, but she shrugged it off. She opened one of the storage areas on the rear of her bike, grabbed her purse and headed to the door.

A buzz of conversation and laughter greeted her as Madge walked inside. People sat at tables drinking coffee and soft drinks. A middle-aged man rose and walked over to her.

"Hi, can I help you?" he asked.

Madge looked around, then focused on the man in front of her. "Yes, I'm interested in finding out about your club. I bought a motorcycle a couple of weeks ago and would like to get to know other riders."

"Oh, great. I'm Lloyd. Welcome to Ogre."

"Ogre?" Madge asked with a crooked little smile.

"Yeah. We just tacked the 'e' on the end of OGR," Lloyd said with a big smile.

"Madge Abercrombie," she said. She stuck her hand out, and she and Lloyd shook hands. "Tell me about the club, what you do, how many members you have, your community plans—do you have a brochure?"

Lloyd scooted over to a messy desk, hunted around, and produced a brochure. Madge noticed the different fonts, the blurry pictures, and a few misspelled words. She shoved it in her purse.

"We have seventy-five active members," Lloyd said.

"How much are dues?" she asked.

"Sixty dollars a year," Lloyd said.

"Is that all?" Madge asked, surprised. She pulled out her checkbook. "Who do I make the check payable to?"

"OGR," Lloyd said, pleased.

Madge completed writing the check and handed it over to Lloyd. He placed it on a duck clip made from wood and a clothespin, on the desk.

"How 'bout I introduce you around?" Lloyd said.

She noticed a poster on the wall and got closer for a better look. It was Marlon Brando from the movie *The Wild One* (1953) and a 1950 Triumph Thunderbird motorcycle.

* * *

MADGE ARRIVED home ninety minutes later, exuding happiness. She parked the bike in the garage and entered the house through the kitchen door.

Carmichael looked up from the stove. "Well, how'd it go at the club?"

"Carmichael, you won't believe it! They're called the Ogres, and it's not that far from Amelia's!" She explained about the club name.

He guffawed. "That's pretty clever."

Madge pulled the brochure out of her purse and showed him. "They really need some help to get organized."

Carmichael studied the brochure. "This is a mess. What are the people like?"

Madge's face lit up. "They're a good bunch of people from what I experienced. First, you have to be at least forty to join. The median age is sixty-two, and almost an equal number of men and women. They seem to be from all walks of life."

"Any big bruisers?" Carmichael asked. His face crinkled in amusement.

"There was one guy with earrings and tattoos, but everyone else seemed to be regular business people, moms, dads—everyday people," she said. "I think I'm going to like this club."

"That's good. You've needed an extracurricular activity since you gave up on most of the boards you were on," Carmichael said.

"I was drowning in those meetings. I should have vacated those positions five years ago!" Madge said.

* * *

TEDDY ARRANGED the throw pillows on the sofa. Tilly spread the throw on the back of the sofa, then moved one corner of the coffee table an inch to get it into alignment. They looked around their new space. The forty-five-inch thin TV was mounted on the wall, and the speakers were inconspicuous.

The wet bar positively glowed with Teddy's mother's old copper beer mugs with brass handles. The café table in the kitchen seated two, and the dining room table seated six without the extra leaf.

"I guess we're as ready as we're ever going to be," Teddy said. More and more of his words were coming out just fine. He figured in another month or so he would be back to talking normally.

"Want to see if they're available Friday afternoon for cocktails?" Tilly asked.

Teddy looked around. "Sure. We can move the rest of our clothes and things over the next few days."

Tilly took out her phone and texted up a storm. "Okay, I sent an invite to my mother and Gray, and Rick and Madge for Friday. Let's see if Gina and Chewie can come over tonight."

"Good idea." Teddy said. He engulfed Tilly is a hug and kissed her deeply. "You have made me so happy."

"If it weren't for you, I'd probably still be on the slippery slope," she said, kissing him back.

CHAPTER TWENTY

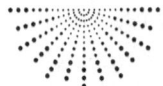

*G*ina and Chewie took the tour of Teddy and Tilly's townhouse.

"This is awesome," Chewie said.

"I love the kitchen," Gina said.

The foursome returned to the living room and settled on the comfortable new furniture.

"My parents and Teddy's brother- and sister-in-law are coming over tomorrow," Tilly said. She went to the kitchen and poured wine from the open, breathing bottle, placed four wine glasses on a tray and returned to the living room and offered a glass to everyone.

Gina and Chewie shared a conspirator glance. "We're moving in together!" Gina burst out.

"Congratulations!" Teddy and Tilly said. They raised their glasses to Gina and Chewie.

"Salut!" They all toasted.

"Your place or Chewie's?" Tilly asked.

"Mine," Chewie said. "It's bigger, and we like it better than Gina's place. Besides, the Alcotts are paying for it as part of my employment contract, so we might as well take advantage of it."

"We're saving up so we can buy a house," Gina said. "Chewie is really good at putting money away, except for his gadgets. I'm trying to curb my shopping addiction."

"You'll be able to take that money you've been paying for rent and apply it to your credit card or car payment to eliminate that debt," Tilly said. "Start with the bill with the lowest balance. You'll be out of debt soon because your rent was pretty steep."

"Wow, that's good advice," Gina said. "I've already given my thirty-day notice at the complex so next month I can start paying off my credit card. That will only take one month's rent, then I can burn off the car payment!"

"We can begin our new life debt-free," Chewie said. "Did you learn that from your classes, Tilly?"

"A local author talked to us about budgeting, and she gave us a discount to her online course," Tilly explained. "It was one of the best courses I've ever taken."

They chatted about the course for a little while, and Gina wrote down the information. "I'm going to look that course up. I definitely need to get more hands-on information on how to get my credit score higher."

* * *

JUDSON ENTERED the motel room with a shoebox filled with odds and ends from the Mercedes. The bed contained shopping bags, a new rolling suitcase, a briefcase, car tools, a change cup, CDs, a box of tissues, a windshield sun blocker, and other mundane things people cart around in their cars.

He had checked the car inside and out for any identifying personal items and wiped down all surfaces. Judson made sure to straighten out the passenger seat floor mat covering the now empty box. Satisfied with everything he saw on the bed, knowing nothing had been overlooked, he locked up the motel room, got in the Mercedes and drove away. Ten minutes down the road, he pulled into a fairly crowded retail parking lot, rolled down the windows, wiped down the steering wheel, door handle, window buttons, and left the keys in the car.

Judson walked away from the car, knowing that within a short period, it would either be in a chop shop or halfway to Mexico. He dropped the old washcloth he had used to wipe away his fingerprints into a trash container by a bus stop, and continued walking for two blocks to a small-time car lot he had passed earlier that catered to the underdogs of society who either had no credit, or their credit was wrecked beyond immediate repair.

Judson strolled through the lot, looking over vehicles for sale. He stopped before a five-year-old Honda Accord. The blue paint job was fairly new. The tires still had considerable tread, so they would last for this trip and beyond.

A hefty man with a shiny bald head, wearing a sports jacket, sauntered over to Judson. "She's a beauty," he said, nodding to the Honda. "Al Duncan." They shook hands.

The windshield showed the asking price of seven thousand nine-hundred ninety-five dollars.

Judson opened the driver's door and looked at the interior. The leather seats appeared to be in excellent condition. "How many miles are on the odometer?"

"Let me go get the keys," Al said. He wrote down the license plate number and hurried back to the office. He returned moments later with the distinct Honda keys and handed them to Judson.

Judson turned the engine over. He noted the mileage from the odometer and listened carefully to the engine. "How much do you want for her?"

Al didn't waste a beat. He started his spiel. "The sticker price is just under eight grand. With taxes, title and insurance..."

"Six thousand cash?" Judson asked.

Al studied Judson closely. "Cash?"

"Cash," Judson said.

"Sold!" Al said.

"I'd like a little modification," Judson said. He and Al walked to the office to conclude the deal.

Forty minutes later, Judson drove the Accord off the lot. Two miles later, he pulled into an auto detailing shop and was met by Miguel.

* * *

ONCE AGAIN, Stacy, Frank, and Chance went through the Munson house. When they stepped over the threshold, Stacy stopped and looked down at the low-pile carpet mat inside the house.

"Hhmm," she said. She opened her kit and withdrew her spray bottle of Fluorescein and sprayed the mat. She opened the door to light up the entryway. The mat lit up a tiny spot of blood. "I love it when someone leaves me presents!"

Frank dug out a bag the mat would fit in and handed it to Stacy. She bagged and labeled the evidence.

"Let's see what else we can find," Chance said as they went on a search for guns. They knocked on walls for secret panels to no avail. Manuela stayed in the kitchen, eating.

After an hour, they met back up in the foyer.

"There's nothing here," Frank stated. "We've been through this house top to bottom, inside and out. If he had guns, he must have taken them with him."

Chance was adamant. "Couldn't have. He didn't even know we were on to him, so he wouldn't have planned. Otherwise, those shoes would have been long gone. I can't believe he was that stupid not to expect to be considered a suspect."

"I think we need to accept the fact that this house is clean," Stacy said. "I've processed his shoes. His wife's blood is on the one shoe, and there's no explaining that away. It was fresh blood, not *the day after* dried blood—say from walking to the crime scene and stepping over the tape."

Chance let out a huff. "I don't think there's enough to prosecute. We need the weapon with his fingerprints on it."

* * *

"LUNA? THIS IS MADGE," Madge announced over the phone. "I'd like to come by and pick up an assortment of chocolates." Madge named off a list of what she wanted.

Carmichael knocked on the doorframe of her home office and walked in with an eleven by fourteen sheet of paper. He folded it over once, then folded it again until what remained was the front page of a folded brochure with crisp, colorful pictures. He held it out to Madge.

"What do you think?" Carmichael asked.

Madge took the brochure and studied the cover and unfolded it, studying each panel. "This looks beautiful, Carmichael. I'll present it to Lloyd at the club. If they want club members posing, or if he sees anything that needs to be changed, I'll let you know.

"I think it should be printed as a brochure with individual pages," Carmichael said.

"That would most likely be best. All this folding would be a major pain to see the details, not to mention getting wrinkled in the process. I'll let Lloyd know what we plan for this," Madge said.

* * *

THE NOUGAT BENTLEY pulled up to the front door of the Ogre club. The lot was filled with motorcycles, all parked in an orderly fashion. Every make, model and color imaginable seemed to be in the lineup, most sporting a little green ogre, which was the club logo.

Madge tooted the horn after she parked the car, then she pressed the button to unlatch the trunk. The front door of the club opened and Lloyd and Tom came outside. Lloyd whistled as he looked over the Bentley.

"So, you're THAT Abercrombie!" Lloyd stated.

Tom's face drew up in question.

"The chocolate people," Lloyd explained.

Tom still didn't have a clue.

Madge shrugged it off. She walked to the trunk of her car and lifted it fully open. Several Alcott Chocolates paper sacks stood waiting with their handles straight up, ready to be transported to the chocolate-deprived.

Lloyd and Tom smiled with delight as they grabbed three bags each. Madge grabbed a Kroger shopping bag and shut the trunk of the car.

"Let's go make everyone happy," she said with glee.

They went inside and Madge took control. "Let's push these three tables together."

Four men volunteered and in no time had the tables aligned and the chairs against the wall, out of the way. Lloyd and Tom set their bags on the table. Madge dug into her bag and removed plates, napkins and disposable utensils.

Tom and Lloyd pulled boxes of chocolates out of the bags and spread them out. When everything was in place, Madge invited the club members to sample the offerings. After the last person served himself, Lloyd went to the front of the room and spoke to the group.

"Guess who our new best friend is?" Lloyd asked the group. He swung an arm toward Madge. "Madge Abercrombie. Her father created the Alcott Chocolate company from the ground up, and we Ogres are lucky to have Madge as one of our own."

The group clapped whole-heartedly. There were a few hoots and whistles among the crowd.

"Come on up here, Madge. Give us a few words," Lloyd said.

Never having had a shy bone in her body, Madge approached the front. She looked around. "You don't have a microphone or sound system?"

Lloyd shrugged no.

"Well, I'll just make do with my voice then," she said. "I'm very happy to be a member of the Ogres, and I've enjoyed meeting everyone at the club." She hesitated, thinking through what she wanted to say. "I've noticed that there doesn't seem to be a structure to the club, and I don't mean that as an insult to Lloyd or the founding members. I was raised with structure, and I've always been involved with clubs, groups, boards, and the like."

The audience sat in rapt attention, listening to their new member.

"I would like to help take this club to the next level and get us involved in things like community projects. Wouldn't it be great to educate people of all ages regarding the joys and the safety issues about motorcycles?"

She had their attention. Madge noticed a lot of head-nodding throughout the room. "We should start by cleaning up this place and getting things like a sound system, a new brochure, and better lighting."

Madge pulled the example of the brochure out of her purse and showed Lloyd. "I took the liberty of redoing the brochure. If there are no changes, I suggest we get some printed up. The treasury has more than enough money for brochures and a facelift to this place. What do you say?"

Lloyd spoke up. "I think you should be our new president! All those in favor say aye."

There was a resounding "aye" throughout the room.

* * *

MANUELA WALKED down the sidewalk from the bus stop to the Munson's house, her giant purse strap across her well-endowed chest. The weight of the world pressed down on her shoulders as she walked around to the kitchen door and unlocked it.

She knew her days were numbered here and didn't know why she kept showing up. No one was going to pay her for being here since Mrs. Munson was dead and Mr. Munson was missing and wanted by the police.

She walked to the butler's pantry and hung her purse on a hook. She noticed a can of peas on the floor and walked a few steps to retrieve it. Manuela gawked at the sight in front of her. A whole section of the pantry stood open, away from the wall, sporting a secret passage. She clasped her hand to her chest and turned. She fled to the kitchen desk, hands shaking, not knowing what to do or who to call.

Manuela grabbed the phone and placed a call. "Amelia, llame al detective! El Sr. Munson ha estado aquí!" *Amelia, call that detective! Mr. Munson has been here!*

Amelia, heart pounding, stared at the disconnected call. She pressed the intercom button. "Lila Mae! Something must have happened next door!"

Footsteps thundered down the stairs. Lila Mae rushed into the kitchen. "What happened?" She gasped out, breathless.

The kitchen door opened and Chiquita came inside, with Louie on her heels. She looked from Amelia to Lila Mae. "What's wrong?"

"Manuela called. I think she said to call the detective. Something happened, but I couldn't understand; she was talking too fast for me to translate."

"Chiquita, call her and find out what happened. I'll call Chance," Lila Mae said.

Chiquita pressed the last call redial button. She sputtered off a string of words and listened, nodding one minute and shaking her head the next.

"She says that Mr. Munson must have been at the house. There's some kind of hole, or doorway that's open in the pantry! She's really freaked out."

Lila Mae grabbed her cell phone out of her pocket and hit speed dial. "Chance, get over to the Munson's house! Evidently, there was a secret room in the pantry."

* * *

LILA MAE, Amelia and Chiquita tried their best to comfort a trembling Manuela.

"Chiquita, get Manuela's contact information. Tell her I'm going to try to find her another job," Lila Mae said.

Chiquita patted Manuela on the shoulder and conveyed the message. Manuela sobbed while blubbering out a few sentences.

"She's very grateful to have good neighbors," Chiquita said.

The doorbell rang and Manuela rushed to the front door with Chiquita, Amelia and Lila Mae on her heels. She opened the door to Chance, Stacy and Frank. They rushed inside and headed to the kitchen while Manuela talked non-stop, with Chiquita translating.

Chance, Frank and Stacy crowded into the butler's pantry and took a look at the open, secret room. It was evident where handguns had been mounted on the wall. Something must have scared Judson into running off and not closing the secret door. Several weapons and boxes of ammo had been left on the floor.

"I'd say one of these was a Ruger," Stacy said. "I wonder if I can capture some shapes to prove my theory."

In addition to guns, there were hunting knives, a couple of fancy switchblade knives, and even some dueling rapiers, and swords.

Stacy let out an 'ooohhh' as she discovered a dagger. "This is a Sykes-Fairbairn Commando Knife from World War II, and look at this! I can't believe it! A Ka-Bar! This was a fighting knife the Marines used in the war."

Chance and Frank took a look at the daggers Stacy pointed out.

"I'd bet he had a SIG Sauer and a Beretta. This guy was a weapons person, that's for sure," Stacy said.

Chance took a look at the boxes of ammo left behind. "May have taken two boxes of hollow-points." He pointed to the dent in the neatly stacked boxes on a shelf.

"Pretty well concealed," Frank said as he studied the frame around the shelving of the pantry. "Don't anyone close this until I figure out where the latch is."

The two investigators and Chance donned gloves. Stacy and Chance poked around and opened cardboard boxes on the bottom shelf in the secret room.

Frank retrieved a stool and started on the top shelf of the opened unit. He moved aside cans and boxes, searching for a concealed unlatching device. The fourth shelf down consisted of all canned goods. He discovered a can of soup that wasn't edible.

"Will you look at this!" Frank exclaimed. "I'd never have thought of using a device such as this. Whoever designed this space was very clever."

Stacy and Chance stopped what they were doing and came out of the room. Lila Mae, Amelia, Manuela, and Chiquita crowded into the butler's pantry to see what was going on.

Frank pushed the section of the pantry closed. It clicked into place. He tested it out by trying to pull on the shelving to no avail. Then he smirked, tilted the can of soup forward, and the unit unlatched.

"Will you look at that!" Stacy said. "I've seen a couple of secret passages before, but nothing with anything as clever as this setup."

Chance studied the setup. "There's no way we would have discovered this on our own, so we should be grateful for whatever made him leave in such a hurry."

"That is so interesting," Lila Mae said. "I wonder if there are other hidden passages or rooms in the house."

Chance stopped in thought. "Maybe we should take another look at the library."

He, Frank, and Stacy nodded in agreement. Chance pulled out his phone and placed a call.

"Mike, I'm going to need Johnson and the team over at the Munson's house," Chance said. He explained the situation with the secret room, his suspicion about the library, and any other room that had shelving.

Chance turned to the women after he ended his call. "I'd think it's pretty safe to say that Manuela's employment is ended. No one's around to pay her, so she might as well leave. Can you ask her if I can have her house key? We might not be finished here."

The women conferred, and Chiquita translated to Manuela. The woman grabbed a dish towel and sobbed into it. She grabbed her purse, dug her keys out and removed the Munson's house key and handed it to Chance. She sobbed as she gathered her belongings, which included an old sweater hanging on a hook in the pantry. Manuela trudged to the front door, followed by Chiquita, Lila Mae, and Amelia, all looking pretty glum.

CHAPTER TWENTY-ONE

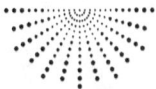

$\mathcal{T}$he party was in full swing at Dorothea's. Joseph looked a little nervous in his new smock, worried he would stain the crisp white fabric. The stains in the old smocks had proven they were permanent, and nothing short of nuclear fusion would get those smocks white again. He tried dyeing them, but the baby burp spots came through, no matter the color of dye chosen.

Joseph and Maria manned the kitchen. Carmichael and Amelia helped with the drinks and canapés, making the rounds in the living area while Chiquita removed discarded plates and empty glasses, chatting with family members as she went about her work.

Lila Mae and Walter were in a huddle, with Lila Mae doing the majority of the talking and Walter nodding and interjecting his thoughts. Madge wondered what was being plotted. Dorothea positively radiated at the complete change of pace in her home, while Bernie and Bambi discussed business.

"You have quite a good business mind, Bambi," Bernie said. "The bowling alley is even more successful than when Jimmy Ray managed it."

"I'm thinking of changing the name to Chaline Family Center, but I'm not sure if that portrays the function of the place," Bambi said. "I'm going to keep working on it, but I think the name Chaline Bowl is outmoded."

"Just keep jotting down notes, and it will come to you," Bernie said.

Chewie and Gina plopped down on the sofa across from Bernie and Bambi.

"You two look way too serious," Chewie said. "What are you planning?"

Bambi explained her dilemma about the bowling alley's name.

"Why don't you completely deviate from Chaline," Gina suggested, as she waved an arm as if pushing something aside. "How about Funtastic Family Center? Then you could have one of those neon signs that listed everything: bowling, restaurant, bar, and arcade? You'd be able to add a neon link whenever you added to the space."

Bambi openly gawked at Gina. "That's a brilliant idea, Gina!" She turned to Bernie. "What do you think?"

Bernie contemplated. "How will they answer the phone?"

Bambi blurted, "Funtastic!"

"You should bring back sock hops," Bernie said.

Bambi, Gina, and Chewie looked at each other for answers. Seeing their lack of understanding, Bernie shook his head.

"The sock hop was a dance at the high school, back in the forties and fifties. You had to take your shoes off and dance in your socks because the hop was typically in the gym and penny loafers and those type of shoes would ruin the gym floor," Bernie said.

Bambi caught on big time. "Wouldn't that be fun! Do you think today's teenagers would like this?" She looked to Gina and Chewie for opinions.

"I think you could have two different age groups on different nights," Gina said. "Teenagers and Tweens. Maybe the ages nine to twelve on one day and actual teenagers on the other day."

"Yeah, you might want to specify junior high/middle school and high school so you don't have college kids showing up," Chewie said.

"Maybe three different venues then," Bambi said. "The nine to twelve group, thirteen to sixteen group, and maybe a more mature group of seventeen to nineteen-year-olds."

"Now you're thinking," Bernie said. "See what a think tank can accomplish? You could use Bill Haley and the Comet's *Rock Around the Clock* as your theme song. Maybe revive some of the original rock and roll."

"Let's Google sock hops and see what they used to do!" Bambi was excited at the prospect of bringing something back from before she was born.

Chance came into the room, spotted Lila Mae and made a beeline to her and Walter. Chance and Lila Mae smooched on the lips. Amelia slipped around people and joined the conversation with Chance and Lila Mae.

"Well, did you find any other secret passages?" Lila Mae asked.

"Just as I suspected, the library had a secret passageway as well," Chance said.

"Really?" Lila Mae asked. "Were there more weapons?"

"A tunnel to the garage?" Walter asked.

Chance pointed to Walter. "Close. There's a fully stocked and furnished bomb shelter under the house."

"Bomb shelter?" Amelia asked. "Are you sure it wasn't a hideout or a safe room?"

Chance pointed at Amelia. "I think you've hit it, Amelia. We're still exploring the place. It's immense with several rooms and closets. Plenty of weaponry down there as well."

"Who would have thought?" Lila Mae asked. "All these years living beside those two. Who knows what went on over there."

Joseph came to the doorway, holding his little gong, and tapped it with the mallet. "Dinner is ready."

Everyone made their way to the dining room where heaping platters of food sat on the side table.

* * *

JUDSON, wearing gloves to hide his fingerprints, finished wiping down an assortment of weapons that lay across the second double bed in the hotel room. A soft tap sounded at the door. He quietly went to the door and looked through the peephole. A burly man stood in front and center, knowing full well he was being observed. Judson opened the door.

"Thanks for coming, Eddy," Judson said. He waved Eddy into the room, then shut and locked the door.

Eddy glanced over at the bed, then looked Judson full in the face. "Where's Kimberly?"

Judson rubbed a hand over his face. "She was assassinated."

Eddy studied Judson. "Who did the hit?"

"I don't know, but I'm a suspect so I had to leave," Judson said. His mouth twitched in a nervous tic as he forced himself to keep focused on Eddy.

"Where will you go?" Eddy asked.

"I thought Vegas," Judson said.

Eddy shook his head. "Too many cameras. Head down to Central America. It's easy to become invisible down there. Don't fly. Drive."

"Okay," Judson said.

"Let's see what you've got," Eddy said, heading toward the bed. He picked up an assault rifle, peered through the scope. The weapon was aimed at Judson. "And Judson, if I find out you had anything to do with Kimberly's death, you'll answer to me."

* * *

STACY WAS busy lifting fingerprints from the horde of weapons that were taken from the secret room in the Munson's house. Two tables in her lab were covered in various guns, knives, and all things weapons, when the fax machine announced an incoming one.

A piece of paper spewed into the receiving tray, then another and another. This went on for several moments. Curious, Stacy crossed the floor and grabbed the pages, and turned the stack over to the first page.

She stared at the various small photo IDs and started reading the accompanying text. The fax machine finally stopped. Stacy grabbed the remaining pages and slipped into her chair. She placed the pages down in front of her and rested her face in her hands as she read, turned a page, and read some more. She skipped ahead, scanning text and photos.

"Wow. Who would have thought?" She said out loud. Stacy texted Chance.

Major news on fingerprints from hidden rooms.

Her phone dinged with his reply. *Be there in twenty.*

Stacy read more of the pages, transfixed.

* * *

CHANCE STROLLED into the lab and slipped into the chair in front of Stacy's desk. "What do we have?"

Stacy looked up at Chance and smirked. "This is better than fiction. You would never believe me without seeing this with your own two peepers, especially where it came from." She handed Chance the dozen or more pages.

He flinched as he saw what the top page displayed. Chance scanned paragraphs, turned pages, and looked up. "Why aren't these pages redacted?"

Stacy shrugged. "I have no idea, but I think the larger question is, why haven't any agencies stormed the doors and taken over the investigation?"

"Can you scan these and email to Mike?" Chance asked. "He's going to have to deal with this."

Stacy scooped up the sheets of paper and went to the scanner and chose email addresses. The machine went to work. "I'm emailing the file to you and me as well as Mike."

* * *

CHANCE CARRIED a tray with two plates of food to the back patio, and Lila Mae followed with a tray of drinks and a bowl of chopped veggies. They placed the trays on the table and unloaded their contents. Lila Mae grabbed the bowl and walked to the edge of the patio and set it on the ground.

Louie and Quack looked up from where they were exploring by the stream and hurried over to see if they were included in the feast. Louie sniffed the bowl of veggies and quickly continued on to the table. He beseeched Lila Mae and Chance.

"Don't worry," Chance said to Louie. "You'll get yours."

Quack waddled up to his bowl and snatched up a piece of zucchini.

"Anything new about my neighbor?" Lila Mae asked. She speared salad with honey-mustard dressing onto her fork and chewed away.

"Were you aware that Kimberly had been with the FBI?" Chance asked.

Lila Mae looked up from her plate. "What?"

Chance grinned.

"Trim and proper trust-fund Kimberly?" Lila Mae asked. "Are you sure?"

Chance explained about the fax Stacy received. "She was recruited in college. Evidently, she was known as a crack shot on the shooting range, and they probably wanted her as a sniper. She had a lengthy career up until her murder."

Her meal forgotten, Lila Mae stared at Chance. "So, she was assassinated?"

"Appears so. Judson may not be the murderer after all. He could be on the run to stay alive," Chance said. "I'm waiting to hear what Mike finds out. We're all puzzled about the file not being redacted."

"Just goes to show that you really never know who your neighbors are," Lila Mae said, lost in thought. She glanced up at Chance. "Why don't you sell your condo?"

Chance stared back hard. "Are you sure?"

"Wouldn't have suggested it otherwise," Lila Mae said.

Chance reached across the table and took her hand.

* * *

BAMBI WAS IN THE PLAYROOM, lying on an exercise mat doing what she called rocking sit-ups. Trevor was lying on her feet, kicking in the air. He squealed with delight each time Bambi curled forward with her hands behind her head. When she curled back down to the mat, she lifted her feet, and her son, which made him very happy.

After completing fifty rocking sit-ups, she eased her feet apart and deposited Trevor on the mat. Then she picked him up and sniffed.

"Someone needs a diaper change!" she said.

He yawned in response.

Bambi went about changing him, then placed him in his crib. "Have a good nap, Trevor. Mommy loves you."

Bambi went to her room, showered, and dressed. She went downstairs and greeted Charlemagne.

"Good morning, Ms. Bambi," Charlemagne said. "Is our boy down for his nap?"

"He almost fell asleep during my exercises," Bambi said.

Charlemagne served Bambi breakfast, which was actually brunch, but Bambi didn't like to eat first thing in the morning. She placed a plate containing a fried egg, surrounded by asparagus, bacon and onions, in front of Bambi on the island counter.

"This is one of my favorite meals," Bambi said as she dug into the scrumptious food.

After she finished eating, she walked outside to check the mail. She raced back into her home office. With shaky hands, she grabbed a letter opener and slit open the official-looking envelope. She pulled out the piece of paper and rejoiced. She took a photo of it and sent a text message to family members:

I just received my certificate in Mommy Defense! Now I can officially teach people!

Congratulations messages rolled into her phone, along with questions about when she took the certification training.

I had taken the class while I was pregnant, and after Trevor was born, I decided to take the certification class. I've been going three days a week for a few months now and finished a couple of weeks ago.

* * *

DOROTHEA WAS FULLY CHARGED after her successful dinner party. No more moping about. She stood at the top of the stairs and looked down. Camilla was in a baby sack at her chest, fretting because her twin was howling up a storm in a baby sack on Dorothea's back.

"Hold on, Haley. Mommy's going to exercise and you two are going to help!"

She grasped the bannister and started down the stairs. Joseph stood at the bottom of the staircase and looked up.

"What are you doing?" he all but shrieked.

"Putting the girls to good use—they're helping me exercise!" Dorothea said.

As she walked down the stairs, Haley sputtered a few more cries, then quieted.

"See, they like the motion!" Dorothea exclaimed. "I'm also going to start walking them in the stroller over to Bambi's. That'll get me back into shape and lift these doldrums."

"Just be careful!" Joseph said. He felt it was his responsibility to look after his boss and the babies.

Dorothea made it to the bottom where Joseph stood. He looked her sacks over and approved. Her house manager watched as she turned around and started back up the stairs. That trip was much slower. By the time Dorothea reached the top, she was huffing and puffing.

"I never realized how out of shape I had become!" she managed between breaths.

* * *

LILA MAE LOOKED around the space on the third floor of the Alcott Chocolates factory. The professional kitchen was taking shape. She glanced at her watch, eager for the appliances to be delivered and installed. The landline phone rang, and she rushed to answer it.

"They're here? Okay, I'll meet them at the freight elevator downstairs," Lila Mae said.

Lila Mae could hardly contain her excitement. She rushed out the door and hurried down the hallway to the freight elevator and stepped inside. On the ground floor, she unlocked the double doors to the back lot and swung one open as the delivery truck backed close to unload. She swung the second door open and made sure there were no obstructions for the equipment to be moved into the elevator.

A big, beefy man stepped down from the driver's side of the truck, clipboard in hand. He and three other men approached her.

"Ms. Alcott?" he asked. "I'm Dennis, and this is my crew. We have your equipment. It's going to take a couple of hours to uncrate, move, and install everything."

"Take as long as you require," Lila Mae said. "Why don't we start off by me showing you the space?"

She led them into the building to the freight elevator, and they rode up to the third floor. They entered the space and looked around.

"As you can see, the designer labeled where everything goes, so this should make things easier," Lila Mae said.

"Yeah, takes out the guesswork," Dennis said. "Okay, we'll get started with the uncrating."

The four men left, and Lila Mae heard the freight elevator take them downstairs. The phone rang again. She rushed to answer it. "Luna? Oh great. Send them upstairs."

Momentarily, the regular elevator dinged and Lila Mae stepped out to greet two men. They carried two covered signs. One sign was for over the door, and the other was for the far wall. This second sign would be visible when someone opened the door to the space.

"The kitchen equipment is being uncrated right now, so you may have to work around the delivery crew," Lila Mae said.

"No problem. We'll be right back," one man said as they carefully deposited the signs on the floor, out of the way. "We're going to get our tools."

They returned with ladders and a rolling toolkit. They installed the first sign over the door, then moved inside to hang the larger sign on the opposite wall.

Lila Mae closed the door and looked at the sign above it. It was perfect. She opened the door, and the larger sign was masterfully even and looked great. She signed off on the documentation, kept a copy, and shook the men's hands.

"Thanks so much. The design came out great, and I can't believe you hung them without using a level," she said.

One of the men laughed. "My brain is like a built-in level. I can tell if something is even an eighth of an inch off."

They chuckled, got in the elevator, and left just as the freight elevator dinged.

* * *

THE NEXT DAY, Lila Mae met the kitchen designer at the space. Boxes and boxes of cooking and baking pans, bowls, and utensils were unloaded into the room to almost overflowing, then the designer barked out orders to his crew.

"Match the boxes with the labels on the cabinets, drawers and shelves," he told his crew.

Boxes were carefully opened and a lot of clanging and banging sounded as cabinets, drawers and shelves were stocked.

Lila Mae walked to the far end of the space, to the laundry area. Manuela, with her new Alcott Industries badge hanging around her neck, snipped store tags off dishtowels, dishcloths, and bar towels, and dropped them into the washing machine. She appeared very happy to be employed again.

A couple of hours later, the grocer supply company arrived. The design people made a path so that the boxes of pantry and refrigerated items could be brought in and stacked by the pantry and the huge refrigerator. The majority of items were organic. Lila Mae borrowed Itsy, one of the line workers who spoke both English and Spanish, to help Manuela and to translate for her.

While the work continued, Lila Mae grabbed a box and opened the walk-in freezer. She hung item signs on the shelf. *Amelia can hang these wherever she wants.* She had bought hanging signs for chicken, turkey, duck, game hens, beef, pork, ham, and sausage.

Finally, the kitchen design crew removed the last empty box and swept up errant peanuts, packing paper, balled up packaging tape and left the kitchen area in spiffy condition. Lila Mae thanked them each with a gift bag of chocolates.

Then she went to check on Manuela and Itsy. She saw that the items had been placed correctly. There was a section for gluten-free flours and other items, as well as a section for regular wheat flour.

Lila Mae inspected the closet that stored various jars and containers that Amelia would be able to use for packaging the recipes she created. Next, she checked out the computer, printer, and labeling system. There were labels for each size jar, preprinted with Amelia's Kitchen, the address, phone number, website address, and an info email address. Lila Mae all but burst with happiness as she looked around the room.

CHAPTER TWENTY-TWO

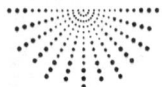

*L*ila Mae sat in Walter's office. "How did you manage to keep this a secret from Gina?"

Walter grinned wickedly. "I password-protected the file. Not only that, but I made it so difficult that even Lawrence couldn't crack the password!"

"That's amazing, Walter. I remember when you couldn't find the button on your first computer to boot it up!"

Walter chuckled. "Some of us have to be pulled, yelling and screaming, into technology."

"So, what's the bottom line with Nathan's estate?" Lila Mae asked.

Walter pulled a sheet of paper out of a file folder. "After gathering all the little tidbits and settling his estate, you're looking at fifty-eight point two million dollars and some change." He handed her a sheet of paper.

"I just can't believe he owned that kind of house and amassed that much money!" Lila Mae said.

"The ladies adored him, and he took advantage of that," Walter said. "So, what shall we do with this? I'm sure you have given it a lot of thought."

"I'd like to give Off the Streets five million dollars," Lila Mae said. "Can I make it from Louie?"

"We'd better identify Louie with his picture so they know he is a dog so you don't start getting mail for Louis Alcott," Walter said with a snicker.

"That dog already gets mail! People are so stupid when they're trying to make a buck," Lila Mae said. "The third floor of the factory is ready to go. I can't wait to see Amelia's face. Her dream came true, and then some."

Walter's face beamed. He loved seeing things come together. "I'm going to suggest to each of your candidates that they look at the prenups I've drawn up and sign up with our tax people. We don't want them to get into financial trouble going out the gate. Handling a sizable amount of money can get people into trouble, especially if they have come from humble beginnings."

"That's a good idea. Amelia and Carmichael are the biggest benefactors since they are engaged. I hope Madge understands if Carmichael leaves her and Rick to help Amelia out," Lila Mae said.

Walter shook his head. "While they love each other, I can't see Amelia and Carmichael working together on a daily basis. They are both used to being in charge in the kitchen, and it could prove to be disastrous."

"How should we proceed?" Lila Mae asked. "Should we have all four of them come at once for a general discussion, then they each have separate meetings with us for their private disclosure?"

Walter tented his fingers. "That would work. When are you going to spring the third floor on Amelia?"

"I thought maybe Amelia could go first, then I could whisk her away," Lila Mae said. "Would that be okay, and would you be okay with the other three? Or should we do this some other way?"

Walter thought for a minute. "Why don't we be sneaky? Let's

set up four different times. I will call each one of them and tell them I would like to meet with them in private regarding a confidential matter, and they must not discuss the meeting with anyone else. That way they won't be able to text or call anyone."

Lila Mae clapped her hands together! "Walter, you are so sly! They're most likely going to think they're going to have to squeal on someone. This is going to be such fun!"

Walter double-tapped his desk. "That's done. Now we can move on to the next part of the equation. When do you want to do this?"

* * *

JOSEPH JUMPED out of the chair when Walter came down the hall and approached him. Joseph went into hyper-emotional over-drive and came close to passing out from preconceived stressful fantasies of why he was called to a private meeting. Walter shook his hand.

"Glad you could come by, Joseph," Walter said. "Come on back to my office and we'll sort this situation out."

Joseph balked. "There's a situation? Is Dorothea mad at me? Have you found out something awful about Eirik, and you have to tell me? Did anything happen to Chewie?"

Walter closed the door behind them. He gripped Joseph's shoulders. "Calm down before you stroke out. Come sit down and I'll tell all."

Joseph noticed Lila Mae sitting in a chair. She held a hand over her mouth to stop from laughing. He glanced from Lila Mae to Walter and back again, trying to understand why she was there for the meeting instead of Dorothea. He figured he wasn't getting fired; maybe she was going to steal him away from her sister?

"Hi, Joseph," Lila Mae said. "Thanks for coming to the meeting. You didn't tell anyone, did you?"

Joseph rapidly shook his head. "No! I didn't even text anyone!"

"Great," Lila Mae said. "Walter, all yours."

Joseph sat rigid with anticipation. He noticed Walter had a file folder and a clasp envelope on the desk. Walter opened the folder.

"As you know, Lila Mae's ex-husband, Nathan, recently passed away and left her his entire estate," Walter said.

Joseph still looked scared.

Lila Mae moved her chair closer to Joseph. She patted his arm. "You know how wealthy the Alcotts are, Joseph. We really don't need a bunch more money because the interest alone supports us nicely."

Joseph nodded again as if in a trance.

"You've been an important part of this family for years, Joseph, and I wanted you to understand just how important your years of loyalty, friendship, and service have been," Lila Mae said. "Therefore, I have made you a beneficiary of part of Nathan's estate."

Walter jumped in. "Joseph, Lila Mae is bequeathing you seven million dollars."

Joseph jumped out of his chair, screeching for joy. "Ohmygod! I can't believe it! I can't believe it!" He continued to jump and scream for joy until Lila Mae latched onto his arm and grounded him.

He pulled her into a hug and cried on her shoulder. "I can't believe it. Thank you so much, Lila Mae!"

Walter cleared his throat to get Joseph's attention. "You're going to have lots of decisions to make in your life. Do you still want to work for Dorothea? Is there something you would want to pursue on your own? Things like that." Walter let that sink in for Joseph.

Joseph calmed down. "I like the fact that I'm now wealthy so I don't have to worry about anything in my future. But I could never not work for Dorothea! She's part of my family, and I love our everyday interactions, including being able to help raise the girls. I'm Uncle Joseph, you know?"

He pondered a moment. "Walter, I want to make sure I'm protected. I don't want anyone to know about the money. Even if I eventually get married, or have a lifelong partner, I'd want to take care of that person in case I died, but money sometimes has a tendency to make people mean—other people who want you for your money."

"Believe me, I learned that lesson with Nathan," Lila Mae said. "You are a wise man to think of those things."

Walter showed Joseph a document. "This is why I have a prenuptial agreement in place for you, which can be changed to be a companion agreement. It is difficult to understand a person's psychology, and it is imperative that you protect yourself. I will also connect you to our tax advisors so they can help you invest the money, in addition to filing your taxes."

Walter handed Joseph the clasp envelope. "All your paperwork is in here. There's a special bank account already set up for you. You'll find a protected debit card in the envelope. I suggest you go to the bank and sign the account. Make sure you have your ID with you so they can verify who you are."

They spent the next few minutes with Joseph signing documents. Tears spilled down Joseph's face. He stood, shook Walter's hand, then turned to Lila Mae and grasped her in a hug. "Thank you so much for your love and trust in me!"

"Joseph, you're our spiritual advisor, and we love you beyond measure," she said. "Go home and collapse for a few minutes—after you go to the bank."

Joseph shut the door quietly behind him.

"That went well," Walter said. "Carmichael will be here in around ten minutes."

* * *

G<small>INA WATCHED</small> J<small>OSEPH LEAVE</small>, sporting a tear-streaked face. She had no idea what was going on and could not understand the secrecy.

When Carmichael arrived, she couldn't answer any of his probing questions. All she could do was shrug. He left in the same state as Joseph, not saying a word.

Then Chewie showed up. Gina was about to go completely bonkers when Chewie left, because her fiancé would not elaborate. She didn't know if it was a massive firing of staff, or something else.

Her intercom buzzed. "Gina, can you come in for a sec?" Walter asked.

Gina grabbed her pad and paper. She hoped she'd get the lowdown on what the heck was going on. She tapped on the door and walked in.

"What in the world has been going on? Everyone was crying, and Chewie wouldn't tell me what happened."

Lila Mae patted the chair beside her in front of Walter's desk. "Come. Sit."

Walter got right to it. "Gina, Lila Mae has made you a recipient of Nathan's estate. You are now the proud benefactor of one million dollars." He explained about the prenup and the taxes, and the financial advisors.

Gina turned to Lila Mae, gaping like a fish drowning on air. "I don't know what to say! You are always so generous! Thank you so much! No wonder Chewie was crying!"

"Why don't you take an extended lunch?" Walter suggested. "Go shopping."

Gina shook her head. "No can do. Chewie and I have talked about my shopping addiction, and it isn't healthy. I'm leaving the money in the bank for our future. We're still young. And don't worry, Walter. I love my work here, so you're stuck with me for the long haul."

Walter came around the desk and hugged Gina. "I wish you

all the best, Gina. No matter what comes down the road in the future. You've got a good head on your shoulders."

Walter and Lila Mae smiled at each other. "Lawrence's turn. Then the big reveal with Amelia. Can't wait!" Walter said. He pushed a button on the phone and they listened to the ringing.

"Lawrence Thompson," Lawrence said.

"Lawrence, come down to my office," Walter said.

"Sure, boss. Be right there."

LILA MAE and Walter returned to his office from lunch. Gina was at her command center, and a frayed Amelia sat in one of the lobby chairs. She jumped to her feet when they shut the door.

"You're not firing me, are you?" The buttonhole side of Amelia's sweater was crinkled from her twisting it relentlessly.

"For heaven's sake, you can be such a drama queen, Amelia," Lila Mae said. "Come into Walter's office."

Gina struggled to keep a straight face. She had to turn away so Amelia could not see her glee.

Amelia followed Lila Mae and Walter into the office. Walter closed the door after her, and they all took their seats. Then Walter dropped the bomb with Amelia's number: twenty-million dollars.

It took approximately seven minutes for Amelia to stop crying, then hiccuping, and totally calm down. Amelia sighed deeply once they had explained everything and handed over the paperwork.

"Wow. Thanks, boss. My head is spinning," Amelia said.

"I'd like you to follow me over to the factory," Lila Mae said. "You need to see something."

"Do we get free samples?" Amelia asked with a devilish expression.

"You bet!"

* * *

LILA MAE AND AMELIA, sporting Alcott security badges, stepped out of the elevator onto the third floor. Lila Mae grabbed Amelia's hand and pulled her to a stop. "I want to show you something, but it's a secret, so you have to close your eyes. I'll lead you forward. Absolutely no peeking!"

Amelia closed her eyes, held out her left hand to avoid crashing into a wall, and let her boss walk her to their destination. Lila Mae made her stop, then she positioned Amelia toward the right.

"Okay, here you go, and look over the door."

Amelia looked up and gasped at the 'Amelia's Kitchen' sign. Her hand flew to her chest. Lila Mae handed Amelia a yellow and pink squiggly key ring that held a couple of keys.

"Open the door," Lila Mae said.

Amelia's hands shook, but she got the correct key in the lock and opened the door.

"Light switch is to your right," Lila Mae said.

Amelia fumbled around, then flipped the switch. The place lit up like daylight. She stepped inside and screamed.

"Are you serious?" She walked around the space, her hands touching surfaces as she passed by.

"Fully loaded and ready to go," Lila Mae said.

Amelia approached Lila Mae and rested her forehead on her boss' shoulder. "I can't believe you did this for me, on top of making me a multi-millionaire."

They parted. Lila Mae looked at Amelia with pure affection. She took a deep breath. "Amelia, you're fired."

* * *

AFTER A WEEK of transitioning from her day job to her new business, Amelia, Lila Mae, and Bernie had several planning sessions. Bernie would mentor Amelia until she felt ready to launch her product line or needed more help. There was a big difference between making out a grocery list and running around to different stores to obtain things and using a grocer supply company.

Amelia had downloaded a blank template grocery list from the supply company's website and compared prices between the big company and warehouse stores like Sam's Club and Costco. There were items that were cheaper at the warehouse stores, so she would use both systems to get what she needed.

Amelia's first big cooking and baking campaign was for her grand opening. The new company sign sat in front of the building, beside the Alcott Chocolate Factory sign, and graced the lobby as well.

The big party was announced with printed invitations and RSVP cards with prepaid postage envelopes. Amelia had paper products printed with her company's name and logo.

UPS arrived with four huge boxes that contained different types of napkins, assorted sizes of paper plates, and bags. Manuela went to work, unloading the boxes and shelving the items.

The feast of delights was almost ready. It had been a couple of days of cooking and baking, with Manuela being the chief dish and bottle washer, scouring pans, bowls, and all the messy things Amelia had used to create each dish.

Amelia had a strict rule that no pans or lids, plastic or wood, would ever go into a dishwasher. She didn't want the chemicals in plastic raining down on everything in the dishwasher. Her cooking teacher had told the class that wood should never go in the dishwasher because the hot water could cause bacteria to enter the wood, and the heated drying phase could cause the wood to split. Pans and lids could lose their sealing ability from the dishwasher, so all of those things were hand-washed.

Ginger beef was sitting in the refrigerator, ready for the lettuce wraps; turkey was cooling for the cranberry-turkey crescent pinwheels; the chicken parmesan roll-ups were complete; and the cocktail sausage balls just needed baking.

The refrigerator held large bowls of cubed cheese, platters of ham and cheese roll-ups, rolled omelets with spinach and cheddar cheese waiting to be sliced, and several dessert offerings including dark chocolate avocado truffles, banana dessert sushi, cheesecake stuffed strawberries and several other delectable goodies.

On the day of the party, Itsy was on loan from the factory. She and Joseph set up tables in the third-floor foyer and draped them with tablecloths. Manuela swapped cookie sheets from the ovens to cooling racks, then transferred the cookies onto plates. Chiquita arranged food artfully on platters, and Carmichael set up a beverage area. Lila Mae placed Carmichael's flower arrangements on tables and counters.

Ninety minutes before the event, everything was in place, and the gang of workers sat on folding chairs and sipped and snacked, getting rested up. To look at the kitchen, you would never know all the activity that had taken place.

"The setup is perfect," Amelia told Lila Mae. "The kitchen designer did a great job with the space, because this was a good test to see if anything needed to be changed."

"It seems efficient," Lila Mae said.

"I swear Madge is going to want to redo her kitchen like this," Carmichael said. "This is the best kitchen I have ever seen. Did you tell me that Rick recommended the designer?"

"Yes, it's one of his friends," Lila Mae said.

"Well, he sure knows commercial kitchens!" Carmichael said.

"I'm going to get changed," Amelia announced. "I love having a laundry, shower and changing area here." She turned to Itsy and Manuela. "Ladies, make sure you change your smocks and put the dirty ones in the hamper."

Joseph stood. "I'm going to get my clothes out of my car. I'll change in the men's room."

* * *

THE THIRD FLOOR was hopping with a steady flow of attendees. Family and friends rubbed elbows with River Oaks hostesses. Everyone was savoring Amelia's Kitchen offerings. Many pocketed business cards and brochures. Amelia wandered around, greeting people and discussing her new business.

Henry and Teddy joined Walter, Lawrence, and Bernie, who were chatting in a corner.

"I locked out all the other floors," Lawrence said. "Guests can only ride to the third floor or go down to the lobby, but workers can use their badges to stop at any floor."

"Good idea," Bernie said. "We sure don't need anyone wandering around."

"This is amazing what Lila Mae did for Amelia," Henry said.

"They're business partners," Walter said. "Lila Mae will make sure Amelia succeeds. We all know that women can cook. I just hope Lila Mae can cope with Chiquita!"

"Everyone's going to be learning Spanish," Bernie said. "Amelia will have to learn to communicate with Manuela, and Lila Mae will have to be able to understand Chiquita when she goes off on a tangent into her native language."

Pecos, Dolly, and Uncle Tito stepped off the elevator. Uncle Tito stood tall in his black cowboy hat, a black vest adorned with silver and turquoise medallions, black fitted jeans fastened with a huge silver and turquoise belt buckle, and hand-tooled leather boots. He carried a custom-painted hand-held drum.

Every single River Oaks hostess watched Uncle Tito. Some gawked in open-mouthed wonder at the magnificent man.

Amelia bounded over to her uncle and they hugged.

"Do you want me to do a blessing now, or should I wait until everyone's gone?" Uncle Tito asked.

"Do it now. Everyone loves your chanting!" Amelia said.

Uncle Tito walked into the kitchen with Amelia. He placed the drum on a counter, took some deep breaths and let loose with his deep timbre voice and chanted. All conversations came to a halt. People gathered around, or stood in the doorway, watching the session. Uncle Tito chanted for a couple of minutes, then picked up the drum and beat out a pattern.

The drumming resonated throughout the space. He walked throughout the space and opened doors and walked into closets and other rooms, pounding on the drum and chanting. He left Amelia's business and walked out the door to the elevator, drumming and chanting away.

When he concluded his blessing, Uncle Tito was swamped by people. Several wealthy hostesses clamored for his attention. Lila Mae, Madge, and Dorothea snickered as Pecos acted as Uncle Tito's business manager.

"I'll check the calendar and we'll schedule a session," Pecos told each person.

He handed out business cards and brochures, and pocketed cards that were handed to him.

CHAPTER TWENTY-THREE

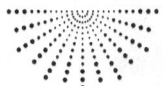

*L*una worked on a spreadsheet, matching shipped orders to faxes received. She felt a sneeze coming on, and her body took over. As her head was in a raised, leaning-back pose prior to the blast, she glimpsed one of the security feeds. She sneezed, grabbed a tissue and blew her nose, all the while staring at one monitor.

She had doubted what she saw, but there it was right in front of her. A plump line worker popped a chocolate into her mouth. Then the woman looked around sneakily and put chocolates in her pockets. Luna snatched up the phone and called Bob Marx.

"Bob, it's Luna. One of your ladies is eating and stealing chocolates off the line!"

She watched the screen as Bob looked around, bewildered. "Are you serious? I'll be right there."

Luna heard the door from the factory floor open, then close as Bob hurried to her station.

"Show me what you've got," Bob said.

Luna pulled up the feed from camera four. She glanced at her watch and determined to look starting with ten or twelve minutes' back since she didn't know what she had missed. She pressed play. Bob watched over her shoulder, and sure enough, the woman was not even working. She was eating chocolates and pocketing them.

"What the heck is going on? Mary has always been a productive worker," Bob said.

"Should you call Dougie or HR?" Luna asked.

Bob thought for a minute. Considering all that the company had been through lately, he decided it might be best to have their manager present. "Yeah, have Dougie call me so we can figure out how to proceed." He left the front and returned to the factory floor. He nonchalantly walked around, greeting and chatting with workers, then headed to his office. Ten minutes later, Dougie entered Bob's office and shut the door behind him.

"I watched the feed, and it seems bizarre. Mary O'Brannigan has been a good worker. There must be something going on that we're not aware of," Dougie said. "Jody's at the dentist. I'll have Luna type up a memo telling everyone we're going to have individual meetings to make sure everyone likes all the changes in the company. They can tell us if there're any processes we've put in place they believe should be changed, or maybe there's something we should consider."

Bob liked his boss and was always surprised how intuitive Dougie was when it came to seeing the whole picture. "That's a good idea. We may even get some good feedback."

"If there's enough time, Luna can pass out the memo at lunchtime, and we can start meeting with people in the afternoon," Dougie said.

The men ended their discussion, and Dougie left Bob's office. He returned to the front and gave Luna the gist of the memo.

"Is Jody coming back to work after the dentist?" Luna asked.

"I don't know. A broken tooth isn't any picnic," Dougie said. "I thought she was going to pass out."

"Poor thing," Luna said. "I'll get right on this."

Dougie rode the elevator to the fifth floor. Ten minutes later, an email from Luna with two attachments appeared: the memo and a form. He printed them out, read the memo, and looked over the form. Dougie left his office, the two pieces of paper in hand, and went to Emily Lewis's office. He figured he'd better have HR take a look at the wording to make sure everything was okay prior to handing out the memo and form.

Dougie knocked on Emily's open door. She invited him in and he brought her up to date with the situation. She watched the footage from security camera four, read the memo and made one change that involved the word choice between can, will, shall, and may. Then Emily looked the form over.

"This is quite clever," Emily said as she looked the form over. "Luna has a knack for communication."

"I'll have her make that change, print them, and hand them out before lunch," Dougie said. He gave Emily a thumbs-up and returned to his office. He picked up the office phone receiver and punched the speed dial internal button for Luna at the front desk.

"Hey," Dougie said. "Emily really likes your memo and form. She wants you to make one small change, though. Do you see where you have the word 'will'? Change it to 'may', then print them up and hand them out."

"Oh, great!" Luna said. "Maybe we should get one of those suggestion boxes so the employees can drop anonymous suggestions when they have a gripe or something. I could order one, then print up a bunch of these forms and keep them in the break room."

"Good idea. Why don't you run that idea by Emily?" Dougie asked. "Love you."

"Love you too," Luna said. "Dougie, I'm so happy now."

"Me too."

* * *

ONE BY ONE, employees were called into the small conference room to have a discussion with Bob and Dougie. The general consensus was they liked the form and liked the idea of the suggestion box.

When it was Mary O'Brannigan's turn, she entered the conference room, closed the door behind her, slipped into a chair and burst into tears. Dougie and Bob exchanged confused looks. Bob excused himself, left the room and returned with a box of tissues and pushed it toward Mary.

"What's wrong, Mary?" Bob asked.

She bawled into a wad of tissues. "I'm going to be deported back to Ireland."

"Why?" Dougie asked. "What happened?"

"My husband's divorcing me, and I'll have to leave," Mary wailed.

"Mary, you've been working here for over a year, so we will have to meet with Mrs. Lewis, the HR lady, and possibly Mr. Branson, the corporate attorney to find out how we can help you," Dougie said.

Bob patted her hand. "Nothing has happened yet, right?"

Mary shook her head.

"We'll find out about work visas until something permanent comes into play, so don't worry," Dougie said. "Are you going to have to move?"

"It's my husband's house," Mary said, her lips quivering.

"Do you have relatives here in Houston? Or close friends— someone you could stay with temporarily?" Bob asked.

"My sister lives over by Meyerland. She said I could stay with her until everything is sorted out. I've been packing my things," she said with another rush of tears.

"Bob, call Emily and see if Mary can go talk with her," Dougie said. He turned to Mary. "It's going to be okay, Mary. The Alcotts take care of their own, and you're part of the bigger family."

Mary smiled weakly.

* * *

TEDDY AND TILLY had their official open house. The entire clan, along with some of Tilly's classmates, perused the rooms. Chance and Lila Mae finished their tour and approached Tilly.

"This is a fabulous floor plan," Lila Mae said.

"We looked at so many places, and in a lot of them, the rooms were all chopped up," Tilly said.

"This place will work for us for several years," Teddy said. His speech was smooth with only an occasional hitch where a word came out garbled.

Tilly looked coolly at Chance. "I'm surprised you didn't question me regarding the most recent murder, Chance."

Chance huffed out a sigh. "Don't be that way, Tilly. Those two times were circumstantial, because of your way of life back then, and you know it."

"Long gone, past," Tilly said. She looked lovingly at Teddy. "If it weren't for Teddy coming into my life, and our odd pairing, I'd probably be on Skid Row."

Teddy wrapped his arms around her. "And if it weren't for you, I'd still be holding my hands at my chest, shuffling and not talking."

"You're a perfect couple." Lila Mae looked at Tilly. "How's school?"

"Great! I love my classes."

Chance thought for a moment. "You should talk with Lawrence Thompson. He works for Walter, and I'm pretty sure you've met him. He's a forensic accountant. I've worked with him on a couple of my cases and he's sharp."

Tilly studied Chance. "Huh, that sounds interesting. I wonder what's required?"

"Probably some legal courses along with specific accounting studies," Chance said. "Lawrence loves what he does."

"I'm going to call him," Tilly said. "That sounds like a much more interesting career path."

"That's something we might consider for a business," Teddy said. "I have my law degree that would protect us." Teddy fully focused on Chance. "We'll need a top-notch investigator on our team."

Chance bobbed his head. "That sounds like a discussion down the road."

* * *

LILA MAE SAT in her big Turkish robe in front of her computer. "It's listed!"

Chance walked into the room, wrapped in his robe, and looked over her shoulder. "Okay! I wonder how long it will take to sell it?"

"You're in a desirable part of town and your square footage is a big selling point for a condo," Lila Mae said. "You'll have to sit tight and see how things go."

"The realtor knows I'm with HPD and may not always be available, so I listed you as an alternate contact," Chance said.

"Do you think it will be weird, us living together?" Lila Mae asked.

Chance regarded her. "What do you mean? We've practically been living together for the past two years. I'm here more than I am at my place."

"I know that, but it's never been permanent because of the condo," Lila Mae said, mildly agitated.

"Are you getting cold feet? I thought the Nathan curse was behind you," Chance said.

"The Nathan curse?" Lila Mae snorted with laughter. "That's a good one. Is that what everyone says?"

"Come on, Lila Mae," he said. "You've been phobic for years. Now that he's dead, you can move on."

They both stood with arms crossed.

"Are we having an argument?" Lila Mae asked.

"Discussion of varying opinions," Chance said. "Come on, I need coffee."

JUDSON MUNSON BEGAN his trip through hell at the US/Mexico border at Brownsville, Texas. He made his first mistake with his uppity attitude while attempting to persuade the border guards with a better way to do their jobs. He discovered that when someone is trying to expedite their US exit, it's best to keep their flopping lips sealed shut. Smiling, nodding, and cooperating went much smoother.

After hours and hours of driving, being stopped by Federales, paying bribes, and watching out for the almost invisible speed bumps, or topes as they are called in Mexico, Judson pulled the car into an Americanized chain hotel. He checked in, dropped his luggage in his room, and went to the restaurant next door.

They had warned him never to drive after sundown, and after everything he had experienced so far on his trip, he heeded that warning. There was no way he'd be able to detect the topes that seemed to be invisibly installed before and after towns, and sometimes in the middle of the towns. He could see from the way things were created that a vehicle could be easily gutted by flying over one at night.

After two margaritas, a meal, and a beer, he headed back to his hotel. He collapsed onto his bed and fell asleep. The next morning, he woke to the sounds of goats bleating, a rooster crowing, and chickens clucking. He showered, dressed, packed up, and left the hotel.

When he returned to his car, he noticed a deep gouge across the driver's side rear door. Someone had keyed the car with a lot of effort. He opened the trunk, stowed his luggage, and walked around the car. He didn't see any other damage.

Three days later, and several hundred dollars less in his wallet due to the exorbitant price of gas, bribes, food, and lodging, he crossed into Belize. Where Mexico was a Spanish-speaking country, the people of Belize spoke English. However, Judson discovered that there were some interpretation issues. He had stopped at a restaurant in Corozal and ordered a hamburger and fries.

What arrived was a hamburger bun with a slab of ham. He laughed it off, ate, and asked the waiter if he could suggest a place to stay. After drawing a map on the napkin and pointing Judson in the right direction, the waiter accepted a nice tip, and Judson was on his way again.

* * *

JOSEPH WAS in complete freak-out mode as he awaited his mother and grandmother's arrival. Eirik watched as Joseph checked and rechecked his watch and every clock in his apartment, looked out the front window, sat down only to spring back up again.

"Calm down," Eirik said.

"What if they don't like you?" Joseph asked, stricken. He looked as if he were about to cry.

A car horn tooted outside. Joseph rushed to the window and saw Chewie and the Bentley. "They're here!"

Joseph threw the door open and rushed outside, chattering in Chinese. Eirik followed. Chewie approached him.

"How's it going?" Chewie asked.

"Joseph is completely freaked out," Eirik said.

"He gets that way sometimes," Chewie said.

They watched as Joseph hugged his mother, then his grandmother, crying all the while. Eirik and Chewie joined them at the car. Chewie popped the trunk, and he and Eirik withdrew the luggage. They rolled everything inside the house. Eirik directed Chewie to the spare bedroom where they deposited the luggage. They returned to the living room.

Joseph prepared tea in the kitchen. Both women hovered nearby, checking out the kitchen, watching what he was doing, and talking in Chinese. Eirik and Chewie joined them in the kitchen area. Joseph placed the tea items on a tray and carried it to the breakfast table.

Then he went to Eirik's side, placed a hand on his arm and made introductions.

"Mother, grandmother, this is Eirik. You have to speak English!" Joseph said. Then he turned to Eirik. "This is my mother, Trudy, and my grandmother, Mei."

Eirik shook both their hands. "It is a pleasure to meet you. Did you have a nice trip from San Francisco?"

Trudy and Mei chatted in Chinese, then Trudy answered Eirik. "Very long flight. One stopover in Phoenix, then we come here and Chewie pick us up."

Joseph motioned for everyone to sit and partake in tea. He dashed to the kitchen and removed a plate of warm, homemade, pan-fried onion pancakes from the oven, which resembled Quesadillas. He grabbed a hot plate mat and set it on the table, then returned to the kitchen for the plates and napkins.

"Sit, sit!" Trudy said to Joseph. "You're making me dizzy!" She grabbed a pancake and took a bite. "This is very good, son!"

Eirik grabbed one and bit into it. "Um-mmm! I like this."

Chewie finished his tea. "I have to go pick up Mr. Alcott and take him to the factory." He bowed to his aunt and his grandmother, then kissed each of them on the cheek. He saluted Joseph and Eirik, then left.

Mei got up from the table and went to the kitchen. She

opened the pantry, perused the contents, then opened the refrigerator. She spied the two flats of eggs and checked out the vegetable bins. Trudy spoke rapidly in Chinese.

"English, Grandma," Joseph said. "I know you speak English, so don't be rude in front of Eirik!"

Eirik kicked Joseph's foot under the table. He scrunched his brows at Joseph. Seeing Joseph's clueless expression, he said, "It's okay. They're old-school and used to speaking their native language. I don't consider it rude."

The ladies giggled as Joseph scowled.

Mei and Trudy had a rapid private Chinese conversation. Then, "Refrigerator stocked well," Mei said. "Make egg drop soup tonight."

Joseph turned to Eirik. "My grandma makes the best egg drop soup. Not that goopy stuff some of the restaurants make."

Trudy got up and went into the spare bedroom. She was gone for several minutes, then returned with two flat, wrapped gifts. She gave one to Eirik and one to Joseph.

Eirik seemed a little embarrassed at all the attention. He unwrapped his gift and stared at the framed picture. It was his name in colorful Chinese characters. "Oh, this is beautiful! Look, Joseph, how my name is in Chinese!"

Joseph opened his and saw his name. He set them side-by-side. He and Eirik studied them.

"This is an incredible art," Eirik said. "Thank you so much!"

"We are glad you like it," Trudy said. "Now I'm going to unpack, then take long nap." She hollered something to Mei in Chinese, and they both went to the spare room and shut the door.

Joseph let out a huge breath. "That went well."

"What were you so worried about?" Eirik asked. "They will be here for a month. There's plenty of time for them to get to know me and vice versa."

Joseph shook his head. "You don't understand. When I told

everyone I was gay, they were all disappointed because I would never have children. Family is very important to Chinese."

"At least they didn't try to force you into a marriage to conform," Eirik said.

"No, they would never do anything like that," Joseph said. "You're the first man I've ever introduced to them."

Eirik looked surprised. "Really? I'm the first? Nothing like putting the pressure on me!" He grabbed another onion pancake and took a big bite. "I love these things. How come you never made these before?"

"By the time they go home, you're going to be sick of Chinese food," Joseph said.

"Wait a week, then make spaghetti or something," Eirik kidded.

CHAPTER TWENTY-FOUR

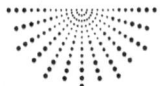

*L*ila Mae and Amelia sat on stools in Amelia's Kitchen at one of the giant islands in Amelia's kitchen. They each had a glass of mango iced tea in front of them, and they nibbled on banana dessert sushi.

Amelia scribbled notes on a yellow-lined tablet.

"I think these three things would be ideal to start with," Lila Mae said. "They were a big hit at the open house." She pointed to the cranberry-turkey crescent pinwheels, chicken parmesan rollups, and cocktail sausage balls on Amelia's list.

"We have to come up with a price list," Amelia said. "Do I price them individually, or so many for so much?"

Lila Mae thought for a moment. "I think you need both. Someone may want to try one to see if they like them, then if they do, they may want a dozen or more."

Amelia jotted notes about prices. "Should we provide bags with my company name to the Alcott Chocolate shops? How would that work?"

"That would be a good way to get your brand out there. Your items will be in their own display case," Lila Mae said.

* * *

A NINE-TRAY DEHYDRATOR sat on the counter. Amelia and Manuela, wearing non-latex gloves that fit like skin, sliced jalapeño peppers and placed them on the trays.

"Make sure you keep your hands away from your face," Amelia said. "I took safety precautions. There's an eye bath solution in the bathroom."

"No, no touch eyes!" Manuela said.

"Tomorrow I can start on the chocolate process and see how these turn out," Amelia said.

The timer on an oven dinged. Amelia peeled her gloves off, dumped them in the trash, and went to the oven. She donned potholders and pulled out two sheets of cocktail sausage balls. She set them on the stovetop grill to cool down. Then she grabbed a baking sheet of cranberry-turkey crescent pinwheels and popped it in the oven on one rack, and bacon-cheddar crescent pinwheels on the other rack. She set the timer for ten minutes.

Amelia grabbed a spatula and removed the sausage balls to a container. She fanned one with the spatula and popped it in her mouth, and chewed. "Oh, these are so good." She placed one on a napkin and brought it over to Manuela. "Try this."

Manuela took a bite. "Oohh. Is good!"

The door opened and Carmichael entered. "Hi, Hon."

"You're just in time," Amelia said. She brought him a sausage ball.

He grabbed it off the napkin and popped it in his mouth and chewed. "These are my favorites! Did you use Italian sausage?"

"My secret." Amelia snickered. "Stick around. I've got two other things coming out of the oven in a few minutes."

Carmichael walked over to the dehydrator. "What are you drying out?" He watched Manuela as she sliced jalapeños. "What are you going to make with these?"

"I'm going to try different chocolate-covered peppers," Amelia said.

"I overheard Rick tell Madge that he's thinking of outsourcing some appetizers to you," Carmichael said.

Amelia gasped. "Really? That would be a great start! I hope he contacts me soon!" She looked at the big clock on the wall. "Manuela, you'd better leave for the bus."

Manuela glanced at the clock, let loose with a string of Spanish and ripped her gloves off. She opened a low cabinet, grabbed her purse, and waved. "I see you tomorrow."

When the door shut behind Manuela, Carmichael sat at the counter. "What do you think we should do with all of this money?"

"I had thought of expanding the house so I could have a larger kitchen with more storage space, but I don't know if I want to go through renovations again," Amelia said.

"Do you want to start looking for a bigger house?" Carmichael asked.

"I think so."

"Do you want to stay in Bellaire, or go to West U, or River Oaks?" Carmichael asked.

Amelia contemplated the question. "Maybe we should start doing an online search for all of those places. I don't want an old house, though, unless it has had major renovations, including plumbing and updated electrical."

"Yeah, those things can really add up, not to mention the inconvenience and nightmares of bad plumbing or wiring. Let's ask Walter who the Alcotts use for a realtor," Carmichael said.

"I really want enough room so I can have one of those squash and gourd arbors built," Amelia said. "I still have the picture that I found online. You can use it for anything that vines or climbs, like green beans, melons and cucumbers."

The oven dinged. Amelia removed the sheets from the oven to cool. "After I clean up, let's go home and start looking!"

Carmichael snatched a pinwheel. "Hot! Hot!" He bounced it in the air. Amelia grabbed a napkin and handed it to him.

* * *

CHANCE SAT on the other side of the desk from his boss. "We lucked out. Munson's Mercedes is being transported back to Houston from San Antonio. He abandoned it with the keys in it and the windows down. If it weren't for the APB, it would have slipped into a chop shop."

"I love it when the system actually works in our favor," Mike said. "Did you get any information out of the perp that stole it?"

"Yeah, he told us where he snatched it from. We've got the San Antonio boys checking out small car lots to see if we get a hit on another vehicle," Chance said.

"What about bank records?" Mike asked.

"He cleaned out one bank account in San Antonio. Munson said he was on his way to Amarillo to help with a church fire," Chance said.

Mike slurped his coffee. "Probably on his way to Mexico, but figured he'd try to throw us off by saying he was heading north. Call someone down at the border and see what you can find out."

Chance stood and headed out the door. He slipped into his office and clicked his computer awake. He logged in and opened a directory of police forces throughout the US. He made arrangements with a detective in Brownsville to take Munson's picture around to the border crossing.

* * *

IT HAD BEEN weeks since Bernie had mentioned it, but the day finally arrived when "the girls," Bambi, Joseph, Carmichael, Amelia, Chewie, Gina, Tilly, and Teddy, stood before Bernie.

The custom order room comprised of large tables, chairs, custom molds, a large chocolate pot, smaller pots for fillings, implements for filling, and other chocolate creation items.

Bernie studied the people before him. "If we ever had a strike, or some other disaster, we would have to take it upon ourselves to fill orders." He let that sink in before continuing. "This is where we fill special orders. When we get a special order, the first thing we have to do is to determine if we have a mold already. If not, we create the design and get a mold made."

He checked to see if everyone was engaged in the talk, and he determined they were interested. "Once all that is taken care of, and we have the molds, we're ready to start hand production. We check the customer's order to find out what type of chocolate they want on the outside, and what they want on the inside. Then we create them."

Bernie clapped his hands, then rubbed them together. "Okay, let's get this custom order started."

He shuffled over to Amelia. "You're the head recipe gal. Carmichael will be your second." Bernie handed Amelia a printed recipe. "Everything you need is in this room."

Amelia and Carmichael conferred over the ingredients and began gathering what they needed.

Bernie stood before the rest of the group. "Typically, there's ten people on board who fill the molds, then release the molds after they've cooled and set. We have ten, including me, so we can get the job done."

He showed them the custom molds. They held fifty squares with a design in the mold's bottom. One mold had a shamrock design, so when inverted, the shamrock would be on top of the candy. The second mold showed a bell; the third mold was a heart. Number four had a ball, and the last looked like an open book.

"We start with filling the design with the color of chocolate the order specifies. Carmichael will make the five-colored choices," Bernie explained. "Then we will fill the remaining square with the chocolate that Amelia is preparing."

He surveyed the group. Everyone seemed on board with their tasks. There was a lot of smiling and hand-rubbing. Bernie let them talk among themselves while exploring their tools. He shuffled over to Amelia and Carmichael to see how they were getting along with the chocolate. Amelia's pot was simmering. Carmichael had the five small pots with the different colored chocolate all set up.

"Two people to a mold, and remember, I'm the tenth person," Bernie said. "So, everyone has a chance to do both the design, and the regular chocolate, the person on the left will start by filling in the design of twenty-five squares, then you will switch places so your partner can have a chance."

Everyone was excited.

"When you switch, the first person will start with the filling of the regular chocolate for twenty-five squares, then your partner will finish up the last twenty-five." Bernie looked the group over. "Does everyone understand what they're going to do?"

Madge and Lila Mae were excited. Dorothea, not so much. "I was never very good at this," Dorothea said. "Madge and Lila Mae had a lot more experience."

"Dorothea, your sisters have not set foot on the factory floor to work in decades," Bernie said in a stern voice. "I think their experience has leveled out and you are all even."

Dorothea grumbled softly.

He went on to explain all the tools and gadgets on the table at each station, and showed how to hold or wield each one. He made them open the drawers and don aprons, and hairnets. They would put on gloves when they were ready to start work.

Two hours later, Bernie appraised the surrounding scene. Different colored chocolate covered the aprons. Faces were dotted and smudged. The tables held globs. In other words, the place and everyone in it was a mess, including himself.

Laughter filled the air.

"Lord help us if I ever need this crew to work here," Bernie said. He removed his stained apron and wiped at his shirt with a napkin, finally giving up.

"Do we get to take some home with us?" Gina asked.

"They have to set, but then we will box them up and everyone gets to take them home," Bernie said. He waved his hand in the air. "Think about this entire process for a minute. This was a small order. If we had an order for hundreds, or if it was something we thought would be popular, we would have had a different mold made, and the order would be relegated to the factory line."

"This was so much fun," Bambi said, licking one of her gloved fingers before pulling the gloves off and disposing them in the trash can.

Joseph glanced at the hamper of colorful stained aprons which was filled to overflowing. Hairnets and gloves filled a small trash can. "If these come clean, I want to know what products were used. Baby burps are hard to get out of my smocks."

DOROTHEA WALKED BRISKLY DOWN the sidewalk, pushing the twins' stroller. She was happy to be making progress on what she called her *figure reconfiguration program*. All her wailing and moaning throughout her pregnancy, not to mention eating everything that was within reach, did her in. And lying around while trying to get through the shock of being pregnant at her age didn't help matters.

After a nice little shopping spree for new workout clothes, including the correct type of shoes to protect her feet, she was two days into her new regime. Wearing a tangerine fitted ruched top with ties at the bottom and matching Capri leggings, she was stylish, even though she felt like a whale. She figured she would be able to tighten the ties on the top as the pounds melted away.

Dorothea was approaching the mid-point where she was to meet Bambi and Trevor, and saw Bambi and her baby carriage approaching at a speed that couldn't possibly be from walking. When Bambi pulled up alongside her, Dorothea noticed the younger woman was wearing inline skates.

"Bambi! You skated?" Dorothea asked. She took in Bambi's cute outfit: a fitted sport halter top and boxer-style shorts. "I don't know how you managed!"

Bambi noticed Dorothea's blushed face and neck. "You need to ditch those leggings and get some shorts. It's too hot for that much spandex. Save it for the winter."

"I can't wear shorts outside!" Dorothea blurted. "I've got all these veins..."

"Dorothea, who cares? You're not big by any long shot, and a lot of women get varicose veins and even hemorrhoids from their pregnancy. You'd look great in shorts like these," Bambi said, grabbing the bottoms of her shorts and holding them out.

"Plus, you'd be so much cooler!" Bambi said.

Dorothea gave Bambi the once-over. "Okay. I'll try to control my thoughts about my body and dress for comfort. Henry doesn't seem to mind. At least he's never mentioned anything."

"That's because he wants to keep his head on his shoulders," Bambi said with a giggle. "Let's go back to your place and see what Joseph is up to."

Dorothea made a wide turn with the twin stroller and they took off down the sidewalk.

CHAPTER TWENTY-FIVE

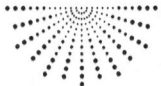

"*I*'ve given this case a lot of thought," Stacy said. She sat opposite Mike, with Chance beside her. "Even though we suspected Mrs. Munson was assassinated due to her history of working for the FBI, all evidence points to Mr. Munson."

Stacy paused for a moment, collecting her thoughts. "The footprints leading back to the driveway. Don't forget the blood-soaked shoes. The drop of blood on the doormat. Then there's the fact that he fled the area and is probably in Mexico."

"I suspect the secret weapons rooms and hideaway were Kimberly Munson's additions to the house because of her work," Chance said. "It was a bonus for Judson to do away with his wife, but we don't have a motive. Granted Lila Mae and I heard them fighting one night, but we're going to have to dig deep to find out what was going on, and to put the blame on Judson."

Mike listened to Stacy and Chance as he sat back in his chair with his feet on his desk. He pulled his feet off his desk and sat up. "We need to find out if someone ordered a hit on her, and why."

* * *

EDDY SAT in the back booth at the bar he frequented in San Antonio, nursing a Corona and eating Mexican food. The door opened, and Pee Wee and Blackjack made their way to the back of the room where Eddy *officed*. They slipped into the booth opposite Eddy.

"Yeah, who are you?" Eddy asked, not impressed.

"Company from Vegas," Blackjack said.

"What do you want with me?" Eddy asked.

"A guy named Munson did his wife in," Pee Wee said. "We understand she was someone special to you."

Eddy set his fork on the plate. "Can you confirm that Munson killed her?"

"My boss, Big Nose Sam, had an agreement about an old debt with Mr. Munson. He wants to know where this guy is hiding," Pee Wee said.

Eddy took a bite of his fajita, chewed while thinking, then swigged beer. "Why do you think I know?"

"It appears you met with him and bought some inventory the lady got from you a while back," Blackjack said.

"If I give him up, what are your plans?" Eddy asked.

"The boss will come up with a plan so everyone is happy," Pee Wee said. "Well, everyone except for Mr. Munson."

* * *

CHIQUITA HELD the door open while Chance carried a box through Lila Mae's kitchen. Lila Mae followed with a suit bag.

"I've got the reading room set up for your office," she told him.

Chance veered off in that direction while Lila Mae climbed the stairs with the suit bag. Chiquita followed several minutes later with shirts on hangers, passing Chance as he went back outside to his Lexus.

After twenty minutes his car was empty. Chance and Lila Mae sat at the kitchen table. "It didn't take long to get a contract on the condo," he said.

"I told you it would be quick," Lila Mae said.

"My office furniture will be delivered tomorrow," Chance said. "I'm not sure if I'll be able to be here or not, so I put sticky notes on the walls where things should go."

"Don't worry about it. Chiquita and I will take care of it," Lila Mae said.

Chiquita disappeared into the bathroom in the butler's pantry. She pulled out her cellphone and sent Amelia a text: *Guess what? Chance is moving in!*

* * *

AMELIA'S PHONE dinged an incoming message. She casually glanced at the screen while she mixed cookie batter. She did a double-take, grabbed a dishtowel and wiped her hands. Amelia snatched up her phone and read the message from Chiquita again. Her heart pounded with the context of the message. She pressed Talk. Chiquita answered on the first ring.

"Are you serious?" Amelia blurted.

"Yes. His office furniture will be here tomorrow! We've brought in some of his clothes. Lila Mae is going to follow him over to his place and they'll get more," Chiquita babbled.

"Holy smokes! This is BIG news! You text Uncle Tito. I'm texting Carmichael and Joseph." Amelia disconnected the call and ran her fingers at Indy 500 speed on the keyboard, texting a larger group than what she first thought about.

Her phone rang. Madge was borderline ranting. "Are you sure? This is too big to be a false accusation. Who is your source?"

Amelia repeated what Chiquita told her.

"Oh, my beating heart," Madge said. "We've waited for this for a long time. We'd better stay calm and let her announce this at her own pace."

* * *

DOROTHEA AND JOSEPH sipped tea while he regaled his stories about his mother and grandmother's visit.

"Eirik is being a good sport," Joseph was saying when his phone dinged. He read the incoming text and girlie screeched like a peacock. Then Dorothea's phone dinged. She looked at Joseph with her mouth floundering.

"Did you get this message?" She shoved her phone at Joseph.

"Yes!" Joseph said, close to tears. "Isn't this wonderful!"

They both joined the texting Indy 500. Phones dinged nonstop with messages from the large family and extended members.

* * *

LILA MAE and Chance were busy loading their cars with more of Chance's hanging clothes, and boxes of t-shirts, jeans, underwear, and socks. Suddenly, their phones went crazy with ding after ding. Chance placed a box of liquor and wine in the trunk of his car and pulled his phone out of his pocket.

"Uh-oh," he warned. "You're not going to like this one bit."

Lila Mae placed the last hanger on her grab bar in the back seat of her Bentley. "What's the matter?"

Chance held out his phone, and Lila Mae glanced at the list of congratulatory text messages. There were even texts from his boss, Stacy, Frank and the team they worked with.

"What the…?" Lila Mae sputtered. "That Chiquita!"

Chance pried the phone from her fingers, pocketed it, and swooped in and wrapped his arms around her.

"Let them have their moment," he cooed. "They're all shocked. Don't be mad at Chiquita, or anyone."

Lila Mae relaxed. "I guess you're right. I expect my phone to blow up with all the messages." She fished her phone out of her purse, and sure enough, there were dozens of texts. Even messages demanding that she respond immediately. "Oh, Lord! Madge is frothing at the mouth, wanting me to call her. I'd better text her and tell her I'll talk to her later."

Chance roared with laughter1. "Yeah, like that will hold her off."

Lila Mae shot daggers at him. "You're enjoying this way too much."

They locked up the cars and returned to the condo for another load. Arms loaded, Chance and Lila Mae returned to Chance's open garage. Lila Mae's Bentley was in back of Chance's vehicle, and Madge was leaning against her nougat Bentley, arms folded. As soon as she spied Chance and Lila Mae, she rushed over to them and grabbed both in a hug.

"I'm so happy for you two," Madge said, sniffling a bit.

Lila Mae struggled. "Thanks, honey, but I'm about to drop my load here."

"Oh!" Madge said. She stepped back and helped Lila Mae with her armful of hangers.

"Thanks, Madge," Chance said.

"What are you going to do with all your lovely furniture?" Madge asked.

"A lot of it is going into storage, then I'll sell it," Chance said. "My office furniture is going to the house tomorrow."

"Once everything settles, we'll see what we can incorporate into my mix," Lila Mae said. "I may get rid of a few of my pieces."

"Really?" Madge said in a gravelly voice filled with surprise.

* * *

THE THREE CARS pulled into Lila Mae's parking area. Three car doors opened. Chiquita inserted the door wedge to keep the kitchen French door open, then she went outside to help with the unloading.

Lila Mae became blotchy with anger until Chance elbowed her. She huffed, then shook off her irritation. "Okay, I give in."

They began unloading the cars. "Follow Chance, Madge. He'll show you where his office is."

* * *

JUDSON MADE it to Orange Walk, Belize. He was worn out, frazzled, and couldn't go one more mile if his life depended on it. The blue Honda was bashed and battered from the crazy Mexican drivers who derived way too much pleasure from *who goes first* down narrow roads and bridges.

There had been one point when he had to throw the car into reverse when a dump truck, bus, or other large vehicle had come barreling down a one-lane road or bridge and didn't slow down when it met his vehicle.

After stopping at a restaurant to soothe his nerves and get a bite to eat, Judson talked with several local people and inquired about an acceptable, affordable hotel. Two people suggested the same place and gave him directions. After paying for his food and drinks, he drove a few blocks to St. Christopher's Hotel on Main Street. At forty bucks a night, it was a step up from the motels in Mexico. The room had air conditioning and its own bathroom, a small desk, and a TV on a wall stand.

Judson brought in his luggage from the car, flopped down on the bed, and practically passed out. After a two-hour nap, he woke up a little disoriented in the strange room, when the sun was going down. Even though he had eaten earlier, he discovered he was ravenous. He changed his shirt, washed his face and combed his hair, then headed out the door.

The Toucan Bar and Grill was a couple of storefronts from the hotel. Judson entered the establishment and took in the ambiance. Paddle fans on the ceiling, hanging lamps that seemed to be made from large gourds, wooden tables and chairs, and a long bar with backless bar stools. He stood in the entrance, wondering if he was supposed to seat himself or wait for someone. After a few minutes, he sauntered in and made himself comfortable at an empty table.

A waitress swooped in and presented him with a menu and took his beverage order. Judson perused the menu, being careful to read the descriptions of the food so he would not make the *hamburger* mistake. He still could not believe the literal difference between a ground beef patty and a slab of ham. When the waitress returned, he chose a seafood dinner.

"This is a lobster tail, correct?" he asked.

The girl looked over his shoulder to where he was pointing on the menu.

"Yes. For a dollar more, you get two tails," she explained.

"Okay, that sounds good. I'll take two, and the baked potato. Does that come with butter and sour cream?" Judson asked.

*   *   *

CHANCE BREEZED into Mike's office. "Got a hit down at the border. One of the border crossing agents recognized Munson's picture."

"Do we know what he was driving?" Mike asked.

"He seemed to think it was a blue Honda, but couldn't be positive if it was an Accord or another model," Chance said. "Luckily, they are going to check their cameras and their license plate readers. They have that face-detection technology in place, so we'll get more than lucky."

"Well, at least we're going in the right direction," Mike said.

"Getting him back may not be so easy," Chance said. "Mexico won't extradite unless the government guarantees that the person of interest will not face the death penalty upon return to the United States."

"We'll let the prosecutor worry about that," Mike said. "Did you get moved?"

"Not one-hundred percent. My office furniture should be there by now, and I've got things going to storage," Chance said. He looked at his watch. "Speaking of which, I need to head out. I'm going to pick up some of my artwork and take it over to Lila Mae's."

Mike chuckled. "It's not Lila Mae's anymore. It's home."

"Yeah, I guess you're right," Chance said. He grinned.

Mike's desk phone buzzed. He hit the speaker button. "Hennessy."

"I have two FBI agents here to see you," Bruno White announced from the lobby.

Mike and Chance groaned. "Send them up."

"Looks like they're going to take over the case," Chance said. "Better call Stacy and Frank."

Mike hit a speed dial number on the phone and connected with Stacy. "Wrap up the Munson case. The Feds are here."

As Mike disconnected the call and stood, two men in black suits appeared in the doorway.

* * *

BIG NOSE SAM'S luxurious office suite held shelves of casino memorabilia from his forty-year career as the owner of Mirrors, a startling casino hotel on the Strip whose mirrored windows played changing scenes on a continuous basis.

Pee Wee and Blackjack sat in front of the desk waiting for the boss to end his phone call. The large portrait of Mama

Vespucci, Sam's mother, looked down on the men with a scathing expression. Pee Wee averted his gaze to no avail. Mama's eyes, unknown to anyone but Sam and security, were ever watchful with tiny cameras.

Sam ended his call on the desk phone and turned his full attention to Blackjack, Pee Wee, and his cigar.

"You wrapped things up in Texas neatly?" Sam asked. He puffed his cigar.

"Yeah," Pee Wee and Blackjack said in unison.

"No loose ends?" Sam asked.

"Nah, we followed the Munson guy to San Antonio," Blackjack said. "We had a talk with a guy he met up with—someone named Eddy."

"We convinced Eddy it would be in his best interest to squeal where Munson ran away to," Pee Wee said.

Sam puffed away, nodding. "Good. Good. The authorities are going to discover a bunch of money in an account, which will look very unfavorable for Mr. Munson. Nobody crosses Sam Vespucci. I don't care how many decades pass. I'm a very patient man."

"Eddy wants this guy dissected," Blackjack said.

"I hope you explained that after he is back home again, in custody, the sky's the limit on his health choices," Sam said.

CHAPTER TWENTY-SIX

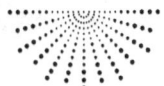

"*I* found your house," Carmichael said as he cradled the phone on his shoulder while arranging flowers in vases in Madge's kitchen.

Amelia was hand-mixing a batch of cookies in a large aluminum bowl, her cellphone on speakerphone. "Oh, yeah? Where?"

"I'll send you a link," Carmichael said.

* * *

COOKIES COOLED on racks as Amelia stared at the monitor. "Oh, wow." She called Carmichael.

"Did you see it?" he asked, bypassing hello.

"Let's go see it!" Amelia said. She was trying hard not to sound like a complete nut job. "It has every feature I've ever wanted! They thought of everything!"

"Thought so. I made an appointment for three o'clock today," Carmichael said. "Figured you'd want to see it."

"This is why I love you so much," Amelia said. "One car or two?"

"I'll pick you up," Carmichael said. "Save me a cookie."

* * *

AMELIA AND CARMICHAEL stood in the driveway, staring at the house. It was more than twice the size of her Bellaire house. The realtor pulled her car into the driveway beside theirs.

"I'm sorry I'm late, I was held up at another showing," she said.

"That's okay," Carmichael said. "We were just taking in the exterior of the house. I'm Carmichael and this is my fiancé, Amelia."

They shook hands with Tracy, who was gussied up to the nines as a modern businesswoman, including her Coach shoulder bag that doubled as a purse and briefcase, and a professionally made-up face that looked spray-painted on.

"The house is vacant. The owners were transferred to Venezuela last month and they are eager to sell," Tracy said.

"Let's look at the outside first," Amelia said. "It looks great online, but it's hard to tell exactly where everything is from the pictures."

The double-wide driveway and parking area in front of the four-car garage were in a pristine condition, without cracks or oil stains. Lush landscaping surrounding the front and sides of the house was evident. Tracy opened the side gate, and they walked into the backyard.

A sparkling pool with a wide seating area of smooth pavers greeted them. There were poles with a tracking system and some type of connection device on one end.

"What the heck is that?" Carmichael asked as he pointed up.

"Wait until you see this." Tracy walked to the pool house, opened the door and retrieved what looked like a TV remote. She pressed a button. A sun filter screen rolled along the track over the pool and the seating area.

"The owners were worried about sunburn and skin cancer, so they had this installed," Tracy explained.

Amelia's mouth hung open. "Wow! I love it!"

"That's perfect for Houston," Carmichael said.

The wide veranda contained a fabulous summer kitchen. There were French doors that opened along the back of the house, similar to Lila Mae's house. As Amelia wandered and scrutinized the property, she noted herb gardens and raised vegetable beds.

"Carmichael, look," she said. "They have an established herb garden. We'll have to find out if they have gone organic, or if we have to redo them."

"They're organic," Tracy said. She handed them several stapled pages with full details regarding the house and property. "It even lists what's planted. Ready to go inside?"

Tracy motioned for them to precede her through the gate to the front of the house. She unlocked the front door and stood aside.

Amelia gasped as she stepped inside. An enormous corner fireplace was to the side of a wall of French doors to the veranda. The living area was open to the large, eat-in kitchen, which was on the right side of the enormous area from her view at the front door.

Carmichael nudged her forward. "Are you in zombie mode? Move."

Amelia stepped forward onto the gorgeous wood floor, the color of caramel. She walked through the living area and veered to the right. "I swear this kitchen was designed for me, Carmichael." She ran her hands over the immense kitchen island. As she walked around it she noticed two large drawers. She opened one and gasped. "Refrigerator drawers!"

She patted her chest. "Be still, my heart."

Carmichael opened a door and discovered the butler's

pantry, which turned out to be about the same size as Amelia's Bellaire living room.

"Look at this!" Carmichael exclaimed. "It's a combination butler's pantry, laundry room, and either craft or sewing center!"

Amelia joined him in the room. "This is fabulous!" She returned to the kitchen and headed to the six-burner gas stove-top, which included a changeable grill/griddle in the middle. She checked the knobs to see if they had a safety feature—she had discovered while looking for her Bellaire stove that some stoves did not have the push-in-and-turn safety feature.

Two ovens and a microwave were mounted on the wall at a height that perfectly accommodated manipulating hot baking pans and dishes. Amelia began opening the cabinets. She discovered vertical storage for baking sheets, cooling racks, and the like.

Carmichael came back to the kitchen, pocketing a tape measure. "Our large stew pots will fit in the butler's pantry with room to spare! There's even a wine cooler." He headed to the full-size refrigerator. "Now this is more like it. We'll have plenty of room for everything, especially with the produce drawers in the island."

Amelia checked out the full-size freezer. There was plenty of shelf room for her canning jars; she froze soups and stews in. Plus, there were roll-out drawers for larger cuts of meat, such as a turkey and roasts. "This is the perfect setup for us, Carmichael."

He stood in the open freezer doorway, looking at the shelves, drawers and bins. "Yeah, even a place for pizza!"

They left the kitchen and explored the rest of the house. The dining room had a built-in buffet side table with cabinets and drawers. There was also an immense dining room table with a dozen chairs in the room.

"If you don't want the table, you can sell it," Tracy said. "They didn't have room for it in their new house."

"We want it!" Carmichael piped up. He turned to Amelia. "We do, don't we? This is perfect."

Amelia ran her hand along the surface of the dark wood. "I can't believe they would leave something so beautiful! You bet I want it! It sounds like we want this house period."

They left the dining room and ventured forth into the rest of the house. There were four bedrooms on one side of the house, all large enough for queen-size beds. On the other side of the house, they found an office, a media room with seating for twenty, and a master bedroom suite that left them speechless.

"I can't take it anymore," Carmichael said. He shaded his face with a hand. "Do you want to see other houses, or is this it?"

Amelia was bedazzled as they walked back to the living area. She stood facing the French doors to the veranda, then walked that way. She opened one set of doors and walked through and stood on the veranda. Then she turned and looked back into the house. She stepped back inside, closed and locked the doors, and faced Tracy.

"How quick can we close with a cash sale?" Amelia asked.

Tracy smiled. "Let's draw up the papers, make an offer, and get everything started."

* * *

AMELIA AND CARMICHAEL sat in Walter's office. He perused the real estate contract.

"They're asking eight-eighty-nine," Walter said. "Since they're already out of the country and want to make a fast sale, and you're offering cash, I'd suggest seven hundred thousand. They'll jump for joy."

Amelia and Carmichael exchanged a silent agreement.

"That sounds fair," Amelia said. "It's a fantastic piece of property."

Carmichael perused the stapled pages from Tracy. "Just over an acre, so we have room to do whatever we want, like having Jingo install that squash and gourd trellis."

Walter double-tapped his desk. "I'll present the offer to Tracy, and she can send it on to the sellers. Let's move on to your Bellaire house."

* * *

AMELIA AND CARMICHAEL climbed into his car at Walter's office building. They sat in stony silence for a minute, then both shrieked for joy. They faced each other, giddy.

"What if they don't accept the offer?" Amelia said, suddenly all worried. "I want that house!"

"They'll make a counteroffer," Carmichael said. "But I think they'll accept. It will be a quick closing with Walter steering the deal. Are we going to pack the Bellaire house ourselves, or have a company pack it up?"

Amelia thought about all of their stuff, especially the crammed kitchenware. "If we do it, it will take a few weeks in between working. If we hire someone to pack for us, they will do it in one or two days. I'd say let's pay someone."

Carmichael backed out of the parking space and headed over to the factory to Amelia's business for her car. "Want to go to Lila Mae's?"

She shook her head. "When they accept the offer, then we'll tell her."

"The first thing I'm going to do is jump in the pool!" Carmichael said.

* * *

Two days later, Carmichael parked his bumblebee car in Lila Mae's driveway. Amelia could barely contain herself. She opened the door just as he shifted the car into park.

"Let's go!" she all but hollered.

They walked to the kitchen door and rang the bell. "Isn't it weird ringing the doorbell instead of letting yourself in?" Carmichael asked.

"I still have my key, but I need to ask about protocol now," Amelia said.

Chiquita rushed to the door and let them in. "Hi. Why didn't you just unlock the door?"

"We were just talking about that," Carmichael said.

"Where's Lila Mae?" Amelia asked.

"Here I am!" Lila Mae called out as she joined them in the kitchen. "I was watching Louie and Quack."

"Hi neighbor!" Amelia squealed. She threw her arms around Lila Mae and hugged her into next week.

Lila Mae pulled back and glanced from Amelia to Carmichael. "Spill!"

"We bought the Tovar's house!" Amelia said, her face alight.

"That sprawling one-story just down the street?" Lila Mae asked.

"Yes!" Carmichael said. "Have you been inside it?"

"As a matter of fact, I have. I thought of buying it before they did," Lila Mae said. "It's a perfect house for you two! And you'll be within walking distance!"

Amelia and Lila Mae jumped up and down in excitement.

Chiquita brought a tray of iced tea to the kitchen table. "Sit! Drink!"

"We saw it two days ago," Carmichael said. "When I saw it online, I knew Amelia would want it. Walter is handling everything."

* * *

CHANCE TIDIED up his new home office after the move. There were boxes and stacks of papers and books everywhere. His cellphone dinged with an incoming message from someone he didn't know. He stopped to retrieve it and read it twice.

Would like to discuss Kimberly Munson in private.

Chance stalled while he thought. He then typed. *Feds took over.*

After a long moment, a dinged reply. *Explanation / closure / why things went to hell. Meet me at...*

Chance thought for a moment. He climbed the stairs to Lila Mae's office and found her sitting in front of her monitor, staring at a spreadsheet.

"Hey, hon," Chance said. "Why don't you enlarge that so you don't wreck your vision?"

"That's a thought," Lila Mae said. "I have no idea why I didn't consider that option." She clicked the plus sign in the corner, and the rows and cells were in the normal range with a twelve-point Arial font. "How about that! All the words are there!"

Chance took a look. "Houston socialites?"

"Yes, I've updated this list monthly for the past decade. This is going to help Amelia's business grow tremendously," she said. "I figured we can email out a campaign for her latest creations, specials, holidays—you know, the whole works."

"Who's going to be in charge of the campaign? Are you going to use one of those special mailing things so you can send everything in one email?" Chance asked.

"I've been researching all that. We're going to outsource to someone who knows how to use one of those email services," Lila Mae said.

"Good. You don't need one more thing on your plate," Chance said. "I may be home very late tonight. I have to go to San Antonio and meet someone about the Munson case."

Lila Mae frowned. "I thought the Feds took over."

"Yeah, they did, but this is a follow-up no one knows about

that will weave all the loose ends together to make sense of the why and the how of the case," Chance said.

"Well, that sounds interesting. You'd better let me in on it when you find out," Lila Mae said.

"You bet." Chance kissed the top of her head, went back downstairs and out the door.

* * *

EDDY AND CHANCE sat in Eddy's *office* in the bar, bottles of Corona in front of them, introductions finished with.

"Kimberly and I were very close before Munson came into the picture," Eddy said with a sour look on his face. "That was when she was known as Delilah Tourance."

"Was that her undercover name?" Chance asked, trying to understand where the conversation was headed.

"No, Delilah Tourance was her birth name," Eddy said. "She was tasked with eliminating a powerful mob person, and her name was changed to Kimberly shortly after that."

"She hit a mob boss?" Chance asked, surprised, but not really.

Eddy snorted.

"How did Munson come into the picture?" Chance asked.

"He worked for Alessandra Vespucci in Vegas," Eddy said. "Munson fell for Delilah and helped her by arranging access to his boss for the hit."

Chance put the pieces together in his head. "So, Judson Munson arranged for his boss to be killed, then disappeared with the hit woman!"

Eddy took a swig of his beer. "Why Delilah ever took up with that bastard is beyond me. Big Nose Sam had a ten-million-dollar bounty out on Delilah, but she went to ground. Someone in Houston spotted her recently, and the ball started rolling too fast to stop."

Chance squinted in thought. He recalled the argument at the Munson's house not too long ago. "Did Munson kill his own wife, or did Vespucci hire it out?"

Eddy snorted. "Big Nose Sam told Judson that if he wanted to continue to see the sun rise into his golden years, he'd better do the deed, or he'd be hunted like the rabbit he was."

"Kind of hard to ignore that promise," Chance said. "But now he's down in Mexico somewhere, so who knows if he'll ever face charges."

Eddy smiled, reached into his pocket, and withdrew a piece of paper. He slid it across the table to Chance. "Depends on who gets here first."

Chance read the name of a hotel and room number in Orange Walk, Belize.

* * *

CHANCE RETURNED to the house after midnight. He let himself in and was thankful that Lila Mae had turned the stove light on and left the light on at the end of the stairs. He walked through the kitchen and down the hallway and almost tripped over a dark hump on the floor.

Quack unfolded himself and quacked at him.

"What in the world are you doing in here, Quack?" Chance asked. "I know for a fact that Lila Mae would not invite you in for a sleepover."

Quack continued to quack. Chance thought the duck was actually raising its voice, maybe in anger.

Lila Mae appeared at the top of the stairs in her robe. "Chance?"

"It's me, and Quack," Chance said. "You didn't bring him into the house, did you?"

"Quack's in the house?" Lila Mae asked in horror as she

descended the stairs. "Quack! How did you get in here? Louie's sleeping."

Chance decided to explore and veered off into the living room. He flipped the light switch and walked to the wall of French doors where Louie's new dog door had been installed.

The flap on the dog door hung cockeyed.

"Uh-oh." Chance kneeled and tried to straighten it out, but it was hung up on something he couldn't determine.

"Oh no," Lila Mae said. She looked around. "I hope he didn't go potty in here. Ducks can be pretty messy."

"You get the door, and I'll get the duck," Chance said. "I'll have to figure out what to do with the dog door to keep him out. Louie will have to be a little inconvenienced until tomorrow."

They put Quack outside, and Chance grabbed a square basket with magazines and placed it in front of the broken flap. Quack pushed to no avail, quacking up a storm. He could not get in.

"Hopefully he'll give up and quiet down," Lila Mae said.

* * *

CHIQUITA, Lila Mae, and Chance sat at the kitchen table sipping café mocha and reading the paper. The kitchen doorbell rang. Chiquita jumped up and ran to the door. She opened the door with a giant smile on her face as she greeted Jingo Jackson. "Hi, Jingo."

"Hi, Chiquita." He was deeply smitten as he looked at her. "Is Lila Mae available?"

"Sure. Come in," Chiquita said, dazzled by his smile.

Jingo stepped inside and followed Chiquita to the table. He gave a little wave. "Hi Chance, Lila Mae."

"Good morning, Jingo," Lila Mae said.

"Lila Mae, I'm going to install Quack's house," Jingo said.

"Wonderful!" Lila Mae said. "He'll be all set now. I can't wait to see what you've come up with."

* * *

A FEW MINUTES LATER, Robert, one of Jingo's workers, pulled a flat cart containing a three-foot long Mallard nest cylinder, a platform and post, and his toolbox. Jingo closed the gate behind the cart.

Lila Mae, Chance, and Chiquita stood by the stream and looked the nest over.

"Huh, that's interesting," Lila Mae said.

"I researched it online, and this cylinder nest is what they like," Jingo said. "I'll have to replace the hay and grass every three years."

Jingo and Robert went about installing the nest. When they were done, Louie and Quack checked it out. Louie sniffed all over the full length of the cylinder, and Quack went inside. When he didn't exit, everyone took turns bending down and taking a look.

"Well, that looks like a success story," Lila Mae said.

Chiquita followed Jingo and Robert as they took the cart and their tools back to the truck.

Lila Mae turned to Chance. "You never did tell me what went on in San Antonio."

"Yeah, Quack threw us off kilter with his little adventure," Chance said. He brought Lila Mae up to date on Eddy's story.

"She killed the mob guy's mother?" Lila Mae asked, horrified. "No wonder he was out for revenge. That worm of a husband of hers. I hope he rots in hell."

"Oh, I'm pretty sure he's going to regret this for however long he lives. There's no protecting a guy with that history," Chance said. "Big Nose Sam will gut him, that's for sure. Not sure if even the Feds can protect him. I turned it over to Mike, and he did likewise."

"Let's hope we get good neighbors once the house sells. I'm pretty sure Judson will have to put the house on the market to pay for his legal expenses when he's apprehended," Lila Mae said.

Chance shook his head. "Could be vacant for a while."

AN UNPRECEDENTED FOUR-WEEK closing on Amelia and Carmichael's Del Monte house was because of Walter's magic. The title company quickly received all the required paperwork, and the inspection revealed no major problems.

Carmichael stood in front of the garage, waving the moving truck up the driveway. Amelia went from room to room, taping colored paper to the door frames that matched the labels on the boxes and furniture, so the movers knew which room to deliver items to.

"Knock-knock," Lila Mae called out from the front door.

"Back here," Amelia yelled.

Lila Mae went in search of Amelia. "Oh, good. You're labeling rooms."

"Yeah, now if the movers will pay attention to the colors!" Amelia said.

"I'll bet Carmichael will remind them," Lila Mae said.

"Yoo-hoo!" Chiquita said as she stepped into the house.

Lila Mae stuck her head out of the hallway. "We're down here."

Amelia and Lila Mae met Chiquita halfway down the hall.

"Do you want me to start unpacking your kitchen things?" Chiquita asked.

"Yeah, that would be great. I just got here and haven't unpacked the refrigerator things," Amelia said.

They all walked to the kitchen where half a dozen boxes were scattered.

"I've got the boxes where I want them to go," Amelia said. "Just ask me about upper or lower cabinet locations."

"I love this kitchen," Chiquita said. "It's so well thought out."

"Everything in this house is like a dream," Amelia said. She grabbed Lila Mae in a teary hug. "Thank you so much for the Nathan funds!"

Lila Mae patted Amelia on the back. "There, there. No time to get emotional now. Start unpacking!"

Two movers came through the front door with furniture.

Carmichael stood to the side. "Look for the color-coded paper on the walls and doors so you get the furniture and stuff in the right room."

CHAPTER TWENTY-SEVEN

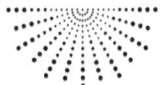

*I*t was blessedly in the high eighties now that the triple-digit temperatures of the summer were behind them. The garage door opened, and Amelia and Carmichael started their brand-new Can-Am Spyder motorcycles. Dark green for Amelia, with Amelia's Kitchen painted on either side of the frame, and royal blue for Carmichael with a cast-iron skillet painted on his ride.

They rode down the driveway, stopped at the street, and turned left. Carmichael took the lead and wove through the streets. They pulled up to Madge's house. Rick settled a helmet on his head while Madge gunned her ride. The four riders took off into the Houston traffic and headed over to the Ogre club.

The End

THE RECIPES

*P*erfect Roast Pork

Cook the Story http://cookthestory.com/

This recipe serves four to ten people. Allow 3-1/2 hours to prepare the roast which includes resting time. It will be juicy and tender on the inside while having a nice brown crust on the outside.

Ingredients:

4-8-pound boneless pork butt or pork shoulder

salt

black pepper

garlic powder

chicken broth

Directions:

1. Allow the roast to sit at room temperature for 30 minutes to an hour.
2. Preheat oven to 300°F.
3. Trim excess fat from the roast but be sure to leave a thin layer.

4. Heavily season the roast all over with pepper and garlic powder. Sprinkle with salt.
5. Put the roast in a roasting pan, fat-side-up.
6. Add at least an Inch of chicken broth to the pan.
7. Bake, uncovered for 40 minutes per pound.
8. Replace the broth as needed.
9. Remove the roast from the oven and transfer it to a plate.
10. Let the roast rest for at least 30 minutes. Use this time to make your gravy.
11. Preheat the oven to 475F.
12. Put the roast in a clean roasting pan.
13. Roast uncovered, for 13-17 minutes until browned.
14. Remove the roast from the oven and carve immediately.

* * *

CHICKEN WITH RIESLING

Food & Wine February 2003
ACTIVE: 30 MIN; TOTAL: 1 HR 10 MIN 4 SERVINGS
5 tablespoons unsalted butter
One 3½ pound chicken, quartered
Salt and freshly ground pepper
1 large shallot, minced
2 tablespoons Cognac
1 cup dry Riesling
6 oz. white mushrooms, sliced
1 tablespoon all-purpose flour
1/3 cup heavy cream

Melt 2 tablespoons of the butter in a large skillet. Add the chicken, season with salt and pepper and cook over moderate heat until slightly browned, about 4 minutes per side.

Add the shallot and cook, stirring, for 1 minute.

Add the Cognac and carefully ignite it with a long match. When the flames subside, add the Riesling, cover and simmer over low heat until the chicken breasts are just cooked, about 25 minutes.

Transfer the breasts to a large plate and cover with foil. Cover and simmer the legs until cooked through, about 10 minutes longer. Transfer to the plate.

Meanwhile, in a medium skillet. melt 2 tablespoons of the butter. Add the mushrooms, season with salt and pepper and cook over low heat until the liquid evaporates, about 7 minutes. Increase the heat to moderate and cook, stirring, until browned, about 3 minutes.

In a bowl, blend the flour and the remaining 1 tablespoon of butter. Stir the cream into the large skillet; bring to a simmer.

Gradually whisk the flour paste into the cooking liquid and simmer, whisking, until no floury taste remains, 3 minutes. Season with salt and pepper.

Return the chicken to the skillet. add the mushrooms and briefly reheat.

* * *

CHICKEN PARMESAN ROLL-UPS
By: Girl Gone Gourmet
PREP TIME: 10 mins
COOK TIME: 30 mins
TOTAL TIME: 40 mins
Thin sliced chicken breasts rolled up with cheese and herbs then topped with breadcrumbs. It's a fun way to do chicken parmesan!
Serves: 2
Ingredients
1 cup tomato sauce

6 thinly sliced boneless chicken breasts (see note)
2 tablespoons grated parmesan cheese
2 tablespoons grated mozzarella cheese
1 teaspoon fresh thyme, plus 1 sprig
1 tablespoon olive oil
1 garlic clove sliced
2½ tablespoons bread crumbs
salt & pepper
Instructions

1. Preheat oven to 350 degrees.
2. Spread the tomato sauce evenly in the bottom of a square baking dish.
3. Season each side of the sliced chicken breasts with salt and pepper.
4. Divide the cheese and herb mixture evenly across the slices and roll each slice up. Place each roll seam side down in the pan.
5. In a small pan heat the olive oil with the garlic and thyme sprig. Let it cook for a few minutes just to infuse the oil with the garlic and herb flavors. Discard the garlic and herbs. Turn off the heat and add in the breadcrumbs, stir to combine with the oil.
6. Sprinkle the breadcrumbs over the tops of the rolls. Bake the rolls at 350 degrees for 25-30 minutes, or until cooked through.

* * *

COCKTAIL SAUSAGE BALLS
Cooking with Dawn Greenfield Ireland
Ingredients
1 lb ground sausage meat (beef, turkey, pork, etc. – your choice, or combine!)

3 C biscuit mix
1 lb grated sharp cheddar cheese
Instructions

1. Mix all ingredients in a large bowl. Roll into cocktail-sized balls.
2. Place on cookie sheet and bake at 300 degrees until lightly browned, approximately 25 minutes.
3. You can freeze these yummy appetizers. I freeze these by a half-a-dozen in pint-size freezer bags for snacking.

* * *

CRANBERRY TURKEY CRESCENT **Pinwheels**
Cooking with Dawn Greenfield Ireland
This recipe serves four. You can double, triple or go for dozens with this easy yummy recipe.
Ingredients
1 Can refrigerated crescent rolls
4 Oz cream cheese
8 Slices oven roasted deli turkey
¼ Cup Dried cranberries, chopped
Instructions

1. Heat oven to 350 degrees.
2. Unroll the dough and separate into rectangles – keep two triangles together. Press the seam to make one rectangle.
3. Spread 2 tablespoons cream cheese on dough within half an inch of the edge.
4. Sprinkle with a tablespoon of cranberries.
5. Top with two turkey slices.

6. Start from the short side and roll up the dough. Press the seam to seal.
7. Slice each roll into 2 pieces.
8. Place cut side down on cookie sheet.
9. Bake 14-16 minutes, or until golden brown.

* * *

GINGER BEEF LETTUCE Wraps
Cooking with Dawn Greenfield Ireland
Modified from Better Homes and Gardens Recipe
The bib lettuce makes a great wrap for this low-carb beef recipe. The beef and vegetables are marinated in a ginger and soy sauce mixture and then all is stir fried until the meat is cooked through. This wrap sandwich is not only healthy, but flavorful.
Minutes to cook: 7
Makes 12 wraps
Serves 4
Ingredients
1 lb beef flank steak or boneless beef top round steak
1 medium yellow or green sweet pepper, seeded and cut in bite-size strips
1 small zucchini cut into thin bite-size strips
½ medium red onion cut into thin wedges
1/3 cup ginger beer or ginger ale
3 Tbsp. soy sauce or Coconut Amino sauce
2 cloves garlic, minced
½ tsp cornstarch or arrowroot powder
2 tsp finely chopped fresh ginger
12 Bibb or leaf lettuce leaves (about 2 heads)
¼ C fresh cilantro leaves
Instructions
Trim fat from beef. For easy slicing, wrap and freeze beef for

30-45 minutes until firm.

1. Thinly slice beef across grain. Place beef in a self-sealing plastic bag.
2. Place pepper, zucchini and onion in another bag.
3. Combine ginger beer, soy sauce and garlic in a bowl. Pour into both bags. Seal bags and turn to coat. Refrigerate 4-6 hours, turning bags occasionally.
4. Drain marinate into bowl. Add cornstarch, mix. Set aside.
5. Heat oil in large nonstick wok or skillet over medium-high heat. Add ginger; stir-fry for 15 seconds. Add veggies. Stir-fry 3 to 5 minutes or until crisp-tender. Remove veggies to a bowl.
6. Add half the beef to wok. Stir-fry for 2-3 minutes. Or until beef is slightly pink in center. Repeat with remaining beef.
7. Return beef and veggies to the wok away from the center.
8. Stir the marinate. Add to center of wok. Cook until bubbly.
9. Toss beef and veggies to coat. Remove from heat.
10. Divide beef and veggy mixture among the lettuce leaves. Top with cilantro and roll up.

SUPER DUPER MOIST **Roast Beef**
By AYLABOO
A great recipe given to me from my Dad which was given to him by a famous chef. Goodbye dry tasteless meat. Hello melt-in-your-mouth yumminess!
Minutes to cook: 150

Serves 12
Ingredients
4.5 lb Beef pot roast
1 tsp salt
1 tsp garlic
1 tsp rosemary
Your favorite spices
Instructions

1. Heat oven to 450 degrees F.
2. Season roast beef with the spices.
3. Place in a roasting pan and roast for 30 minutes.
4. Reduce heat to 350 F and continue to cook for 90 minutes (20 min per pound).
5. Remove the roast and wrap tightly in aluminum foil (shiny side facing meat).
6. Place wrapped roast on a plate or cutting board for 30 minutes. (The roast will continue to cook in its own juices in the foil.)

* * *

Sweet Potatoes Hasselback with Cilantro & Lime

When I first saw these potatoes, I thought they were lobster tails! What a surprise, and they are yummy!

Ingredients:
3 Sweet Potatoes
5 garlic cloves, sliced
2 T chopped Cilantro
3 T oil (coconut or olive)
Zest of 2 Limes
1/4 tsp Salt
Directions:

1. Preheat oven to 425 degrees.
2. Place potatoes on a cutting board and cut a 1/4-inch slice from the bottom of each potato so they will lay flat.
3. Place two long wooden chopsticks on each side of the potato, lengthwise
4. Slice the potatoes crosswise, about 1/4-inch apart slices, cutting vertically, down to the chopsticks.
5. Place garlic slices in between the slices.
6. Mix together cilantro, oil, lime zest and salt.
7. Brush mixture on the potatoes.
8. Place in oven for 40 minutes.
9. Increase oven temperature to 450 and bake another 15 minutes.

Adjust this recipe for the number of guests.

BEVERAGES

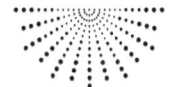

Pumpkin Spiced Martini
By Chad Tackett
http://fitera.com/

Ingredients

6 large ice cubes
4 ounces chilled coffee or espresso
1 shot Baileys
1/2 shot vanilla vodka
1/2 teaspoon pumpkin pie spice
Pinch of cinnamon

Directions

1. Combine the first 5 ingredients in a cocktail mixer, shake vigorously, and pour into a martini glass or over ice in a cocktail class.
2. Sprinkle cinnamon on top and enjoy responsibly!

Nutritional Info
Calories: 118
Fat: 1 g

Protein: 0 g
Carbs: 8 g
Fiber: 0 g
Sugar: 2 g

Note: this recipe is from Chad Tackett's *Top 100 Delicious Fat-Burning Recipes* book, which you can get for just $7 here!

* * *

TIRAMISU **Martini**
By: The Cocktail Lady
www.ayearofcocktails.com/
Ingredients
1 1/2 ounces vanilla vodka
1 1/2 ounces crème de cacao
1 1/2 ounces coffee liqueur
3/4 ounces Irish Cream Liqueur
chocolate syrup
cocoa powder
Instructions

1. Drizzle chocolate syrup around the inside of a martini glass.
2. Stick the glass in the freezer to firm up the chocolate.
3. In a shaker, add ice, vanilla vodka, crème de cacao, coffee liqueur and Irish Cream Liqueur. Shake well.
4. Take martini glass out of freezer and rim with more chocolate syrup and then rim that with cocoa powder. Strain cocktail into the martini glass and enjoy.

DESSERTS

*D*ark Chocolate Avocado Truffles
Cooking with Dawn Greenfield Ireland
Total time: 2 hrs 30 mins
Makes 20 balls
Prep Time: 30 mins
This is a messy recipe, but the end results are so worth the mess! And, there's no sugar involved!

Ingredients
1 ripe avocado
½ cup dates, soaked (3 hrs.) and drained
¼ cup dark cocoa powder - plus - 2 T for dusting
1 ½ Tbsp. melted coconut oil
1 ½ Tbsp. coconut flour
dash of sea salt

Instructions

1. Place first 6 ingredients in a blender/food processor. I use my Ninja.
2. Blend on high until silky smooth.

3. Use a scraper to scrape down the sides of the blender and blend once more.
4. Sprinkle a chopping mat, waxed paper, or cutting board with the cocoa powder for dusting.
5. Scoop one tablespoon of the batter and roll through the cocoa powder to form a ball.
6. Place on a plate when completely dusted.
7. Repeat until all batter is rolled into balls through the cocoa powder.
8. Refrigerate balls 2-3 hours until hardened.

* * *

Banana Dessert Sushi

Alejandra Ramos of Always Order Dessert shares her quick and easy dessert option that's packed with healthy monounsaturated fats or MUFAs. Try it with your favorite nut butter and sweet toppings for an indulgent treat every day.

Ingredients

1 banana

2 tbsp unsweetened natural nut butter (such as cashew butter, peanut butter, or almond butter)

1/3 cup total of your favorite crushed or chopped nuts and seeds (such as almonds, pistachios, sesame seeds, chia seeds, flax seeds, unsweetened coconut flakes, etc.)

Directions

1. Spread a thin layer of nut butter on the entire banana.
2. Spread chopped nuts and seeds on a shallow plate and roll banana over it, pressing lightly so that the nuts and seeds stick to the banana. Slice covered banana into 1-inch thick slices. Eat immediately or place in

the freezer until solid and then transfer to a zipped bag to store.

Optional additions: unsweetened cocoa powder, ground cinnamon, raw cacao nibs, sea salt

Note: Each daily serving is 1/2 banana (or approximately 3-4 sushi pieces).

BONUS STORY!

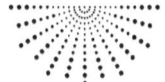

*R*ead a short story about Bernie and Chewie!
Chewie escorted Bernie out the front door of the Lake Sides Assisted Living Center off the 610-Loop near the Galleria. Bernie was gussied up in a summer-weight pale green jacket, black slacks and a gold and green patterned shirt—trying for a 92-year-old Don Johnson of the Miami Vice era look.

They walked to the curb at the horseshoe driveway skirting around residents and guests coming and going to lunch. Chewie opened the rear door of the dark brown Bentley and helped Bernie inside, then he got behind the wheel.

The Bentley wove through traffic for a couple of miles and pulled up to valet parking at the Men's Club on Sage Road off Richmond. Chewie disengaged the ignition key and fob from the large key ring, and handed over the small key ring to the valet as soon as he had Bernie and the walker deposited at the sidewalk by the front door of the establishment.

They went inside and were seated. After their order was taken and iced tea was delivered to the table, Chewie excused himself. "I'll be back in a minute. I'm going to wash my hands. Don't do anything embarrassing!"

Bernie was mesmerized by the scantily clad waitresses passing by the table. "Uh-huh."

"Behave!"

Bernie scowled.

Chewie shook his head and left the table. When he returned, Bernie's chair was empty, but the walker was there. Chewie stood at the side of the table and looked around the club, confused.

No Bernie. No commotion.

Trying to keep panic at bay, Chewie turned to the occupants of one of the tables close by.

"Excuse me. I'm so sorry to interrupt your lunch, but did you happen to see where my employer went?"

Two business men looked Chewie over. He was impeccably dressed in his custom Kato of Green Hornet suit. "The old man in the green jacket?"

"Yes, sir. Did you see where he went? I don't see him here, and he couldn't have gone far without his walker," Chewie said. He indicated the walker by the table.

"Yeah, he left with his friends," the man said.

"Friends?" Chewie balked. "He doesn't have any friends here!" Chewie ran through the club and out the door. He looked around the parking lot to no avail. "Oh my God! Where is he?"

The two businessmen exited the club; one still had his linen napkin in hand. They approached Chewie.

Chewie took out his cell phone and frantically clicked through contacts. "Chance? I think Bernie's been kidnapped!" He listened attentively, then told Chance where he was. The call ended, and he pocketed the phone.

One of the men put his hand on Chewie's shoulder. "We got a good look at the guys with your boss. Did you call the cops?"

Chewie fanned himself with his hand. "Yes, Detective Walker will be here momentarily."

"Who's your boss?" the other man asked.

"Bernie Alcott," Chewie replied, freaked out.

"The chocolate millionaire?"

"Billionaire," Chewie corrected. "I hope they don't hurt him!"

* * *

SIRENS APPROACHED FAST. Chance's Lexus and two police cars screeched to a halt by the front door. Chance bolted out of the car and rushed to Chewie followed by two policemen. Another car pulled up and Detective Sergeant David Johnson got out and approached Chance.

"What do we have?" Johnson asked.

Chance held up his hand. "Just got here." He turned to Chewie. "Start from the beginning."

"Less than half an hour ago I pulled up right here for the valet. I escorted Bernie into the club, we were seated at a table, and we ordered our steaks," Chewie said. "After the girl brought the iced tea, I went to the restroom to wash my hands. I wasn't gone more than five minutes, and when I returned, Bernie was gone, but his walker is still by the table."

Chewie turned to the two men. "These gentlemen were sitting adjacent to us, and I asked them if they knew where Bernie went."

The first man stuck his hand out to Chance. "Elroy Frickenstein."

Chance stared the man down.

Elroy held up his hands. "I was tormented all through school."

Elroy's friend introduced himself. "Robert Banks. As soon as the Asian fellow left the table, these two guys went and talked to the old man, then they left."

"Did you get a good look at them?" Chance asked.

"Yeah," Elroy said. "One guy has a large brown mole on his cheek." He stopped and held his right hand out toward Chance.

"His right cheek. I always have to do that to make sure I know my right from left. Anyway, the guy with the mole had on a brown suit with a silky tan shirt with palm trees on it. Very tacky. Probably polyester."

"He was about six feet tall with a slight build," Robert said. "The other guy was shorter, stockier and probably fifty. He had on a black suit, pretty worn, and an off-white shirt."

Chance and Detective Johnson looked hard at Elroy and Robert.

"You two seem to have a knack for details. Is there something you want to tell us?" Chance asked.

"Oh! We run an investigation business. You know, divorces, child custody—stuff like that," Elroy said. He dug a cardholder out of his pocket and extracted cards and handed one to Chance, one to Johnson and one to Chewie.

"Details are second nature for us," Robert said. "The guy with the mole was about 45."

Chewie stared at the card. The name of the company, Eyes Wide, was displayed in bold, along with a big blue eye. A phone number was the only contact information on the linen card.

Chance turned to the two policemen. "Go and see if you can track down the drinking glasses or dishes—anything those two men may have touched. I'll get Stacy and Frank with CSI out here to see if they can gather evidence."

"You two," Chance pointed to Elroy and Robert, "We need you to look at pictures downtown. See if you can recognize these two guys." Chance handed each of them his card.

He put his hand on Chewie's shoulder. "I know this is nerve-wracking. You're going to have to call a family meeting. Call Lila Mae and get that started. Have her call Walter and Henry. Go over to her house right now. We don't know who these guys will contact if this is a kidnapping for ransom."

Chewie stared right through Chance as if he were in a

trance. "I hope they don't hurt him!" He snapped out of it, shook himself slightly, and approached the valet station.

Johnson followed Chewie. The valet was nowhere to be found.

* * *

CHEWIE STOOD at Lila Mae's kitchen door hand ready to knock. The door flew open and Lila Mae grabbed him in a hug and pulled him into the kitchen.

"Oh. My. God." Lila Mae said. She fanned herself with her hand. "Let's all stay calm. Everyone is on the way."

Amelia took one look at Chewie and went into high gear. She extracted him from her boss and led him to the kitchen table. "Sit."

She hollered to Chiquita. "Fill the teapot and make some chamomile tea!"

Madge's Bentley screeched up the driveway. She all but leaped out of the car and dashed to Lila Mae's door. She grabbed Lila Mae into a hug. "It's okay. It will be okay. We'll pay the ransom. Everyone stay calm."

Amelia intervened while the teapot shrieked. "Why don't you sit down and help Chewie. I think he's in shock." She guided the distraught sisters to the table.

A loud crunch sounded in the driveway. Amelia stretched her neck to witness Bambi's yellow Bentley bashed into Bernie's car. Bambi didn't even acknowledge the accident. She flung open the car door and marathon-ran to the kitchen door, barefoot. Her face was wild with fright. She was out of breath. She started crying.

"Pay the money! Tell them we'll give them a bonus if they don't hurt him!" she bleated in her squeaky voice.

Amelia ushered Bambi to the table. She patted her back. "It will be okay. Chance is on it."

More tires screeched to a stop. Dorothea barreled through the door in complete disarray. Lila Mae and Amelia stared at the pink and white smock top with monkeys, green checked wrinkled cotton Capri pants, and mismatched shoes their sister wore.

"Has anyone called Walter to make arrangements for the ransom?" Dorothea shouted.

Madge stared in horror at her baby sister's appearance. "Dorothea, are you okay?"

"Am I okay? What kind of question is that, Madge?" Dorothea yelled. "Of course, I'm not okay. Daddy is out there with a bunch of lunatics and God knows what's going on!"

Bambi cried a river and soon started hiccuping. Chiquita grabbed the box of tissues from the kitchen desk and plopped it in the middle of the table. She returned to the counter and placed tea bags into cups, then poured the water. She rummaged around until she found a tray and delivered the steaming cups to the table.

Madge looked at the tea. "I need a shot of whiskey, not tea!"

"This is not a time to get sloshed," Lila Mae hollered.

"Are you serious? Think about it... this is the worst crisis we've ever experienced. I say that deserves serious liquor!"

Ever so quietly Chewie agreed. "Liquor... please."

Gina all but ran through the door, stopped and looked around. She spotted Chewie surrounded by women and rushed over to him. "Honey, are you okay?"

Chewie stood. They hugged tightly. He started crying. "All these black belts and I could not protect him!"

* * *

JAN WHEELER, a reporter detested by the Alcott clan, stood broadcasting in front of the Men's Club. "Chocolate billionaire Bernie Alcott has been kidnapped..."

Stacy and Frank arrived at the Men's Club. The walkway to the door had crime scene tape stopping curious people from crossing the line. A police officer lifted the tape and waved the CSI team inside. The news camera followed their progression to the front door. The music had been muted. Wary men sat at tables,les unable to leave without police permission.

Stacy spotted an empty table and made a beeline for it. She set her cases on the table and looked around.

"Let's see how Chance wants to handle this. We could have each group come to the table and take their fingerprints, then send them on their way," she said.

Frank checked his cell phone. "Johnson sent me a text. Said they thought they had the beer glasses from our two suspects. Let me go track those down." He took off toward Johnson.

Chance was talking to three men at a table. Johnson was taking information from four men at another table. Two policemen were at different tables, taking information. One of the policemen left his table of people and approached Chance.

"Detective Walker, one of the men I'm gathering information from doesn't have any ID."

"Nothing at all?" Chance asked. His brows scrunched in question.

Chance held his hand up to his group and walked with the policeman back to his table. A man jumped to his feet, worry etched across his face. "I left my wallet on my desk at work! I swear I had nothing to do with this kidnapping!"

Chance looked at the others at the table. "Are you willing to vouch for this man?"

The men stumbled over each other, talking at once. Chance held up a hand.

"As long as you know you're on the line if he doesn't prove who he is and appears to be someone of interest in this case."

They all turned their focus on their friend.

Frank and Johnson walked to a table that was wrapped in crime scene tape where two beer glasses and plates sat.

"These are the suspects' lunch settings. Hopefully, you can get some fingerprints," Johnson said.

"Maybe even some good DNA," Frank said. His face creased into a grin, and he rubbed his hands together. He set his case down and got to work.

Stacy approached Chance. "Hey, Chance. How do you want to process all these people? We can have the occupants of each table come over to my table." She pointed to where her cases were.

"Sounds good. I'll have one of the team escort each table over. We're going to have to come up with a system so no one tries to sneak out without being processed," Chance said.

"I've got just the thing in my car." Stacy left and returned in a few minutes with a roll of tickets.

"What's that?" Chance asked.

"Drink tickets for the BBQ next month, Stacy said."

"It's for a good cause," Chance said.

* * *

AFTER THE ROOM was cleared of customers and the staff had been processed, Chance approached the manager.

"Who's in charge of the valet parking?" Chance asked.

The manager was sweating bullets. "I hire the valet staff."

"What happened to the guy who checked in the Bentley?"

"I have no idea where he went," the manager said. "He's so fired! And I'll send his picture and info out to the community so no one hires him."

"Show me what you have on him. Especially the photo," Chance said.

The manager and Chance went to his office, and the manager unlocked a file drawer. He flipped through manila folders with names neatly written in block letters. He tipped one folder and extracted the folder in front of it and placed it on his desk.

He flipped through the paperwork until he came to an employment card. A photo was in the upper left corner, and information was filled out in different fields. A signature was at the bottom of the sheet.

The manager handed the sheet to Chance. "I can make you a copy, but I can't give you the original. You know how it goes."

Chance looked over the sheet. "This is good. Yes, please make me a copy."

The manager opened the top of the all-in-one printer and made Chance a copy.

Chance handed the manager his business card. "Call me if you hear from him, or if you or any of the staff remember anything pertinent to this case." They shook hands, and Chance walked outside.

He walked to his Lexus and opened the trunk. He placed the employment record on the floor of his trunk, took out his phone and took a picture of the record. Next, Chance uploaded the photo and sent it to his boss, Captain Mike Hennessy. He typed a message to be sent with the photo:

Need APB on this person of interest in the Alcott kidnapping case.

Within moments his phone dinged with a response:

Probably halfway to Mexico, but we'll give it a try.

IRV PICKED the large brown mole on his face while Tim stuffed French fries in his mouth.

"I don't know why you had to choose lunch to pull this off," Tim complained. "I'm starving and burger-doodle isn't exactly what I had in mind for a great meal."

"For crying out loud, will you shut up! Sometimes opportunities come at inconvenient times," Irv said. He swatted Tim alongside the head—not in a playful way.

Bernie sat on a straight-backed chair with duct tape across his mouth and hands tied behind his back. His hair stuck straight up on top of his head and out to the sides like a clown's. He muttered loudly through the tape.

"Give it a rest, will you?" Irv asked, looking Bernie's way.

Bernie kept up the racket. He nodded his head in the direction of an open bathroom door. Finally, Irv caught on.

"You have to go?"

Bernie made a long muttering noise.

"Okay, but you try anything, you're dead meat, got it?"

Bernie sighed and nodded.

Irv untied Bernie's hands and stood him up. Bernie rubbed his arms, took a step forward, and teetered on shaky legs. Irv grabbed Bernie's arm and led him slowly to the bathroom.

"Don't try anything funny."

Bernie shuffled forward and closed the bathroom door. He sat on the toilet, patted his pockets, and pulled out his cellphone. He tapped some buttons, sent a message, and pocketed the phone. Then he worked on the tape over his mouth. He stood, lifted the lid, unzipped and peed.

After a minute or so, Bernie flushed, then turned the water on in the sink. He worked the tape some more, freeing part of his mouth, then yanked for all it was worth. He pounded the counter as his skin turned bright red.

"You two have no idea the havoc you've brought upon yourselves," he muttered. He turned the water off, opened the door, and shuffled a few steps. Irv took in the missing tape. He looked mad.

"Exactly how much trouble do you think a 92-year-old man is going to cause?" Bernie asked. "You left my walker behind!"

"Oh, okay. No tape. You just sit tight until we get some ransom money from your family," Irv said.

"Shouldn't Pedro be back by now?" Tim asked.

"Yeah," Irv said. He looked through the mini blinds.

A knock sounded on the door.

Tim went to the door and looked through the security viewer in the door. He stepped back and opened the door. Pedro sauntered in, dressed in his valet uniform.

"Did you do it?" Irv asked.

"Yeah. I went to the big house and left the ransom note," he said.

"Did anyone come outside and see you?" Tim asked.

"Naah."

"Okay. Now we wait," Irv said.

"Which house did you go to?" Bernie asked.

"Mind your own business," Tim said.

"Unless there were a bunch of cars there, no one might be home for hours, smarty pants," Bernie said.

Irv, Tim, and Pedro shared a look of disbelief.

"If everyone was not gathered at that house, they are all at another house, get it?" Bernie said.

* * *

CHANCE PULLED into Lila Mae's empty driveway. He was surprised that the crowd was not there. He got out of the car and walked to the door and let himself in.

"Anyone home?"

Louie trotted up to Chance and jumped against his legs.

Chance stooped and picked up the dog. "Where'd everyone go?"

Louie panted. He did not appreciate being left behind.

Chance set Louie on the floor and left the house.

* * *

THE LEXUS PULLED out onto Del Monte in Houston's luxurious River Oaks and meandered over to Kirby Drive. Chance drove to Madge's ostentatious house and pulled into the driveway. Carmichael's yellow and black Mini Cooper was there along with two Houston police cruisers.

"Now what?" Chance said.

He hurried out of the car and went to the door. He was about to knock when the door opened and Carmichael greeted him.

"That was quick," Carmichael said. "I didn't think they'd called you yet."

One of the CSI vehicles pulled into the driveway and Frank got out.

"What's going on?" Chance said. "I was just looking for everyone. No one's at Lila Mae's."

"Brick came through the window. Has a ransom note tied to it," Carmichael said. "I called the cops. They called it in and talked to your boss. He's the one who called the CSI."

Chance waited until Frank got to the door. "Let's go see the evidence."

Chance and Frank followed Carmichael through the house to the dining room. Glass was all over the floor where a window had shattered. A red brick was on the floor amid the glass with a note rubber-banded to it. Chance and Frank turned their heads to read the part of the note that was visible.

If you want to see your father alive, bring $5 million in a rolling suitcase to the Presideo shopping center on S McGregor Way tomorrow night at midnight.

"Well that doesn't make much sense," Frank said. "That's a big abandoned shopping center."

"No one ever accused any kidnappers they were too smart for their own good," Chance said.

Chance's phone beeped, dinged, and rang. "What the heck?"

He looked at the text message displayed on his iPhone. It was from Lila Mae.

We've got him!

Chance took the call. "Walker." His normally controlled face showed disbelief as he listened. "I'm on my way." He looked at Carmichael. "They've got Bernie! Come on!"

Carmichael looked at the window, Frank and the cops, then he left with Chance.

"Where are they? Who's got him?"

Chance turned on his red and blue official lights and the car screeched out of the driveway. Carmichael tightened his seatbelt and held the side of his seat.

"Seems these stupid criminals didn't search Bernie, and he texted Chewie where he was being held. The entire family took their fury out on these three guys."

"Oh, wow," Carmichael said. "I'd hate to be on the receiving end."

"Isn't that the truth," Chance said. He and Carmichael shared a knowing look.

* * *

THE ALCOTT CARAVAN screeched into the cracked parking lot of the Sunshine Motel, where weeds outnumbered patches of blacktop. A rainbow of Bentleys and a Mercedes pulled up in front of unit eight-A. The residents—glazed-eyed drug addicts and prostitutes, along with hangers-on—gawked in open-mouthed surprise as the angry occupants of the cars exited the vehicles.

Chewie approached the door with the crooked door number at a run and high-kicked the weathered wood with peeling paint. The door crashed to the floor, splinters flying.

Irv, Tim and Pedro jumped to their feet.

"Told you this was a bad idea," Bernie said. "No one can help you now."

Chewie and Bambi flew into the squalid room, whirlwinds of kicks, chops, punches and jumps. Bambi grabbed a frying pan off the tiny cooktop and bashed Tim alongside the head.

The Alcott sisters, Amelia, Chiquita, Gina, and Walter, plowed into the room after the two living tornados.

The girls and Walter ran to Bernie.

"Daddy!" Lila Mae, Madge, and Dorothea screeched. They grabbed him in a group hug, tears flowing like fire hydrants flooding the street.

"Bernie! Are you alright?" Amelia, Chiquita, Gina, and Walter barked out. They joined the group hug.

"You're smothering me!" Bernie yelled. He tried to extricate himself from his distraught family and loved ones.

Madge patted Bernie down, checking for anything broken.

Dorothea tamed his wild hair with her fingers.

Lila Mae kissed his cheek. "Oh, Daddy!"

Finally, Walter and Dorothea helped Bernie outside to his chocolate-colored Bentley.

Madge turned her fury onto a battered Irv. She bashed him with her purse a couple of times.

Lila Mae swung at Pedro and clipped him in the jaw with her purse.

Amelia slapped Tim's face in rapid-fire succession while Chiquita grabbed Pedro after Lila Mae finished with him. She shook him like a dog with a rat and screeched a long line of what Amelia guessed were X-rated cuss words.

Gina grabbed Chewie into a hug and kissed him stupidly.

Tim, Irv, and Pedro huddled together on the floor in fear for their lives.

* * *

THE ONLY THING Chance noted that was sunny about the Sunshine Motel on South McGregor Way was the sun beaming down a steady ninety-eight degrees on the faded, peeling structure with the cockeyed blue shutters.

He and Carmichael immediately spotted the familiar Bentleys and Mercedes that boxed in a faded red Honda Accord and a Caddy with a busted taillight. The drug addicts and prostitutes hung back from the deranged family, but looked on with keen interest.

Chance noticed the crushed bumper and Bernie's legs sticking out from the rear seat of the dark brown Bentley. He parked his car, and he and Carmichael got out. Chance headed over to Bernie, and Carmichael headed to Amelia, where a lot of loud conversations were heard.

Bernie was quite subdued as he sat sideways on the seat. Chance noticed a wide, red mark across Bernie's mouth.

"What'd they do, tape your mouth?" Chance asked.

Bernie looked up. "This has been an experience." He rubbed his mouth. "Hurt like hell to tear it off, but I managed. You'd better go clean up after Chewie and Bambi. Chewie knocked the door in. Those guys didn't stand a chance! Then my angel went momentarily crazy, and finally, the girls like to have beat them to death with their purses."

"Okay. Sit tight. You're going to have to provide testimony once this settles." Chance couldn't stop the smile that spread across his face. With his long experience regarding the sisters and extended family members, he knew exactly how this played out.

"I'm not going anywhere," Bernie said.

Chewie came over to the car, Gina hanging on his arm. "Are you still okay? Do you need bottled water? An aspirin?"

"I'm okay. A little embarrassed that I was taken advantage of, but I'm grateful you came to my rescue."

"How did they get you to leave the club?" Chance asked.

"Told me the car was on fire! They all but dragged me out the door to show me," Bernie said.

"Well, they can't get out of this. One of them threw a brick through Madge's window with a ransom note attached," Chance said.

"That would be Pedro," Bernie said. "He returned, all proud of his good deed."

"Has anyone called this in?" Chance asked.

"I don't know," Chewie said. He and Gina made eye contact. She shook her head.

Chance walked over to the family. He approached Lila Mae. They smooched real quick.

"Has anyone called nine-one-one?"

Lila Mae frowned. She turned to the family. "Did anyone call the police?"

There was a murmur of questioning among them along with a bunch of shaking heads.

"Doesn't look like it," Lila Mae said.

Chance pulled out his phone and placed a call as he walked through the open doorway of unit eight-A. "Mike, call off the APB. We've got three suspects, one of whom is the valet parking attendant." He briefed his boss about the latest adventures of the Alcott clan, including the brick.

"Sounds like a tidy package to me," Captain Hennessy said. "I'll send the troops."

Chance looked around the dismal motel room. The cheap coffee table was broken in two, chairs over turned, the café table and chairs in the kitchenette were destroyed, a Teflon frying pan was dented and discarded on the floor, and the three perpetrators were huddled on the floor cringing in fright from the petite blond who attacked them with a vengeance.

"Don't you ever disrespect a senior citizen again, understand?" Bambi vented to them.

Three bouncing heads, like rear-window dogs, affirmed their understanding.

Chance approached Bambi, stifling a smile. "Good job, Bambi. I'll take it from here." He looked down and noticed she was barefoot.

"Everything happened so fast I jumped off the sofa and ran to the car," she explained.

* * *

LILA MAE, Amelia, and Chiquita were dragging on their feet, nerves played out. Amelia cut sandwiches and piled them on a single plate.

"Take this to the table," she said.

Chiquita grabbed the plate. She put some napkins on a stack of three plates and brought them to the kitchen table. "You people sure know how to take care of business."

Lila Mae poured lemon and cucumber-infused water into three glasses. She picked up all three glasses and brought them to the table. "We do get a little exuberant at times."

Amelia opened a bag of Original Terra Chips and poured them into a bowl. She headed to the table and plopped into a chair. She rested her head in her hands. "You think so? I am so drained from this ordeal," she said.

"Thank God those men were stupid. If they had searched Daddy, we might have had a different outcome," Lila Mae said.

"That Chewie guy is something else!" Chiquita said. "Did you see how he kicked in that door? And Bambi! She was like a tornado!"

Lila Mae and Amelia snickered. "You should have seen her four months ago. She saved Dorothea and took down a murderer, then gave birth!"

The End

SNEAK PEEK - BOOK 4

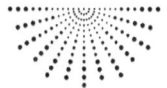

*G*et your next batch of the Alcott family adventures with Book 4, Nutty Chocolate!

The characters you loved in *Hot Chocolate, Bitter Chocolate* and *Spicy Chocolate* are back, and just when you thought things couldn't get any nuttier with the River Oaks Alcott clan, along comes Book 4, Nutty Chocolate.

Lila Mae and the girls are busy planning Bernie's 93rd birthday party. For an old geezer, it didn't appear that he was slowing down anytime soon. Expect Bambi to clobber him a time or two, and for Chewie to keep him in line.

Now that the chocolate factory was back online with great management, thanks to Dougie Vey and Bob Marx (with Luna running the front end), the Alcotts can breathe easier.

While things are all lovey-dovey with several of our favorite people (Pecos and Dolly lead a string of nuptials), there's a mighty unrest among the clan—a lot of flux with old jobs and businesses. Risks are weighed and taken.

Henry walks in on an unethical situation with a client and her soon-to-be ex-husband's attorney. He had harsh words with his law firm over the incident. One of his law partners ends up dead. All fingers point to Henry.

This is the second time the Divine household has been subjected to a murder investigation. Dorothea and Joseph are strung out on raw nerves with the accusations, all the while with the twins teething and screaming in stereo.

Chance has to tiptoe through the murder investigation, or move to a temporary location until Henry's name is cleared. His boss offered his sofa, but Chance and Lila Mae had an unspoken truce. And there's one thing the Alcott family stands for: solidarity! They will get to the bottom of this murder and clear Henry's name.

ABOUT THE AUTHOR

Dawn Greenfield Ireland, also known as D.E. Greenfield & DG Ireland, is an award-winning author of 22 novels, (5 series: cozy mystery, sci fi/fantasy, billionaire shapeshifters, and dystopian), and a stand-alone sci-fi romantic adventure.

Most of her 7 nonfiction books have won awards. Dawn has adapted a few of her award-winning screenplays into book format, and several of her books into TV series format. She also created over 50 themed notebooks.

She had two screenplays optioned, and she worked on a screenwriter-for-hire project. Dawn has a certificate from the Professional Program in Screenwriting from UCLA (2002), and a certificate from ScreenwritingU (2023).

Dawn writes full-time. She lives among dreams and fantasies with two cats and moving boxes. Her head is filled with stories. She doesn't suffer from writer's block. Every word she has written and published is from her noggin (brain, in case you don't know what noggin means). Her fiction is all make-believe from the deep dive into her imagination. Her nonfiction has been researched until her brain has numbed.

Dawn's business, Artistic Origins, has been around since

1995. Besides writing, she coaches writers, edits, formats, and publishes clients' books. Her former day job as an award-winning technical writer played a major role in her fiction writing. She is detailed-oriented, the organizational queen of the known universe, and never misses a deadline.

If you need an editor, formatter, or someone to publish your book, give her a holler.

Leave a review on your favorite retailer's website. Reviews help authors sell books!

You can find her on social media.

facebook.com/dawn.ireland.18
x.com/dawnireland
instagram.com/dawngreenfieldIreland
goodreads.com/dawnireland
linkedin.com/in/dawnireland